The Dare Before Christmas

The Daring Daughters Book 15

By Emma V. Leech

Published by Emma V. Leech.

Copyright (c) Emma V. Leech 2022

Editing Services Magpie Literary Services

Cover Art: Victoria Cooper

ISBN No: 978-2-492133-62-6

All rights reserved. Without limiting the rights under copyright reserved above, no part of this publication may be reproduced, stored in or introduced into a retrieval system, or transmitted, in any form, or by any means (electronic, mechanical, photocopying, recording, or otherwise) without the prior written permission of both the copyright owner and the above publisher of this book. This is a work of fiction. Names, characters, places, brands, media, and incidents are either the product of the author's imagination or are used fictitiously. The author acknowledges the trademarked status and trademark owners of various products referenced in this work of fiction, which have been used without permission. The publication/use of these trademarks is not authorised, associated with, or sponsored by the trademark owners. The ebook version and print version are licensed for your personal enjoyment only. The ebook version may not be re-sold or given away to other people. If you would like to share the ebook with another person, please purchase an additional copy for each person you share it with. No identification with actual persons (living or deceased), places, buildings, and products are inferred.

About Me!

I started this incredible journey way back in 2010 with The Key to Erebus but didn't summon the courage to hit publish until October 2012. For anyone who's done it, you'll know publishing your first title is a terribly scary thing! I still get butterflies on the morning a new title releases, but the terror has subsided at least. Now I just live in dread of the day my daughters are old enough to read them.

The horror! (On both sides I suspect.)

2017 marked the year that I made my first foray into Historical Romance and the world of the Regency Romance, and my word what a year! I was delighted by the response to this series and can't wait to add more titles. Paranormal Romance readers need not despair, however, as there is much more to come there too. Writing has become an addiction and as soon as one book is over I'm hugely excited to start the next so you can expect plenty more in the future.

As many of my works reflect, I am greatly influenced by the beautiful French countryside in which I live. I've been here in the South West since 1998, though I was born and raised in England. My three gorgeous girls are all bilingual and my husband Pat, myself, and our four cats consider ourselves very fortunate to have made such a lovely place our home.

KEEP READING TO DISCOVER MY OTHER BOOKS!

Other Works by Emma V. Leech

Daring Daughters

Daring Daughters Series

Girls Who Dare

Girls Who Dare Series

Rogues & Gentlemen

Rogues & Gentlemen Series

The Regency Romance Mysteries

The Regency Romance Mysteries Series

The French Vampire Legend

The French Vampire Legend Series

The French Fae Legend

The French Fae Legend Series

Stand Alone
The Book Lover (a paranormal novella)
The Girl is Not for Christmas (Regency Romance)

Audio Books

Don't have time to read but still need your romance fix? The wait is over...

By popular demand, get many of your favourite Emma V Leech Regency Romance books on audio as performed by the incomparable Philip Battley and Gerard Marzilli. Several titles available and more added each month!

Find them at your favourite audiobook retailer!

audible

an **amazon** company

audiobook ***chirp***

Acknowledgements

Thanks, of course, to my wonderful editor Kezia Cole with Magpie Literary Services.

To Victoria Cooper for all your hard work, amazing artwork and above all your unending patience!!! Thank you so much. You are amazing!

To my BFF, PA, personal cheerleader and bringer of chocolate, Varsi Appel, for moral support, confidence boosting and for reading my work more times than I have. I love you loads!

A huge thank you to all of Emma's Book Club members! You guys are the best!

I'm always so happy to hear from you so do email or message me :)

emmavleech@orange.fr

To my husband Pat and my family ... For always being proud of me

Table of Contents

Family Trees

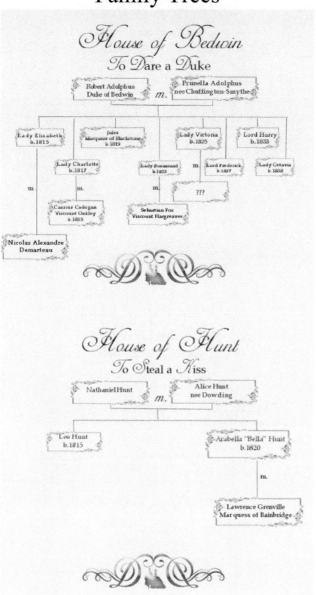

House of Bedwin
To Dare a Duke

Robert Adolphus
Duke of Bedwin

m.

Prunella Adolphus
nee Chuffington-Smythe

Lady Elizabeth
b.1815

Jules
Marquess of Blackstone
b.1819

Lady Victoria
b.1825

Lord Harry
b.1833

Lady Charlotte
b.1817

Lady Rosamund
b.1823

m.

Lord Frederick
b.1827

Lady Octavia
b.1838

???

m.

m.

m.

Cassius Cadogan
Viscount Oakley
b.1815

Sebastian Fox
Viscount Hargreaves

Nicolas Alexandre
Demarteau

House of Hunt
To Steal a Kiss

Nathaniel Hunt

m.

Alice Hunt
nee Dowding

Leo Hunt
b.1815

Arabella 'Bella' Hunt
b.1820

m.

Lawrence Grenville
Marquess of Bainbridge

House of Cavendish
To Break the Rules

| Silas Anson | | Aashini Anson |
| Viscount Cavendish | *m.* | aka: Lucia de Feria |

Twins

| Ashton Anson | | Vivien Anson |
| b.1816 | | b.1816 |

m.

August Lane-Fox

House of Trevick
To Follow her Heart

| Lucas Baxter | | Kitty Baxter |
| Earl of Trevick | *m.* | nee Connelly |

Conor Baxter	Lady Aisling	Lady Cara
Viscount Harleston	b. 1817	b.1824
b.1815		

| | *m.* | *m.* |

| Mr. Sylvester Coote | Wulfric de Vere |
| | Viscount Latimer |

2

House of St Clair
To Wager with Love

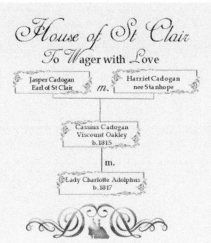

Jasper Cadogan
Earl of St Clair — *m.* — Harriet Cadogan
nee Stanhope

Cassius Cadogan
Viscount Oakley
b. 1815

m.

Lady Charlotte Adolphus
b. 1817

House of Cadogan
To Dance with a Devil

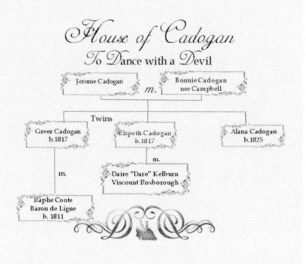

Jerome Cadogan — *m.* — Bonnie Cadogan
nee Campbell

Twins

Greer Cadogan
b. 1817

Elspeth Cadogan
b. 1817

Alana Cadogan
b. 1825

m.

Daire "Dare" Kelburn
Viscount Roxborough

m.

Raphe Coote
Baron de Ligne
b. 1811

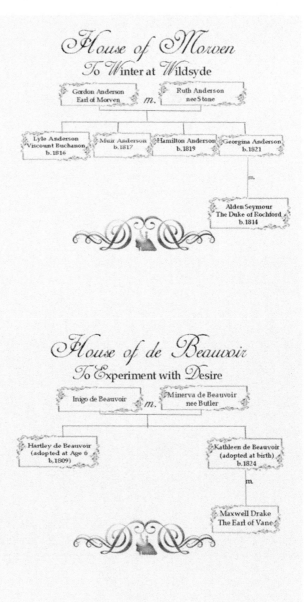

House of Morven
To Winter at Wildsyde

Gordon Anderson
Earl of Morven

m.

Ruth Anderson
nee Stone

Lyle Anderson
Viscount Buchanon
b. 1816

Muir Anderson
b. 1817

Hamilton Anderson
b. 1819

Georgina Anderson
b. 1821

m.

Alden Seymour
The Duke of Rochford
b. 1814

House of de Beauvoir
To Experiment with Desire

Inigo de Beauvoir

m.

Minerva de Beauvoir
nee Butler

Hartley de Beauvoir
(adopted at Age 6)
b. 1809

Kathleen de Beauvoir
(adopted at birth)
b. 1824

m.

Maxwell Drake
The Earl of Vane

House of Rothborn
To Bed the Baron

| Solo Weston
Baron of Rothborn | m. | Jemima Weston
nee Fernside |

Larkin Weston
b.1816

Grace Weston
b.1821

m.

Mr Sterling Oak
b. 1813

House of Knight
To Ride with the Knight

| Gabriel Knight | m. | Lady Helena Knight
nee Adolphus |

Florence Knight
b.1817

Evie Knight
b.1822

Felix Knight
b.1824

Emmaline Knight
b.1826

m.

Henry Stanhope
b.1799

Louis César de Montluc
Comte de Villen
b.1812

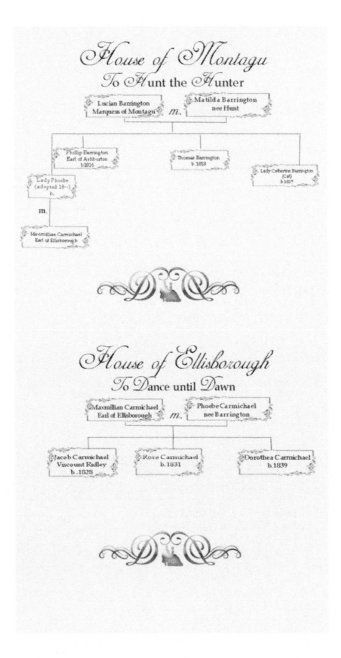

House of Montagu
To Hunt the Hunter

Lucian Barrington
Marquess of Montagu

m.

Matilda Barrington
nee Hunt

Phillip Barrington
Earl of Ashburton
b.1816

Thomas Barrington
b.1818

Lady Catherine Barrington
(Cat)
b.1827

Lady Phoebe
(adopted 18--)
b.

m.

Maximillian Carmichael
Earl of Ellisborough

House of Ellisborough
To Dance until Dawn

Maximillian Carmichael
Earl of Ellisborough

m.

Phoebe Carmichael
nee Barrington

Jacob Carmichael
Viscount Ridley
b.1828

Rose Carmichael
b.1831

Dorothea Carmichael
b.1839

Prologue

Dear Emmeline,

Thank you so much for coming to stay with us. I miss you already. Dot, Emily and little Izzie were so sad and are expressing their displeasure by being as annoying as possible. Do come back and save me from them soon. Ridley is also sorry you have gone, though he would never say so, being 'a boy' and an older brother too. He's horrid ninety percent of the time anyway so it's hard to tell when he's stomping about what the problem is. I think he's sweet on you, though, not that he will admit such a shocking thing. To be fair, he's sweet on any pretty girl in his vicinity. Papa says it is normal and I'm not to tease him so, but it's rather irresistible. I have promised to try.

Our piano misses you most of all. I don't think I shall ever be as proficient as you, no matter how I practice. I never heard such lovely music before in my life.

Have a wonderful Christmas, dear Em, and send your family much love from us all. We shall hope to see you again in the New Year.

—Excerpt of a letter to Miss Emmeline Knight (daughter of Lady Helena and Mr Gabriel Knight) from Lady Rose Carmichael, age 13, (daughter of Phoebe and Maximillian Carmichael, The Countess and Earl of Ellisborough.)

5th December 1844, The Duchess of Bedwin's Christmas Ball, Beverwyck, London.

Lady Victoria Adolphus looked out over a sea of colourful swirling silks, each one revolving around the ballroom in the company of an elegant sweep of black-and-white as the men guided their partners. Viewed from above, her mother's famous Christmas ball was a dazzling affair. Everyone who was anyone was here, the cream of the *ton*. It was the event of the season and, no matter where people were or what commitments they had, no one would miss it. Beverwyck, already a magnificent backdrop, was dressed in splendour for the festive season. Vast swathes of greenery studded with red berries and apples and thick scarlet ribbons wound around the vast marble pillars of the ballroom, the fresh scent of pine and bay and rosemary perfuming the air.

Torie ought to be down there. Right at this moment, she ought to be dancing with… someone. She couldn't remember who. It didn't matter, anyway. The only man she wanted to ask her to dance hadn't and wouldn't, and she didn't know why. Barnaby Godwin was simply the nicest man in the world. He was handsome and kind and sweet, the kind of man who would never let you down, never forget your birthday, and never leave you standing in a corner of the room whilst he went off to enjoy himself elsewhere. Yet Barnaby Godwin didn't like her. Every single man in this room who was not a close friend or related to her vied for her attention. Men fell over themselves to dance with her, flirt with her, or fetch her refreshments, all hoping to marry the daughter of a duke with a vast dowry. It was rather depressing to accept that she had all but begged Barnaby to court her, and he had run a mile.

"Are you hiding?"

Torie jumped as a deep voice spoke close to her ear.

"Oh, Jules!" she protested, scowling at her big brother as he appeared beside her shoulder. "You startled me."

He shrugged, looking unrepentant, and leaned against the wall, staring down at the party as she had been doing.

"Shouldn't you be dancing?" he asked, taking a drink from the crystal glass he held. It wasn't the champagne everyone else was drinking; the tawny liquid suggested he'd opted for brandy instead.

"Shouldn't you?" she retorted.

Jules smirked at her and raised the glass. "Touché."

They stood in silence for a moment. Up here they were hidden from view, the private balcony shadowy and unlit and only accessible from the family wing of the grand house.

"Why aren't you down there, dancing and having fun, then?" Jules asked.

Torie looked up at him, seeing concern in her brother's eyes. For all his teasing ways, he was a good brother, kind and caring, and never too busy to spend time with his younger siblings. Torie knew he was gaining a shocking reputation, something over which he and their father were increasingly at loggerheads. Yet it was hard to align the wicked Marquess of Blackstone who was forever in the scandal sheets with the man before her. They seemed entirely different people.

She shrugged in response to his question, uncertain how to answer. She would have to return to the party before Mama missed her too and began asking the same thing.

"I don't know. I'm just not in the mood for dancing, I suppose."

Jules quirked an eyebrow. "I bet your dance card is fit to bursting."

Torie snorted. "Well, that's hardly an astonishing feat of deduction, is it? I bet you're hiding up here from all the marriage-hungry young ladies eager for you to dance with them."

"You would be right," Jules replied dryly.

"How long do you think we've got before Mother comes to fetch us?" Torie asked.

Jules leaned over the balcony and sighed. "About five minutes. I think she's on her way up."

Torie groaned and hurried to the door. "Come along. If she finds us up here, we'll be in the basket."

Jules pushed off from the wall and followed Torie as she made her way back to the main staircase so they could return to the party.

"Are you sure there's nothing wrong, sis?" Jules asked.

Torie glanced over her shoulder and gave him a sad smile. "Nothing anyone can do anything about. But I'm not giving up yet."

"That sounds ominous," Jules observed, his dark eyebrows tugging together. "You're not getting into any mischief, are you? Where's that blessed hat at the moment?"

With a laugh at her brother's dark tone, Torie shook her head. "I think Aggie has it, but no. I've not taken a dare. Not yet, at least."

Jules studied her face as they made their way towards the top of the stairs. "Be careful, Torie, won't you? Don't do anything daft."

Impulsively, Torie turned and kissed her brother on the cheek.

"Of course not," she said with a smile, and then took a breath, steeling herself and walking down the grand staircase and back into the fray.

Barnaby glanced at the lady beside him and wondered what she was thinking. Miss Ada Robinson was the daughter of a wealthy merchant, and a woman whom Barnaby had given serious consideration to courting. Though not a great beauty, she was pretty in a china doll way, a diminutive creature with large blue eyes and slender shoulders. Her complexion was fair, her eyes fringed with pale lashes and her blonde hair the colour of ripe wheat. So far, she had seemed pleased with Barnaby's attention, and no one else appeared to be in the running for her affections, which was something. The trouble was, Barnaby did not know what was in her head. Conversation was one-sided as he rattled on, trying to entertain her. The lady smiled and nodded, and either laughed or made encouraging noises as the moment warranted, but rarely spoke herself. Though they had met some weeks ago, Barnaby still had little idea what she was interested in, or what her likes and dislikes were, though she was certainly a good listener. A little too good.

"Would you like to dance?" he asked her, gaining an appreciative flash of wide blue eyes filled with pleasure.

"I would," she said, nodding and making her golden ringlets bounce.

Barnaby held out his arm to her and guided her onto the dance floor.

It was a country dance, one where you had to change partners several times, and once they had gone through the moves of the dance, Barnaby turned to receive his new partner, and was startled to discover Lady Victoria before him. For a moment, he couldn't breathe. She was undoubtedly the most beautiful woman here tonight, not that he'd allowed himself to look. Her dark hair was glossy and thick, styled in soft waves about her face, her porcelain skin flushed from the heat of the room. Dressed in a gown of opulent gold satin, she shimmered like a Christmas angel, and Barnaby felt his heart give a frantic kick behind his ribs.

Ignore it, he told himself fiercely. She was not for the likes of him.

"Good evening, Mr Godwin," she said, her voice soft as she touched Barnaby's gloved fingers with her own and spun away.

The dance returned her to him a moment later, and they held hands again as they danced down the length of the room together. Her hand seemed to burn against his, the contact electric even through their gloves. As they got to the end, the lady glanced up at him before they parted again, and Barnaby's breath hitched at the look in her eyes.

Barnaby had seen the devastating effect his good friend the Comte de Villen had on women often enough to know what a come-hither glance looked like. Never had he seen one turned in his direction, though. Longing hit him square in the chest, the desire to follow that look and see where it led. It almost hurt to ignore it, to push it back into the dark recesses of his mind where useless hopes and dreams belonged. Yet, ruthlessly, he forced the sensation back down, determined to erase her from his mind. He was done chasing after women with whom he hadn't a hope. The ill-fated affair with Lady Millicent had been a humiliating and crushing experience, and he was not about to repeat it. The younger son of a mere baron, and with three older brothers, Barnaby had no title to inherit, no fortune at his disposal, nor any expectation of one. He had a tidy little home that provided a decent income, and he was comfortably well off, but for the daughter of a duke… he might as well be a road sweeper. Oh, no. No more chasing heiresses, or women whose sights were set on marrying up. Millicent had got her earl and good luck to her. Not that it was entirely her fault. Her father had been determined for her to make a good match, and Barnaby understood that, but it wasn't as if she'd put up anything resembling a fight either, and that had rather stung.

Not that he was heartbroken. He'd seen people in love and knew he had not experienced it himself, especially after having watched Louis drown under the force of the emotion for some considerable time. It had not been love he'd felt for Millicent, but it had been an affectionate friendship that he had hoped... but never mind. It was not to be. Besides, he had Miss Robinson to consider now. It was early days, but perhaps she could be the one, if only she would deign to share a little of herself with him, so he could get to know her.

The dance ended and Barnaby held out his arm to the lady, who looked flushed and pretty after their exertions. Barnaby smiled at her, and she laughed.

"That was fun."

"It was," he agreed readily. "You dance very well."

She returned a shy smile and looked pleased by the compliment. Guiding her off the floor, Barnaby cursed as he crossed paths once again with Lady Victoria on the arm of her brother, the Marquess of Blackstone. He wondered what on earth she was doing dancing with him, when the ballroom must heave with men clamouring to fill her dance card, but it was none of his affair.

"Godwin," Blackstone said, startling Barnaby, who had not been expecting to be noticed. Though they'd been introduced and had spoken a few times, they were not exactly friends. "How do? Enjoying the crush?"

"Indeed, my lord," Barnaby said with a smile. "The duchess has excelled herself as usual. It is a magnificent affair."

"I'm so glad you're enjoying it, Mr Godwin," Lady Victoria said, returning his smile, though her green gaze drifted to Miss Robinson with curiosity.

A sharp little elbow dug at Barnaby's ribs, and he looked around in surprise to see Miss Robinson widening her eyes at him. Oh, of course, an introduction was required. He sighed inwardly.

"My lord, Lady Victoria, might I introduce Miss Ada Robinson? Ada, Lady Victoria Adolphus and Jules Adolphus, the Marquess of Blackstone."

To Barnaby's astonishment, Miss Robinson lit up as Blackstone took her hand.

"A pleasure, Miss Robinson," the marquess said politely.

"Oh, the pleasure is mine, I assure you," Miss Robinson gushed, her blue eyes brilliant with excitement. "Such a wonderful evening, and the dancing... so delightful. Do you enjoy dancing, my lord? It's such a pleasure to dance at such a fabulous event. I believe the waltz is next. My favourite dance, though my father still thinks it scandalous. Can you imagine? He's rather old-fashioned, I'm afraid. Do you like to waltz?"

Barnaby stared at the woman in shock, astounded to see her so animated. That was probably the most conversation he'd heard from her in the past sennight. Blackstone's expression had cooled, however, and Lady Victoria seemed uneasy.

"Oh, my brother rarely dances, Miss Robinson, but who have you got on your dance card for the waltz?"

Before Miss Robinson could reply, Blackstone cut in.

"If you would excuse me, I see someone I must speak to. Please enjoy the rest of your evening, Miss Robinson, Mr Godwin. I'll see you later, Torie," he added, a look passing between him and his sister before he walked away.

Barnaby glanced at Miss Robinson, noting the bitter frustration in her eyes with regret, but no surprise. Another young lady hunting a title. Ah well. Better to figure it out now.

"Mr Hardy is next," Miss Robinson said with a dejected sigh. "Oh, and here he is. Excuse me, Mr Godwin," she added, before hurrying away to her new partner.

It left Barnaby standing beside the one woman in the ballroom he did not want to spend time with. He could feel her gaze upon him and racked his brain for a polite way of extricating himself from the situation.

"I expect your dance partner will be here soon," he said, giving the lady a polite smile.

"No, actually," Lady Victoria said, a hopeful glint in her eyes he could not mistake. "I... I kept the waltz free, in case...."

She blushed and looked at her feet.

"I beg your pardon, my lady," Barnaby said desperately, knowing he could not possibly dance with her. Far, far too dangerous. Regret struck at his heart as he saw the flash of hurt in her beautiful eyes, but he ploughed on regardless. "There's my aunt. She'll have been looking for me this age. I'll be in the suds if I don't show my face. Must dash. Apologies. Have a lovely evening."

Feeling like an utter blackguard, Barnaby hurried away towards the corner of the room where his aunt was speaking with the other Viragoes she was friends with. Not that he had the least intention of spending time with them. He'd pay his respects, and then he was getting out of here and going home. Though naturally buoyant of spirit, he felt utterly deflated, tired and dispirited, and he needed to get away from everyone else who seemed to be having so much fun. At least for a while. Perhaps with a few days' peace he'd feel more the thing. He'd best hope so, for Louis and Evie had invited him for Christmas, and the last thing he wanted to do was ruin it for them by being a wet blanket. Well, he'd best buck himself up and stop being such a misery then, but not tonight. Tonight, he was heading home to a decent bottle of cognac, and he intended to make enough inroads into it that he could consign Miss

Robinson and Lady Millicent firmly in the past and keep them there. And as for Lady Victoria… well, he'd best not think of her at all.

Chapter 1

Dearest Evie,

We are so excited to be with you at Heart's Folly for Christmas. Only three more days and we shall be together again. Mama and Papa are looking forward to it immensely, and even Felix has been busy Christmas shopping and you know how hard he tries to be indifferent to everything these days. I think he believes he looks like an overgrown schoolboy if he seems too enthusiastic, the daft creature. Though he's been so morose these past weeks, I'm certain he's in love again. No idea who it is this time, but there is a lot of gazing into space and sighing. It's most provoking.

I had a wonderful time with Phoebe and Max and their brood. Rose is turning out to be quite a beauty, very much like her beautiful mama. Montagu visited whilst we were there, and he and Matilda sent their love to you and hope you and Louis will visit them at Dern soon. It's close to Heart's Folly, I think?

Well, I had better get back to wrapping presents. Have you finished all your shopping yet? I must still find something for Felix, for he is so troublesome to buy for. I don't have the least clue what will please him these days.

Much love and see you very soon!

—Excerpt of a letter to Evie de Montluc, Comtesse de Villen (daughter of Lady Helena and Mr Gabriel Knight) from her younger sister, Miss Emmeline Knight.

15ᵗʰ December 1844, en route to Heart's Folly, East Sussex.

Torie stared out of the carriage window. It was a rather dismal day, which suited her mood. It had rained on and off for much of the journey and she rubbed her gloved hand against the glass to remove the fog. It made little difference, for a frail mist clung to the countryside, draining the colour from everything until it was damp and wreathed in grey. She sighed, and the glass fogged up again. Closing her eyes, Torie tried to summon some enthusiasm for the coming days, but it was hard. Mr Godwin would be here and, though there must be at least twenty guests, including the children, she would be in his company every day. Not so long ago, that had been something to look forward to. Torie had hoped it would be a chance to let him see she was not a stuck-up creature, nor unkind or frivolous, or whatever it was he believed her to be that made him rush to be out of her company. Also, she adored Evie and had so been looking forward to getting to know her new husband better and exploring their wonderful home, but now she could only remember the way Mr Godwin had snubbed her, leaving her standing on the dance floor all alone, when he must have realised that she wished to dance with him.

Perhaps she had acted badly and given him a disgust of her, for usually he was so unfailingly polite and kind. Perhaps she had been as crass and obvious as Miss Robinson, who had gazed up at Jules with such blatant interest and prattled on about how much she loved the waltz. Torie had cringed for her, knowing just how

Jules would react to such an obvious manoeuvre. He'd fled, just as she'd known he would—far too used to being hunted by ladies with marriage on their minds—and just as Barnaby had done moments later.

"Why's it called Heart's Folly?"

Torie opened her eyes, jolted from her thoughts by her brother, Fred. At seventeen, he was nearly two years younger than her, but in the past months he had grown terrifically and was now a full head taller. He was almost as tall, though not yet nearly as broad, as Jules, who was five and twenty. Indeed, he seemed all arms and legs these days.

"Don't know, don't care," Jules muttered, yawning and not bothering to open his eyes.

"I wasn't asking you," Fred said irritably. "You're not interested in anything unless it's got petticoats."

"Fred!" Torie exclaimed, glaring at him and jerking her head towards Harry, who, at eleven years old, was their youngest brother. Their youngest sibling, little Octavia, was riding in the carriage ahead of theirs with their parents, thank heavens. At five years old, the little minx was a terrible fidget.

"Oh, don't fuss, Torie," Harry complained, folding his arms. "I know all about Jules. Everyone knows all about Jules. He's a rake and a libertine."

"Harry!"

"What?" Harry demanded indignantly. "He is too."

"You see the trouble you cause?" Torie demanded of Jules, who just cracked open a bleary eye and closed it again without bothering to answer. She huffed and tried to remember what the question had been.

"Evie told me a Mr Heorot Payne named Heart's Folly," she said, remembering the letter Evie had written her. "He built the house for his wife, whom he adored, but it was so expensive that he almost bankrupted himself. I believe there's some story to do with Mrs Payne and Oliver Cromwell, too, for Mr and Mrs Payne were staunch royalists."

"Well, that's all very interesting," Harry said, "But I still don't see why it's called Heart's Folly."

Fred rolled his eyes at his little brother. "Heorot is Old English for a hart or stag. It's a play on words."

"Then why isn't it Hart's Folly with an a, not ea?" Harry demanded.

"Because of the love story, I suppose," Torie replied with a sigh, gazing out of the window.

How romantic it was. To think, Mr Payne had built the house expressly to please his beloved wife. That the man had so wanted to make her happy that he spent far too much to make the house as beautiful as he could.

"Well, I don't think it's very romantic to spend all their money on a house they can't afford," Fred retorted, pragmatic as usual. "What's the use of it if they can't afford to live in it?"

"Oh, but they did live in it. Somehow Mr Payne turned his fortunes around. I don't know how. They were happy here for generations until the name died out towards the end of the last century. At least, that's what Evie said. The place was in a shocking state when Louis bought it. There's been a huge amount of work done, though Evie says part of the house is still untouched. It's a vast place. I bet there's lots of secret rooms and hidey holes."

Jules stirred, opening his eyes to give Torie a curious glance. "That being the case, why aren't you beside yourself with excitement, desperate to explore? Surely you've been dreaming about mad monks and Gothic horror stories with such a delicious backdrop as that?"

Torie shrugged, but Jules knew her too well and continued to study her. Until recently, Torie *had* been desperately excited, but now her pleasure in the coming days was diminished by the knowledge that Barnaby Godwin did not like her. Now she must spend the entire Christmas period in the company of a man she esteemed above all others, knowing that he despised her. It was a most lowering experience. Torie did not believe she had a right to his love or attention, and she could have accepted him not feeling the same way, but such an obvious rejection from a man known for his kindness and good manners… well, that hurt.

Torie looked up, finding Jules watching with concern. Well, let him. She was not about to explain herself any more than he would do. They both had their secrets. So she turned away and concentrated on watching the countryside change as they grew closer to Heart's Folly.

Louis César lounged on the bed and watched with pleasure as his wife dabbed a little perfume behind her ears. It was an expensive scent he had bought for her whilst they were in the south of France. Evie turned to smile at him and got up from before her dressing table, holding a box of jewellery in her hands.

"Would you help me, Louis?" she asked.

He stood and moved closer, smiling as he saw the exquisite set of emeralds he had given her for her birthday a few years ago. She had not known he was in love with her back then, and had been blissfully ignorant of what kind of man he really was. So much had changed, and he counted his blessings every morning he woke beside her.

"I'm glad I don't have to hide them any longer," she said, her eyes sparkling.

Louis fastened the heavy necklace in place, amused as she shivered at the touch of the cold jewels. Sliding his arms about her waist, he bent and kissed the sensitive spot beneath her ear, making her shiver again.

"I'm glad we don't have to hide any longer, or this might be awkward," he murmured, smoothing his hands over the burgeoning swell of her stomach.

Evie's hands covered his, and she chuckled.

"A little more than awkward, but I don't think anyone is unaware of our marriage now, not after the amount of scandalous headlines and prints we've generated over the past years."

Louis pulled her closer, inhaling the scent of long hot summers, remembering making love to her in the beautiful gardens of the house they'd bought overlooking the Mediterranean sea. Desire simmered beneath his skin and, as much as he was looking forward to their first Christmas at Heart's Folly, he rather wished their guests elsewhere for the moment.

"Stop it," she scolded, though she was laughing still.

"Stop what?" he demanded, all innocence, though he knew she could feel his reaction to her proximity through layers of silk and petticoats.

"You know very well what," Evie chided him, turning in his arms. "We have guests, so there's no escaping dinner and going to bed early. You must behave, husband."

He sighed heavily, staring down at her. "If I must."

"You must," she said firmly, but pressed a kiss to his lips before moving away and sitting back down at her dressing table to add the earrings and hair clips that went with the necklace. The emeralds glittered in the lamplight against the smooth perfection of her skin. "Barnaby is unhappy."

Louis nodded, sitting down on the mattress again as he waited for her to finish her toilette.

"*Oui,* of this I am aware. The hopes he had for Miss Robinson were dashed, it appears. I did not like her, as you know. Rather an insipid creature. Apparently, she took one look at Blackstone and made her interest abundantly clear. Another young lady in search of a title."

"Well, you did warn him," Evie said with a sigh. "Oh, the poor man. But really, why is he being so stubborn about the young lady who admires him so? Won't you tell me who it is, Louis?" she asked for the tenth time.

He laughed and shook his head. "I cannot, *mon amour*. I promised him, so you must guess. But Barnaby believes she is too far above him and does not wish to tread the same path he did with Lady Millicent. He's afraid of being labelled a fortune hunter but, more to the point, I believe he already has feelings for the lady and fears he might get his heart broken if it went wrong this time."

Evie huffed with frustration. "Oh, poor Barnaby. But can't you at least give me a clue?"

Louis shook his head, enjoying her exasperation. Teasing her was always a delightful pastime.

She wrinkled her nose in consternation. "Well, what do you think? If the lady is someone we know, you must have an opinion."

"Of course I do," he said, getting to his feet and taking her hands, pulling her from the stool before the dressing table and into his arms. "I believe the lady is in love with him, and we must do all in our power to throw them together as much as possible."

"But how can we, if—" Evie broke off, staring at him. "She's here!"

Louis' eyes widened in mock surprise. "I never said that. However did you surmise such a thing?"

"Oh!" Evie squealed, kissing him hard. "She is! She's here. Well, in that case, it's Victoria or Emmeline. They are the only marriageable women here, and my sister would surely have mentioned something, at least dropped a hint, and…. It must be Torie," she said, beaming at him.

Louis returned his most guileless expression and shrugged. "I could not possibly comment."

Evie snorted and shook her head. "Wretch," she said fondly. "But now I know, I can help. We shall sit them together at dinner, and send them off together when we gather the greenery to decorate, and—"

"Have a care, Evie," Louis said, reaching out to caress her cheek. "A man does not like to be forced into things against his will. Barnaby has his pride. If we try too hard, he might dig his heels in."

Evie pursed her lips. "Perhaps, but Torie needs the chance to make him see he's being an idiot, and she can't do that if she's not in his company."

"Also true," Louis replied. "Well, let us see what we can do, for I have every intention that Barnaby shall be as happy as we are."

"Oh, yes. He deserves it, for being such a good friend to you."

Louis smiled and nodded. "I owe him a good deal, but he is not the only one I wish to see settled. His aunt also needs a husband, I think. She has been alone for far too long. Such a remarkable woman needs a companion, for I believe she is lonely. Not that she would ever admit such a thing."

"Lady Balderston? You're not serious, Louis? But who…?"

Louis shook his head and guided Evie to the door. "All will be revealed, *amour de ma vie*. Just wait and see."

Torie felt her heart sink as she sat down at the dinner table that night, to discover Mr Godwin beside her. Across the table Emmeline, who knew of her predicament, sent her a look of deep sympathy but there was nothing to be done but endure.

"Good evening, Lady Victoria."

"Good evening, Mr Godwin," Torie replied, not looking at him. Instead, she turned towards the Duke of Axton on her left. "How did you find the journey, your grace?"

Torie let Axton's words wash over her, only listening with half an ear, too aware of Mr Godwin sitting so close beside her as she stirred her soup around with little enthusiasm. She had no appetite tonight, her stomach tied in a tight little knot. How she was supposed to do justice to what she had no doubt would be a splendid dinner, she did not know.

The arrival of Henry and Florence Stanhope—Evie and Emmeline's older sister—midway through the meal sent everyone into a flurry. They turned up late, exhausted after a difficult journey beset with a broken carriage wheel, with a wailing baby and Henry carrying his three-year-old son asleep on his shoulder. With apologies for disrupting everyone, they disappeared up to their room with promises to do better tomorrow.

Afterwards, everyone settled back down to their meal, and several courses came and went. Torie did her best to do justice to them, but anxiety made every bite stick in her throat and she could only wish the evening would end quickly. She toyed with the idea of feigning a headache, but that seemed a rotten thing to do to Evie when she had worked so hard to make everything lovely for her guests. It *was* lovely, too. The room was large and elegant, a fire burning in a huge ornate fireplace, and the table was beautifully arranged, silver and crystal glittering in the candlelight. Sweetest of all was the happiness shining in Evie and Louis' eyes. That this was a match made in heaven was perfectly obvious to all, and Torie had to fight to squash a little sliver of envy. Evie deserved everything that was good, and she was so happy for her, but… well, no matter. She dared a glance at Mr Godwin. He was turning his wineglass in his hand and frowning at the elegant table setting of Christmas roses in the middle of the table. He didn't appear to have eaten much more than she had.

Perhaps sensing her gaze upon him, he turned his head, and their eyes met. Torie felt a fierce blush rise to her cheeks and looked hurriedly away. Her breath caught as she experienced the same wash of humiliation as she had when he'd walked away from her at the ball, and she cursed under her breath. She might as well paint a sign on her head that read *I love you, Mr Godwin* if she was going to be as obvious as that. The indignity of it burned. If only she could just pretend he wasn't there, but every nerve ending seemed unwillingly oriented towards him.

Axton was now deep in conversation with Louis César and Emmeline was talking to Jules, so she could do nothing more than turn her attention back to her plate and do her utmost to pretend everything was fine. Determinedly, she speared a tiny, perfectly golden roast potato and stared at it. Her throat was so tight she felt certain it would choke her.

"Are you well, my lady?"

Mr Godwin's voice was quiet, filled with concern.

"Quite well," she replied, aware she sounded stiff and cold and unable to do a thing about it.

Torie raised the little bite-sized potato and put it in her mouth. She chewed, relieved this would put an end to any expectation of a fuller reply. She chewed and chewed, too anxious to swallow.

Oh, do stop acting like such a ninny. He's just a man. He doesn't have to like you and you don't need to get in such a tizzy about the fact he doesn't. For heaven's sake, pull yourself together.

Torie swallowed. A mistake. The potato lodged in her throat and her stomach churned. She sat very still, breathing hard. No. No, this was… not good.

"Excuse me," she muttered, and fled the table.

Barnaby accepted another glass of wine, knowing that he had better eat a bit more or he would have the devil of a head in the morning. Why he couldn't eat was something he did not wish to consider, but there was no escaping the guilt that sat in his guts like a lump of lead, cold and heavy and dashed uncomfortable.

Lady Victoria had clearly got the message he had delivered so cruelly at her mother's ball. She had barely spoken to him above the merest civility and refused to look his way. Except for a moment ago. Her lovely skin had been pale—too pale, he'd thought—until the moment their eyes met, when her cheeks blazed scarlet, and she had looked hurriedly away.

Barnaby had heard her breath hitch. He'd thought he'd heard her curse under her breath too, but likely he had imagined that against the lively chatter that filled the dining room. Everyone was having a marvellous time… well, except for him and, it appeared, Lady Victoria. He had an awful suspicion he was to blame for the lady's unhappiness, which seemed ridiculous. Why on earth should she care for what he thought? But… But she'd told him why, hadn't she? She had written him those lovely words which had made his chest ache, made him dream of impossible things…. Well, he'd dreamed of impossible things before, and look how that had ended.

"Excuse me," the lady said, her voice strained as she shoved her chair back and hurried from the room.

Barnaby watched her go with consternation and then looked around to see Louis glaring at him. His friend jerked his head towards the door the lady had just departed through, his meaning obvious.

Barnaby hesitated but Louis glared harder.

Oh, damn and blast.

Reluctantly, Barnaby pushed to his feet and followed the lady out. A footman pointed him in the direction the lady had fled, and Barnaby hurried after her. The sound of a door closing had him changing direction as he came across a door that led outside to the gardens. She had pulled the curtain back and the chill night air still lingered in the room. Barnaby stepped out into a frosty December night, his breath clouding around him.

The skies were clear now, studded with stars, the day's rain and cloud all vanished and promising a brighter day tomorrow. Barnaby blinked in the dim light, sensing movement at the far end of the terrace he found himself on. Cautiously, he followed.

The lady was standing at the corner of the terrace, staring up at the stars. His heart clenched as he took in the sight of her bathed in moonlight. She was heartbreakingly beautiful, the kind of woman a man would fight duels for, would go to the ends of the earth for, if he were fool enough to fall in love with her. Barnaby did not want to be that fool. A man like him was ill-equipped to be her knight in shining armour. Yet it was hard to see her like this, so exquisitely beautiful and so unhappy. Her slender arms were bare and wrapped tightly around her middle, and she was shivering.

"Lady Victoria?"

She jumped at the sound of his voice and spun around.

"I'm sorry, I didn't mean to startle you," he said, holding out his hands as if to show he meant her no harm.

"M-Mr Godwin, what are you doing here?" she demanded, sounding none too happy about the fact he had followed her.

"I was worried you were unwell."

"I already told you I was not," she said curtly. "I just needed some air, that's all. Please, do n-not let me k-keep you," she added, her teeth chattering.

Barnaby shrugged out of his coat, and she took a step away in alarm.

"W-What are you doing?" She glared at him.

"You're freezing, and you'll catch pneumonia if you stay out here like that," he said firmly, moving closer and putting his coat around her bare shoulders.

"There's n-no need," she said crossly, but he heard the catch in her voice and guilt sliced deep in his chest.

"Yes, there is."

"Now *you'll* catch pneumonia," she retorted.

Barnaby gave a huff of laughter. "Well, that would serve me right."

She glanced at him, her gaze uncertain. He looked steadily back, offering her a tentative smile. The lady turned away and put up her chin.

"You had best go in. If you're found alone with me, you might have to marry me, and you wouldn't want that."

There was more bitterness in her voice than Barnaby could have expected, despite what had passed between them.

"My lady," he began, needing to say something, anything, but he did not know what.

"Oh, please go away," she begged, turning back to him, her beautiful eyes shining too brightly in the darkness. "I know you don't like me and you're only here because you're a kind man, but please… please…."

"I do like you," he said, unable to let her believe that, unable to bear her unhappiness when it was his fault.

She snorted, and the sound was so unlike anything he expected to hear from the untouchable duke's daughter that he could not help but smile.

"It's true, and I was never more surprised nor touched by your words, my lady. I… I am very aware of the honour you did me in writing such a letter, and in return I have behaved very shabbily towards you. Please forgive me."

"You left me standing in the middle of our ballroom feeling like a fool," she accused him, the quaver returning to her voice and making him want to drop to his knees and beg her forgiveness. She deserved so much more than that. Lady Victoria deserved the moon, but he was not the man to reach it for her.

"I know," he said, turning away from the hurt in her eyes and looking out at the gardens, bathed in eerie silver moonlight. "I panicked."

"What?"

He glanced back at her, aware of her incredulous expression.

"It's no good," he said in frustration. "What is the point of me spending time with you, dancing with you, when everyone knows you'll marry a duke or a marquess or an earl, or at least some fellow with money to burn? I'm a younger son, I've no fortune, no vast estate, and I'll not put myself through all that only for you to realise what I knew from the start, once it's too late. Your estimation of my character is too generous, and thoroughly undeserved, but I am honoured by your regard for me, more than I can say. But I shall not act the fool, my lady, not when all the world knows it would be a shocking *mesalliance*. Not again."

"Not again?" she repeated, staring at him in confusion. Suddenly, her expression cleared. "You mean like Lady Millicent. You think I'd treat you so poorly?"

"It was not her fault, but my own. I ought not to have pursued her. In the end, she had no choice," Barnaby said, not wanting the lady maligned for circumstances beyond her control.

"Perhaps," she admitted, her voice softer. "But she knew of her father's plans to marry her to that man months ago. I know because the earl spoke to my father about it recently, about how she had accepted his decision earlier in the year, knowing she was gaining title and wealth in return for what she would lose. They did not make the engagement public because she asked to be allowed to enjoy one final season before she married. I do not wish to speak ill of her, for I cannot know what was in her heart, but at the very least it was unkind of her to lead you on when she knew it would come to nothing."

Barnaby stiffened, the words cutting deep. He shook his head. "That's… She wouldn't. I know she…."

But as he saw the compassionate look in the lady's eyes, he knew she was telling the truth.

"I'm sorry, Mr Godwin, but I did not tell you to cause you pain, but only to illustrate the difference in our situations. My father only wishes for his children to be happy. Obviously, he would be delighted if we married well, but he knows what it is to be trapped in a marriage that makes you miserable, and he would never do that to any of us. We shall all marry for love, or not at all. So, you see, your fears are baseless."

Barnaby sucked in a breath, letting that information sink in. Millicent had known it was going nowhere, but she had still led him about by the nose, let him believe there was hope. She knew he had been in earnest and she… she had been toying with him. Why? Why had she done it?

As if he had spoken the words aloud, Lady Victoria answered his question.

"I promise you, I did not know it then or I would have found a way to warn you. I can only imagine she wanted to spend as much time with the man who would have been her choice if things were different, while she still could. I suppose I cannot blame her for wanting that, though I would not have hurt you for the world, if the choice were mine to make."

He nodded, seeing sincerity in her eyes, though humiliation seethed beneath his skin that she should know this—that others had known this, perhaps even at the time—and they had seen him making a cake of himself.

"You have nothing to feel embarrassed about," she said, her voice surprisingly firm. "It is Lady Millicent who should bear any shame for behaving so thoughtlessly. You were… you *are* honourable and good, Mr Godwin. If I were lucky enough to be in Lady Millicent's position, I should consider myself fortunate indeed."

Barnaby stared at her, startled by the uncompromising words. A faint blush stained the lady's cheeks but, other than that, she looked utterly composed, as if she had not just laid her heart bare before him. Words crowded his mouth, but he could find nothing to say. His heart felt bruised, his confidence shaken by what she had told him. How could he have so misjudged Lady Millicent? To have been so taken in by her, by her smiles and confidences and flirtation, made his stomach churn with mortification.

"Victoria?"

They both jumped as a deep voice cut through the silence.

"I'm sorry, Papa. I wasn't feeling very well," she said, shrugging Barnaby's coat off her shoulders and handing it back to him.

She hurried over to her father, who gave Barnaby a hard look.

"Really? And are you well now?"

"Yes, quite well now. I just needed some air. Mr Godwin was worried about me when I left the dinner so suddenly, and was good enough to look after me, but I'm feeling much better. Have I missed the dessert?"

"Not yet," the duke said, taking his daughter's arm. "Come along, then. It's bound to be something extravagant, if Evie has had a hand in it."

They left the terrace, the duke sending Barnaby one last dark look before the door closed behind them.

Barnaby put his coat back on, wishing the lavish perfume of otto of roses didn't linger upon the fabric, wrapping itself around him and invading his senses. The scent served as a forceful reminder of why the woman was out of his reach, no matter her words. It reputedly took one hundred roses to make just one drop, which was why it was shockingly expensive. The lady would have to give up such extravagances, would have to resign herself to not having every luxury, the finest gowns and jewels, the best carriages, houses teeming with servants and… and what was the point? He did not want that for her. He did not want to take from her in order to make her his own. She thought she wanted him, and though that was a difficult enough concept to wrestle with, it was nothing more than a young woman's romantic dream. The truth would be a terrible disappointment to her, for it was neither sensible nor realistic. She had got some daft notion into her head about him from heaven alone knew where, but soon enough she'd realise she'd made a mistake. Well, Barnaby would not go out on a limb only to find himself set aside again, or left at the altar, or worse still, married to a woman who grew to resent him for everything he had taken from her.

No. Lady Victoria was far above his touch. The sooner she accepted that, the better. Yet the vision of her standing bathed in the moonlight lingered in his mind, and a burst of longing made his chest ache. *Pack it in, you bloody fool,* he told himself. *Forget it. Forget her.*

It was the only way.

Chapter 2

Dearest Emmeline,

I said goodbye to Oliver Cootes today. I am torn between sobbing my heart out and such relief that I feel horribly guilty. He was my dearest friend, but I know now that I have only ever regarded him that way, or as a brother, and it would have been cruel of me to allow him to believe otherwise. It was foolish of us to get engaged so young and I thank heaven that we never made the news public. I have spared us both that humiliation, at least.

I think once he has spent time away from me, he will realise he, too, made a mistake. I do not believe he ever loved me as one ought to love the person you marry. It was simply that we were such dear friends, and I was familiar and, frankly, close at hand. The new position he has taken up in Hertfordshire has excellent prospects for him and I know he will do wonderfully well. I pray he meets a lovely girl and tumbles head over ears in love with her. As for me, well, I do not know what the future holds, but I'm in no hurry. I spent so many years assuming I would marry Ollie that I've never looked about myself for other possibilities. My future is suddenly an unknown quantity, and I am terrified and excited all at once. My sisters both found happiness, and I must hold tight to the belief there is the same chance awaiting me, if only I am patient enough.

Raphe has been very kind, for I feared he might be cross with me for causing his brother hurt, but he understood and even thanked me for being brave enough to make my feelings clear. He said it was never easy to cause another pain, even if it was the kind thing to do. I'm afraid I turned into the most appalling watering pot, but he endured it very stoically. He's a lovely man and a wonderful brother-in-law.

I hope you have a lovely Christmas, Em, dear. I look forward to seeing you in the New Year. We shall face the season together and see what excitement 1845 will bring us.

—Excerpt of a letter to Miss Emmeline Knight (daughter of Lady Helena and Mr Gabriel Knight) from Miss Alana Cadogan (daughter of the Hon'ble Mr Jerome and Mrs Bonnie Cadogan).

16th December 1844, Heart's Folly, East Sussex.

"Isn't it a beautiful place?" Emmeline said with a sigh, tilting her head up and closing her eyes as the weak winter sunshine warmed her skin. There had been a hard frost last night, and the grass sparkled white, a perfect winter vista.

"It's wonderful," Torie agreed, staring back at Heart's Folly with pleasure though she tugged her cloak a little closer, for it was bitterly cold. It was worth braving the icy morning, though, for the views of both the house and the surrounding countryside were magnificent.

The Elizabethan manor house was set on high ground and had commanding views over the Weald and Sussex Downs. Built of local flint and stone, it was very much part of its environment and looked as if it had stood forever and would never do otherwise. Yet, despite the strength of its walls and its grandeur, it was a pretty place; the sunlight glinted on the leaded light windows and invited you in. Torie longed to explore, but she was trying to behave herself. Mr Godwin was already vastly intimidated by her father being a duke. If he discovered she delighted in running about exploring hidden doors and searching for ghosts, he'd run away even faster than he was currently doing.

"What are you going to do about Mr Godwin, then?" Emmeline asked, sliding her arm through Torie's as they carried on walking.

A chill wind tugged at their skirts and bonnets and the frozen grass crunched beneath their feet with each step.

Torie shrugged. "Bide my time," she said with a grin. "He admitted that he liked me last night, after all. It's only the inequality in our positions that holds him back. I think Lady Millicent hurt him very deeply."

"The poor man," Em said, her expression full of sympathy.

Torie nodded. "I could shake her. She looked like butter wouldn't melt, did she not? And yet all the time she was batting her eyelashes at Mr Godwin, she was engaged. Surely she could see he was in earnest? I could," she added bitterly, for it had been terribly hard, watching him courting another lady when she could not do or say anything.

"Have you liked him for a long time, Torie? Why did you never say before?" Emmeline asked with a touch of reproach.

"I didn't know myself to begin with," Torie admitted ruefully. "He was often around in company with Evie, for where Louis goes, he goes. They're very good friends. And he was always so much fun, and so kind and polite. He never has a bad word to say about anyone and never boasts or makes people laugh at another's expense. I am so often surrounded by men puffing themselves up and trying to outdo each other by telling me how wealthy they are, how clever, what perfect shots, and fine horsemen… it's exhausting having to pretend to be impressed all the time."

Em laughed and squeezed Torie's arm. "Poor darling. How glad I am Mama married beneath her, according to those fools who view things in such a way. Papa is ten times better than most of the noblemen out there, for he earned everything he has. It wasn't just handed to him. But at least I must only deal with fortune hunters, not those snobs seeking to elevate their position. I can imagine how Mr Godwin shone out amongst all those conceited peacocks."

Torie nodded. "I didn't realise at first, but I was always so relieved when he appeared, glad to have someone sensible to talk to who wouldn't fall over themselves to impress me. He was always so honestly himself, and… and then I began to miss him when he didn't appear, and then I realised how handsome he was. I mean, I know he's not beautiful like the comte, nor a golden Adonis like Pip, but he *is* handsome, and he has the loveliest eyes, Em. They're a sort of golden hazel, and so warm, and…."

She blushed as she noticed her friend's expression.

"Oh, Torie, you are in a bad way."

Torie threw up her hands. "I know!" she wailed, and then laughed as Em hugged her tight.

"Come along, you poor lovesick goose," Emmeline said, tugging her back towards the house. "I'm starving and I don't want to miss breakfast."

Torie huffed. "Aren't you at least in love with someone? You usually are. At least I could feel we were both suffering together."

"No, there's no one," Em said cheerfully, only snorting with amusement as Torie scowled at her.

"Haven't you met *anyone* interesting?"

"Oh, interesting, certainly," she replied, grinning. "But I'm not in love with him."

Torie pounced all the same. "Who?"

With Em, it was probably only a matter of time. She had the most romantic heart and longed for a grand passion to sweep her off her feet in the most dramatic way possible.

"Wrexham," she said, as they retraced their steps back towards the house.

"The Marquess of Wrexham? Oh, of course. You sat next to him at Mama's dinner for Lord Latimer." Torie said, screwing up her nose. "His father, the duke, is a horrid old man. I cannot help but pity him for that."

"So do I, and for all the things people say about him, but Wrexham is not the least bit mad, which is what I'd heard, though he is rather a devil," Emmeline said thoughtfully. "His being blind makes the stupid *ton* uncomfortable, though, so all those people who were once his friends would rather not speak to him. It makes me furious on his behalf, for it must be dreadfully isolating. I didn't know it that night, but Aunt Prue said his father practically keeps him a prisoner since he lost his sight."

Torie nodded. "Mama told me Sefton *insisted* she invite him. Can you imagine the audacity of asking that of Mama in the first place? But she said he only did it hoping to humiliate the poor man by forcing him to endure a formal dinner."

Emmeline's face darkened. "I didn't know that. What a vile man to do that to his own son! But why? Why would he want to humiliate his heir in public like that?"

Torie shrugged. "I don't know, but Mama says they despise each other. I'm so glad we weren't born into such awful families, Em. I mean, Harry can be a bit of a trial and I could cheerfully murder Jules on occasion, but I love them dearly and would never want them to be the least bit unhappy."

"We are lucky indeed," Emmeline agreed thoughtfully and then exclaimed, as the sound of her stomach rumbling became perfectly audible.

Torie snorted. "Come along. We had best feed you before you swoon."

"Very best of cousins," Emmeline said happily, and the two of them ran together back to the house.

"Well," Evie said, staring outside as the wind howled past the window later that afternoon. Though the skies remained clear, the temperature had dropped further, and the wind picked up, making staying outside an uncomfortable idea. "I was going to suggest we gather greenery and choose a Christmas tree for the entrance hall today, but I think I'd rather stay indoors."

"I second that," Lady Balderston said, giving a little shiver at the thought of leaving her comfortable seat by the fire.

"A third from me," Florence added. She looked rather weary but happy, sitting with her baby daughter, Mabel, sleeping in her arms whilst Emmeline entertained her nephew, Oscar, with a wooden Noah's ark laid out on the floor in front of the fire.

"It doesn't look like a day for tramping about in woodland," Mr Godwin agreed sympathetically.

"What would you like to do instead, then? How about a tour of the house?" Evie suggested.

"Oh, yes, please!" Torie exclaimed at once, earning a grin from Evie.

"Well, I knew you'd say that," she said with a snort. "And I'll get Louis to tell you about the ghosts. I won't listen to his stories, they're too disturbing."

Torie widened her eyes in delight. "Ghosts? As in, more than one?"

"Well, you needn't look so delighted," Mr Godwin said. "I know you enjoy all that Gothic drama, but it gives me the creeps."

"Oh, but don't tell me you're afraid of ghosts, Mr Godwin, for I shan't believe it of you," Torie said, a little wickedly.

He sent her a look that suggested he knew her game before he replied. "Not afraid," he said with dignity. "But I'm in no hurry to meet with one either, and I don't reckon you would be if you thought about it for above a minute."

"Oh, don't bank on it, Barnaby, old man," Jules said, not taking his nose from out of the book he was reading. "Show her a dingy cellar or a secret chamber and she's in alt, unnatural creature that she is. I'd bet a walk in a graveyard on All Hallows' Eve would be her idea of a fine time."

Torie glowered at her brother and reached over, plucking the book from his hands. "The Vampyre, by John William Polidori," she read aloud. "Well, there's the pot calling the kettle black."

"Give that back," Jules grumbled, snatching it from her. "I was just getting to the good bit."

"There's no such thing as ghosts, nor vampires," Lady Balderston said firmly. "Stuff and nonsense."

"Quite right, Hester," the Duke of Axton said, nodding his approval. "Glad to see you've gained a bit of sense over the years."

"Oh, more than a bit, Axton," the lady shot back, glaring at him.

Axton just grinned and settled himself in the chair more comfortably, apparently satisfied at having riled her.

"Well, who is coming, then?" Evie asked, giving her husband a nudge. "Louis, you'll give them some of the history, won't you?"

"If it would please our guests," he replied easily, setting the book he'd been reading aside. "If you want to gather everyone who is interested, I shall be in the entrance hall in twenty minutes. Does that suit?"

"Perfect," Evie beamed. "Torie, come and help me see who else wants to come."

Twenty minutes later, Louis led Torie, Barnaby and his Aunt Hester, Axton, Jules, Aggie and Fred on a tour of the house. Torie listened in fascination as he showed them around the magnificent building, explaining about the work that had been done, which was extensive. It was a splendid home, grand and yet welcoming, with plenty of cosy places to curl up and be comfortable with a good book, as well as opulent public rooms, meant to impress. But she was most captivated of all when they came to the west wing, which had yet to be renovated. Louis told them all sternly that they were not to come here unescorted, for parts of the building were unsafe and best avoided. It was gloomy with no lamps lit, which only added to the sombre atmosphere. Holland covers draped the remaining furniture, giving the rooms a ghostly aspect that made the hairs on the back of Torie's neck prickle.

"Are there any secret tunnels or priest holes?" she demanded of Louis, who smiled.

"Certainly, though I suspect we've not found them all yet. There is a priest hole hidden in the library, and a tunnel that goes from the dining room to the site of the original kitchens. According to local lore, there are more, though. There is said to be a ghost that guards the entrance to one tunnel, that of a loyal servant. There are stories about the courageous chatelaine, Mrs Payne, too. She still watches over the house she loved so much, and can be seen standing on the front step at dusk... not that we've seen her ourselves. Not yet, anyway. Mrs Payne's husband was fighting for the Royalist cause, and she was left alone here with her daughters.

One day, soldiers arrived to take the house. She, her children, and all her staff, armed themselves and defended Heart's Folly against the Parliamentarians, who did their utmost to take the property and destroy it. Her courage in the face of such opposition is quite staggering, for they were only sixty in all against three hundred men, but she kept the property safe from Cromwell's forces for many months, until her husband and his men came and relieved them. It is said she hid her most precious possessions to keep them from Cromwell during the civil wars. The story goes that the lady promised God she would never retrieve them if he kept her people safe, and she never did. So, if the legend is true, there is a treasure hidden somewhere on the property, but no one knows where."

Torie stared at Louis. Her expression must have been a picture because he gave a snort of laughter. "Do you want a shovel, my lady? I shall speak to the head gardener."

Torie was so entranced by the story she did not even protest at his teasing.

"Treasure?" she whispered in awe. "Hidden by the lady who fought off Cromwell's men?"

"Well, now you've done it," Jules said, shaking his head. "I hope you don't mind company, for you'll not get rid of her now. Not until she's poked about in every corner, opened every door, looked under every floorboard. A dog with a bone is our Torie once she gets an idea in her head."

Torie glared at him. "Just because you don't have a romantic bone in your body, Jules. Oh, but just imagine it. The lady desperately hiding the things she held most dear whilst the enemy gathered outside the walls, determined to destroy her home and take anything of value. However did she do it, I wonder? Can't you imagine her taking up arms with her daughters beside her? It's… It's inspirational," she said, feeling quite emotional.

Louis nodded. "I quite agree, Cromwell's men were fools to underestimate her. In my experience, there is no more formidable sight than a woman intent on keeping those she loves safe. I can imagine Lady Balderston in such a role, with no difficulty whatsoever."

Barnaby's aunt grew a little pink at the compliment but inclined her head. "Thank you, Louis, and I believe you are correct. I should have no difficulty in shooting anyone with the temerity of believing they could breach *my* walls," she said coolly, skewering Axton with a look no one had any difficulty interpreting.

Louis' lips twitched, and he moved them hurriedly on, but Torie lingered, moving to stare out of the window, her imagination running riot as she conjured the vision of Mrs Payne standing in this exact spot, spying the lines of soldiers in the distance, and steeling herself to do battle.

After dinner, everyone lingered in the parlour Evie and Louis had adopted as their favourite place in the house. In daylight hours it was a large, sunny parlour, but of an evening, once the curtains were drawn and the fire blazed merrily in the hearth, it was cosy and intimate, with lots of comfortable furniture and footstools, soft cushions and cashmere throws for anyone feeling a chill. A peaceful atmosphere reigned as the guests chatted, played cards, or read, as was their preference. Barnaby was not in the mood for cards and had settled himself down with a book, though so far he'd read the same page three times and still didn't have the foggiest idea what it had said.

Behind him, Aggie and Fred were talking, though the conversation—which they clearly did not know he could hear—was becoming somewhat heated.

"She *is* an idiot," Fred said firmly. "I never heard of such a hare-brained thing in all my life."

"How is it hare-brained for her to go off alone, and not for you?" Aggie demanded.

There was an impatient tut from Fred. "For one, I'm a man."

Aggie greeted this comment with a sceptical noise unlikely to endear her to her friend. Sure enough, Fred's voice was terse as he carried on.

"For another, I was not setting off merely to amuse myself, but in order to keep a good friend from behaving like a lunatic."

"I was not behaving like a lunatic, and you know as well as I do that I have far more experience of being alone in dangerous places than you do," Aggie countered furiously.

There was a taut silence before Fred spoke again. "You have no idea how much I wish that were not true, Aggie," he said softly. "But that was a lifetime ago now. You're a lady, remember, with people that love you, and you must not put yourself in such danger again. Promise me?"

Aggie sighed, her anger dissipating. "I'll try not to give anyone who cares for me such a fright again, Fred. I promise, but I do think you are a little hard on Cat. She only wanted an adventure of her own and she was awfully unlucky."

Fred snorted. "She could have been a deal unluckier, and that we have Kilbane to thank for getting her home safely beggars belief."

"Well, Cat insists he's not as awful as everyone says. Perhaps she has a point."

There was a choked sound and Barnaby could well imagine Fred fighting to bite back a scathing comment.

"No. She does not," he said succinctly. "And don't you go imagining otherwise. Now, are you playing this wretched game, or aren't you?"

"Yes, but it's your turn," Aggie retorted. "Do pay attention."

Barnaby hid a smile and, despite his best intentions, his gaze drifted to the other side of the room. Lady Victoria was poring over an enormous book which was propped on her knees and Mr Felix Knight, sitting close beside her, was doing likewise. Their dark heads were close together, the two of them whispering. Felix lifted his head and laughed, his green eyes sparkling with amusement as Torie grinned at him.

Barnaby smothered a surge of irritation, reminding himself they were cousins and more like brother and sister, before scolding himself soundly for even caring. Lady Victoria would marry someone else, not him, and so he had no business getting all possessive and jealous when she would never be his. That idea only made him increasingly irritable, and so he got up and paced to the window. He tugged the curtain aside and looked out.

"The wind has dropped," Louis observed as he came to stand beside Barnaby, holding out a glass of cognac.

"Thank you," Barnaby replied. "Yes, a calmer day tomorrow, I think."

Louis moved closer and lowered his voice. "*Alors,* what do you know about your aunt and Axton? I think there is history there, *n'est-ce pas*?"

Barnaby nodded. "That's right. Though Aunt Hester never speaks of it. Mother told me, though. They were close once, when they were young, I mean. Everyone thought she'd be his duchess. Even Hester, if my mother is to be believed. Mind, she's jealous of Hester, if you ask me, so I can't be certain it wasn't said out of spite."

"Perhaps it was, but I suspected as much," Louis replied with a thoughtful nod. "What happened?"

Barnaby shrugged. "From what I heard, the old duke and duchess stepped in and told Axton Hester was beneath him and he needed to remember his duty. Axton's pa had betrothed him to some other duke's daughter from the cradle, by all accounts. So they forced him to marry his father's choice of bride. The lady in question didn't like the arrangement any more than Axton did as it

45

turns out. They were at daggers drawn until the day she died, and Axton and Hester never spoke again."

"And he has loved her all these years," Louis mused, considering Axton, who was snoring gently in the chair by the fire.

Aunt Hester was stabbing a needle into an embroidery hoop with rather more violence than was perhaps necessary, glowering at the duke at intervals.

"Well, now I don't know about that. She's only just begun speaking to him again and the two of them fight like cat and dog these days," Barnaby said, shaking his head. "I don't reckon my aunt ever forgave him. Can't say I blame her, either."

"Ah, but Barnaby, do you not remember hearing what Lady Bainbridge had to endure when she encountered her husband's grandmother? The old harridan treated her most cruelly. I can only imagine how she would have dealt with her own son. I think perhaps you underestimate the pressure brought to bear upon Axton."

"But if he loved her…." Barnaby protested.

Louis raised an eyebrow at him and smiled in such a way that Barnaby paused.

"What?"

"Mon ami, I think perhaps you should listen to your own advice before you make a terrible mistake."

Barnaby scowled at Louis. "It's not at all the same thing. I am not in love with the lady, nor her with me. I am being sensible and ensuring we do not get ourselves in such a… a bind, by stopping things before they begin."

Louis sighed, giving him a look of such fond exasperation that Barnaby only felt increasingly irritated. "But the heart is not a sensible organ, Barnaby, and you cannot force it to do something it does not wish to. Perhaps this is something you must learn for yourself, though."

"Oh, pack it in, Louis," Barnaby said with a huff. "I'm not some green boy, you know. I promise you, I'm happier for you and Evie than I can say but I've had about all the romantic nonsense I can take for one day, thank you very much. I'm going to bed."

With that, Barnaby downed what remained of his cognac, handed the empty glass back to his host, and bade everyone goodnight.

Chapter 3

Dearest Aggie,

I have finally been allowed to write to you again. You cannot know what agony it has been not to correspond with you or anyone else. Thank you so much for the letters you sent. I was even forbidden to read those for the first sennight after the 'incident', such was the depths of Papa's fury. I have never seen him so angry, though I know of course it was because I scared him half to death. Unfortunately, it coincided with a rare visit from Pip, where he and Papa had rather a fierce row. We have hardly seen my brother of late, and he is so secretive I know my parents fear he is in trouble, but Pip will not ask for help, nor confide in Papa. I think this hurts Papa very deeply, but I hope he understands it is not a lack of trust, it's just that none of us can bear to disappoint him. I can well imagine if Pip is in a fix, telling Papa will be the last thing he wants to do. Oh, Aggie, it is such a terrible thing to see that look in his eyes, far worse than his anger, which is always short-lived. Of course, Mama was upset — which makes Papa wretched too — and she begged

Papa to intervene, which he will not do. He says Pip is a man and if he does not ask for help, he cannot take matters into his own hands, much as he would like to.

So, you see, my little adventure only added fuel to a fire already burning, and the results were hardly surprising.

Yet, for all the trouble I have caused, I do not regret it. The talking machine was so fascinating, but that was not the most thrilling part of my adventure, and it was an adventure, Aggie, but I dare not write it in a letter, dear friend. If ever I am allowed out of the house again, I shall tell all, but for now, I wish you the merriest of Christmases and a happy New Year.

—Excerpt of a letter to Miss Agatha de Montluc (adopted daughter of Louis César and Evie de Montluc, Comte et Comtesse de Villen) from Lady Catherine 'Cat' Barrington (daughter of The Most Hon'ble Lucian and Matilda Barrington, Marquess, and Marchioness of Montagu).

17th December 1844, Heart's Folly, East Sussex.

The next morning the wind had dropped, and the residents of Heart's Folly woke to a glorious winter's morning. After breakfast, Torie stood on the front steps next to the dogcart and helped little Oscar feed a lump of sugar to the sturdy pony that was waiting patiently for the guests to gather. Though they weren't going far, they would need the cart to bring back the Christmas tree and the larger boughs of greenery that would decorate the fireplaces. They had provided smaller baskets for gathering the mistletoe and holly. Torie brushed the lingering grains of sugar from her gloved fingers and picked her basket up as Henry gathered up his son.

Louis and Evie stood on the steps, dictating who was going with whom to gather what. Most everyone had already set out, and Torie's heart fluttered as she still had not been directed and Mr Godwin had not yet appeared. Though they stood a little distance apart, with the pony between them, Victoria could still hear the conversation when he finally arrived outside.

"Barnaby, at last. I had almost given up hope," Louis said, greeting his friend. "As you are finally here, you will collect mistletoe, please, and escort Lady Victoria."

Torie's heart skipped until she heard the gentleman's response to this idea, which she ought to have expected. His irritation was quite audible.

"Louis, pack it in, now. You are not helping. There is no way on God's green earth I am escorting that woman through the woods alone."

"You're not alone, Barnaby," Evie protested. "We're all going down there. Indeed, we shall walk with you, we were only waiting for you—"

"No." His response was firm and unequivocal. "I do not wish to accompany the lady and that's an end to it."

Torie could not help but glance over at them, to see his expression as he said such a thing, and at that moment Evie noticed she was there.

"Oh, Torie, love," she said, clearly horrified that Torie had overheard the exchange.

Torie's cheeks burned. It was obvious Louis and Evie knew of her feelings and had been trying to help, which was sweet of them, but nonetheless mortifying in the circumstances. However, she was a duke's daughter, and she knew how to behave in the face of embarrassment. She put up her chin and buried her hurt feelings.

"It's of no matter. I shall go on my own. I believe I can manage such a task all by myself," she said, aware that her tone was too brittle but unable to soften it for fear of revealing the depths of her humiliation.

She turned before they could say another word, striding across the gardens, hurrying as fast as she could to get away from Mr Godwin, and Evie and Louis' sympathetic expressions.

"Nicely done, *mon ami,*" Louis said, glowering after the lady as she strode away, head held high, shoulders stiff.

Barnaby muttered a curse. "That was entirely your fault," he retorted. "If you hadn't been playing matchmaker, I would not have had cause to say such a thing."

"Oh, do stop squabbling," Evie said impatiently. "Barnaby, I do not care a jot who you blame, but now you simply must go after her and apologise. Did you not see the hurt in her eyes?"

A shaft of regret skewered his heart at Evie's words. Yes, he had seen the flash of pain before she had masked it so completely. That he had caused such feelings made him feel rather nauseated, though that he had the power to inflict such harm still seemed extraordinary. Perhaps because he had always been overshadowed by his older brothers—who were louder and dominated any conversation or gathering with the force of their presence—or perhaps because of late he had become used to standing in Louis' shadow, he was unaccustomed to being the centre of attention. To be the focus of Lady Victoria's regard seemed so farfetched he hardly knew what to make of it, but it seemed the lady was in earnest, and he had just stamped all over her feelings like the veriest lout.

"Fine. I'm going, but I will thank you to stop meddling between us, for you are not helping in the least," he said, regretting his terse words at once but too anxious to follow the lady to stop and amend them. So, he left his friends standing on the steps of Heart's Folly and hurried off after Lady Victoria.

She had already travelled a fair distance from the house, and Barnaby broke into a run to catch her. He could not help but admire the picture she made set against the frozen winter scene. Her warm winter gown was a pale green with a matching bonnet, though the satin ribbons were a deep forest green, making his imagination picture her as some delicate woodland creature running back to the safety of her home. A thick, dark green shawl striped in blue, pink and yellow, was wrapped tightly about her slender shoulders, the multicoloured fringe dancing as she hurried on.

"My lady," he called. "Lady Victoria, please wait."

She did not turn, though he knew she had heard from the stiffening of her shoulders.

"Victoria!" he tried again, wondering if this less formal approach might gain better results.

Suddenly she stopped, swinging around to face him with a huff. "Mr Godwin, you've made your feelings quite obvious to all. I promise you, I have received the message loud and clear. I shall not foist my company on you again."

Barnaby caught her up and blew out a breath of frustration. "You know that is not how things are, or why I prefer to keep away."

She snorted at that and walked off.

"Fine, then do as you wish and leave me alone. As I said, I shall not bother you again."

"You know I cannot do that," he protested, following her as she took the path that led into the trees. Ahead of them they could hear the faint sounds of laughter from the others, so Victoria turned to the right, plunging into the woods in the opposite direction. "Everyone else went that way," Barnaby pointed out, earning himself a glare of annoyance.

"Then do go and join them," she said, with icy politeness.

Barnaby sighed, with little choice but to follow her. He watched as she picked her way through the overgrowth, for there was no well-worn path here and her skirts hindered her passage. Barnaby kept close, afraid she would trip on a fallen branch, and then found himself hastily looking away as she lifted her skirts to step over a rotten log, giving him a tantalising glimpse of slender ankles.

"I really think we ought to join the others, Lady Victoria," he said, hoping to cajole her into turning back as the woodland was becoming thicker and less friendly. "It is a Christmas party, after all. We're supposed to be sociable."

She turned and shot him a volcanic look that felt as if it singed his skin, such was its impact.

"Or we can carry on stumbling into the wilderness," he added. "That is a perfectly valid option." A completely idiotic option, he thought inwardly, though he was sensible enough to keep that observation to himself. Barnaby sighed as a bramble caught at his coat and stopped to untangle the blasted thing, only to hear a gasp and a muffled thud.

"Oh, drat and bother!" the lady exclaimed.

Tugging free of the thorns, not heeding the damage it did to the fabric, Barnaby hurried to the heap of skirts and petticoats now decorating the forest floor.

"Victoria! Are you hurt?" he demanded, doing his utmost to ignore the long, elegant stocking clad legs on show as she'd sprawled in an undignified heap.

"Only my p-pride," she said crossly, though the hitch in her voice told him how mortified she was.

"Here, up you come." Barnaby reached down, grasping her hands in his and helping her to her feet.

Her bonnet had fallen off, dangling from her neck by its ribbons, and there were leaves in her hair, her cheeks flushed a beguiling pink from the cold and embarrassment. Barnaby felt a rush of tenderness towards her, needing to take away the sad glitter in her eyes, his heart aching as he saw the fierce way she held herself together, though her lip trembled slightly.

"Are you hurt?" he asked softly.

She shook her head, a sharp movement that was as brief as it was unconvincing.

"Show me," he urged.

Slowly, she swallowed and then raised her gloved hand. The tender skin between the edge of the glove and her sleeve had been badly scratched, blood staining the lace edge of her gown.

"Ouch," he said with sympathy, reaching for his handkerchief.

Carefully, he inspected the wound, removing any dirt with care, and then wrapped his handkerchief about her wrist.

"It's clean," he assured her with a wry smile.

She made an impatient sound, but she seemed less likely to burst into tears now, so that was something.

"Shall I take you back to the house?" he asked cautiously.

She shook her head, not looking at him.

Barnaby sighed. "Victoria—"

"What?" she demanded, turning to glare at him, her green eyes so fierce, so full of pride and uncertainty that he longed to take her in his arms, to kiss her until all those hard edges softened and he could make her smile again.

But that was foolishness. *That* was the road to destruction.

Yet, despite his instincts screaming at him to get away from her and fast, he could not leave her here, all glittering pride and hurt feelings. So, though a voice inside yelled at him to stop, he reached up and carefully removed the bits of leaf and debris from her thick, dark hair, smoothing an errant curl back behind her ear before reaching for her bonnet. He put it back on her head, untangling the knot of ribbons as she stood still for him, her gaze wary. He lifted her chin and tied a neat bow, as if she were a little girl, not a full-grown woman.

"There," he said quietly. "Almost as good as new."

"Almost," she repeated, the ghost of a smile at her lips, her tone rueful.

Barnaby held her gaze, aware of the glimmer of amusement in the green of her eyes. Her father had eyes that colour, peculiar to the Adolphus clan. The blood staining his handkerchief now might as well be bright blue, for eyes that deep shade of green marked her as being so far above him he felt giddy considering it.

Barnaby let out a breath and took a step back.

"Well, if not back to the house, where to, my lady?" he asked, too aware of the way the light in her eyes died as he broke the intimate moment, as he stepped away and returned to the formality between them upon which he insisted.

Her jaw tightened, her chin going up, and she looked around. Her dark eyebrows drew together. "What's that?"

Barnaby turned to look in the direction she was staring, seeing nothing but a thickening tangle of bramble and ivy amongst the trees.

"Trouble," he replied, losing patience with the idea of tramping farther into this unkempt wilderness. Louis had made great strides with the house and garden, but he needed people in here sooner rather than later to thin out this mess, which was doing none of the trees any good as they crowded together, blocking out the light.

Victoria ignored this and walked on.

"I really think—"

"Oh, do hush," she said impatiently. "I know what you think. You think we should all keep to our places and behave just as we ought, never stepping off the path or doing anything that might make people think badly of us."

"Oh, now, that's not fair," he said, stung by the accusation.

"Isn't it?" she demanded, quirking one elegantly arched eyebrow. "Prove it, then. Step off the path, Mr Godwin."

With challenge in her eyes, she turned away from him and walked purposefully onwards, tugging her skirts free of brambles with each step she took.

Barnaby clenched his hands, indignation and annoyance simmering within him. He was very tempted to leave the dratted creature here and go back to the house by himself, except… that was a big fat lie. What she actually tempted him to do, he really did not want to think about, because it was far, far too dangerous.

However, he could not leave the vexing woman out here alone. As much as he needed to put distance between them as soon as possible, his instincts would never allow him to leave her unattended, so he swallowed his ire, battened his less gentlemanly impulses firmly behind bars of iron self-control, and followed her deeper into trouble.

Though her wrist was stinging and throbbing horribly, she was certain there was something buried beneath the thick canopy of ivy. It looked as if there had been something solid there once, more than simply a thicket of trees and brambles.

"Ouch!"

Torie cursed as her foot plunged into a hole beneath the dense layer of dead leaves and bracken. Before she could even begin to overbalance, Mr Godwin's arm shot out, snatching her about the waist and hauling her back, saving her from falling again. She squealed in shock as she found herself held tight in his arms, her hands grasping his biceps to steady herself. Startled, she gazed up at him, suddenly viscerally aware of something she had not really noticed before: Mr Godwin was remarkably strong. Though she had admired the breadth of his shoulders, she had been ignorant of the depth of muscle she now discovered, hard and unyielding beneath her fingers. Her heart did a peculiar little dance behind her ribs, making her increasingly breathless.

"Just how many times must I pick you up before you give this up as a bad idea, you stubborn creature?" he demanded, his voice at once frustrated and amused.

Torie couldn't answer, could barely breathe, as the object of her desires for so many months held her tight in his arms. If she were bolder, she might have taken the opportunity to kiss him. Her sisters would have. Lottie and Eliza and, shockingly, even well-behaved Rosamund had been brave enough to reach out and take what they wanted, but they had been wanted in return and Mr Godwin... well, he didn't want her. Not enough to fight for her, anyway. Victoria had all the pride a duke's daughter might be entitled to, though it was only just enough not to throw herself into the arms of a man who kept rejecting her.

As she stared up at him, too shocked and beguiled by his nearness to move away, Mr Godwin stilled, his grasp on her waist firming, his hazel eyes lowering to focus on her mouth. Torie licked her lips nervously and his gaze darkened, tracking the movement avidly.

"Victoria!"

They both leapt as an imperious voice cut through the undergrowth. It was some distance off, but broke the spell quite effectively. Torie blushed and stepped out of Mr Godwin's embrace.

"Coming, Mama!" she called, aware of the breathless quality of her voice as she hurried off towards her mother and the rest of the gathering.

Chapter 4

Jules, you devil, where have you gone to ground this time?

Certain young ladies have been asking after you. You're in trouble, my friend, and none deserve it so richly. When are you back in town? I propose a club meeting of the Sons in the New Year. It's been too long since we took a head count and caught up with each other. You'll be pleased to hear that the club is thriving, and membership is up, despite you doing your utmost to drink the profits. Hades is a fitting name for our venture, but you need not try so very hard to play King of the Underworld. Others have this covered, believe me. Kilbane, for example, who turned up three nights ago. I toyed with the idea of denying him entry, but decided it would be more interesting to let him in. He's a wicked sod, but where he goes, it tends to get lively. It did, incidentally. You missed quite an evening.

You'll not believe this, but I bumped into Felix Knight the other day and he was badgering me to let him join us! In the first place, the last time I saw him, I swear he was about twelve years old, yet it can only have been a year or two ago, and now the fellow tells me he's twenty! How the hell did that happen? I felt positively ancient, Jules, old man. In the second, his father would have us by the balls if we let him anywhere near Hades, let alone inducted him as one of the Sons. How did he hear about us, though? That's what I want to know. Find out will you? I don't want our privacy jeopardised by curious children.

Is it true you and your family are spending the next few days with the Knights at Heart's Folly? In which case I might call in one morning. It's an easy enough ride from my parents' house, where I have promised to spend some time before they head off to Arabella's for Christmas, and I have some business to attend to in Lewes. So, I'll see you soon. You've been warned.

—Excerpt of a letter to Jules Adolphus, The Most Hon'ble Marquess of Blackstone (eldest son of Robert and Prunella Adolphus, Their Graces, The Duke and Duchess of Bedwin) from Mr Leo Hunt (eldest son of Mr and Mrs Nathanial and Alice Hunt).

18th December 1844, Heart's Folly, East Sussex.

"Are you sure you won't come?" Emmeline said, staring at Torie with concern in her eyes.

Torie shivered and wrapped her thick wool shawl tighter about her. The temperature had plummeted further overnight, and ominous clouds hung low in the sky. She wondered if they'd have a white Christmas this year, for snow did not seem unlikely.

"Quite sure," Torie replied, smiling at her friend. "I have things I want to do. I'll be quite content on my own, I assure you."

Torie kept her attention entirely on Emmeline, though she could feel Mr Godwin standing a little to her left, his gaze upon her.

"Shall I stay too?" Emmeline asked, which was typical of the dear creature, who would happily sacrifice her own pleasure for a friend without the slightest hesitation.

"No!" Torie exclaimed. "You've been looking forward to this trip, and you've still shopping to do, remember? I was lucky in finding the last things I needed before we came, so I'm all done."

"Well, if you're sure. I do still need to get a few things," Emmeline admitted.

"I am sure. I'm looking forward to doing some exploring on my own," she whispered so no one but Emmeline could hear.

"Oh!" Em said, her expression clearing. She frowned. "You'll be careful, though?"

Torie nodded, taking her hands. "I promise."

Their conversation halted at the sound of hooves on gravel, and everyone turned to look at the man riding up to the front of the house.

"Good morning!" called a cheery voice.

Torie gasped as she recognised the handsome rider. Tall, broad-shouldered and blond, with an irrepressible twinkle in his eyes, Leo Hunt was the image of his father.

"Leo!" Emmeline cried, as she and everyone else rushed to greet him.

He laughed and, handing his reins down to a groom who hurried forward, jumped to the ground with athletic grace.

"Prue, darling, you look more beautiful than ever," he said, enveloping the duchess in a warm embrace.

"Oh, you!" Prue said, laughing and pushing at his shoulders. "Put me down, you big lummox. How undignified."

"Oh, don't pretend you haven't missed me," he said, grinning at the way her cheeks grew pink.

"Well, of course we've missed you, you wicked boy, and whose fault is that? If you weren't so busy with all your wicked goings on, you might have time for us. And *must* you set Jules such a dreadful example? It isn't as if he needs the help to go to perdition."

"Mother!" Jules groaned, rolling his eyes.

Leo laughed and patted his friend heartily on the shoulder. "Well met, Jules. How do?"

"Marvellous," Jules replied dryly. "And dreadfully sorry to inform you, but we're off out Christmas shopping in Lewes. So, sadly, we cannot offer you tea and crumpets."

He pouted and made a sad face that had Leo snorting with amusement.

"I can see you are devastated to miss out on my visit, so I shall come with you. I told you I had things to do in Lewes, did I not?"

Jules groaned. "Fine, but do not gossip about me to my mother. She has quite enough information about my tarnished soul. Believe me, she needs no more."

"There's more?" Prue said, her gaze narrowing.

"Er...." Jules said, sending Leo a panicked glance.

Leo held out his hands. "Well, you walked into that with no help from me."

"We really should be going, Mother," Jules began, when Mr Godwin walked up to them.

"Leo?" he said in confusion. "Leo Hunt, is that you?"

Leo's eyes grew wide. "Oh, my word, Barmy Godwin! It's been an age. I keep seeing you in the distance at events, but never seem to track you down. How the devil are you?"

"*Barmy* Godwin? You two know each other?" Louis César asked, looking between them with interest.

"How do, Monsieur le Comte," Leo said, shaking Louis' hand with a smile. "Oh, yes, we go way back. At school together. Barnaby was two years below me, but he was the school's secret weapon."

Louis' eyebrows went up. "Secret weapon? *Barmy* Godwin? This I need to hear."

Leo laughed, a rich, infectious sound that had everyone's attention riveted upon him. "Sports. Barnaby's an absolute fiend. Ruthless, I tell you. Won more games for us than I can recall. Don't let those soulful eyes and that mild manner dupe you. Put him on a horse, on a football field, cricket pitch, or God help me, try sparring with him. He's an entirely different beast when there's a competition afoot."

Everyone swivelled to stare at Barnaby, their surprise so apparent that Torie felt quite annoyed on his behalf. The poor man turned pink, sending Leo a look of irritation.

"What nonsense," he muttered, tugging at his cravat.

"Oh, ho! Tell my mother that," Leo replied with a snort. "She's still not forgiven you for knocking me out cold that time. Lord, I had that shiner for weeks."

"Barnaby?" Louis said, staring at his friend as if he'd never seen him before. "I do recall you saying you were good at sports, but… is this true? Have you been hiding your light under a bushel all this time?"

"That was a long time ago," Barnaby said with a huff before glancing up at the sky. "If we're going, I think we ought to hurry. The sky is looking rather ominous."

"Also adept at changing the subject," Leo remarked with a smirk. "But we'll leave him be for now. Always was modest about his talents, old Barmy."

Barnaby returned a warning glare and walked towards one of the waiting carriages.

"Come along Leo, there's room with us," Jules said, waving him to follow them. "The groom will take care of your horse."

With an easy nod, Leo followed his friend and Torie turned her attention back to Emmeline.

"Well, it seems you're in for an entertaining day with Leo and Jules together," she said dryly.

Emmeline snorted. "Provided they don't start a riot. By the way, did you have any idea... about Mr Godwin, I mean?"

Torie thought about that. "No, not exactly, but I've always known there's far more to him than he lets people see. Leo is right: he's modest, not the sort to shout about himself or want to be the centre of attention. He's always making certain everyone else is happy and entertained rather than trying to make himself look good. It's one of the things I've always admired most about him."

"Ah, Torie. If I get to speak to the man today, I shall tell him how wonderful you are and—by the time he gets home—he'll be thoroughly in love with you."

Torie gave a squeak of alarm. "Don't you dare! He's already got the comte pushing him in my direction, which has naturally set him even harder against the idea. If you do it too, he'll likely run away and never be seen again. No," she said with a sigh. "Just leave it be. I'll not set my cap for a man when he's made it so obvious he doesn't want to get involved."

"Oh," Emmeline said with a dejected sigh. "Shall I stay with you? I don't like to leave you all alone when you're sad."

"I'm not the least bit sad," Torie said at once, forcing a bright smile. "A little disappointed, that's all, but I have a mystery to unravel and treasure to find. Who on earth could be sad in those circumstances?"

"Well, probably not you," Emmeline conceded with a wry smile.

"Exactly. Now, run along before they go without you. I shall see you later."

"If you're sure, then?" she asked.

Torie nodded and Emmeline hugged her before hurrying to the waiting carriages.

Mr Godwin hesitated, standing outside of the carriage he was sharing with Evie and Louis.

"You're not coming?" he asked, something that looked like suspicion lurking in his hazel eyes.

"No," Torie said succinctly, not seeing why she ought to explain further.

"Why not?" he pressed.

She let out a sound of irritation and folded her arms. "I would think you'd be pleased. You're free of my presence for a whole day. Why not enjoy it?"

"That's what I'm asking myself," he grumbled. "But I have this prickling feeling down my spine that tells me you're up to no good."

"How very unpleasant," she said coolly. "But none of your affair, unless you have changed your mind and wish to spend the day with me?"

She quirked an eyebrow. He sighed, and she wondered if that had really been regret in his eyes and if she were very wicked for wishing it had been. He was only doing what he thought was best, after all, no matter how muddle-headed his thinking.

"Have a good day, Lady Victoria," he said politely, and took his place with the others.

Victoria stood on the doorstep and waved them off before hurrying back inside and collecting her bonnet and gloves. She had exploring to do.

Barnaby sat back against the squabs, quite unable to shake the sense of unease that nagged at him. The lady was up to something, he was certain of it. No doubt the moment their backs were turned she'd be off investigating the unrestored parts of the building, despite Louis' warnings to stay clear, or plunging back into the woods in pursuit of whatever it was she thought she'd seen.

His thoughts returned to that moment yesterday, with her in his arms, and he wondered what he would have done had the duchess not called for her when she had. He snorted inwardly, well aware of what he would have done. He'd been within moments of plunging headlong into catastrophe and kissing her. God, but it had been tempting, the way she had licked her lips, as if anticipating the touch of his mouth, the taste of his kiss. His skin tightened at the recollection, and he forced himself to think of something else… like the fact she might go into the woods alone and break her ankle, and not be found until tonight, when they returned, if the staff didn't notice she was missing. He tried to force the feeling away, telling himself he was being ridiculous. She was a strong-minded young woman, but by no means daft. Yet, the temperature was dropping, and he could not shake the vision of how enchanted she'd looked when Louis had told her about the treasure. She had been utterly spellbound. The chances of her not going off exploring were nil.

"Hell," he muttered.

Louis turned to look at him, frowning. "What is it?"

"Stop the carriage," Barnaby said, unable to hide the impatience in his tone.

Evie sat forward in her seat, regarding him with alarm. "Barnaby, whatever is the matter?"

He hesitated, wondering if he was being ridiculous, but he could not shake the sense of unease nagging at him. "I'm not going with you."

"Whyever not?" Evie asked, her face filled with concern.

"It's your fault," he told Louis irritably. "You ought never to have mentioned that dratted treasure. She'll be off tearing the place apart, you mark my words."

"Oh." Louis' expression cleared and grew remorseful. "Indeed, had I known what an imagination the young lady had… but too late now. I suppose she'll be so intrigued she'll be tempted to explore the unrestored parts of the house. That might not be wise."

"Exactly!" Barnaby snapped, rapping on the roof of the carriage.

"Oh, but Louis, since you spoke to Mr Trencher yesterday, he said it's not so—"

"Safe. Not so safe as it could be," Louis replied firmly. "Not for a young woman alone. Anything might happen. You had best ensure she's not up to mischief, my friend, though I shall regret losing your company. Is there anything I may purchase for you as you are missing the trip?"

"Yes, something for my aunt, drat you, Louis. The last thing I need is a day in Lady Victoria's company, but I shall spend the entire day imagining her falling through rotten floorboards or in a frozen pile, lost in the woods if I don't ensure she's not up to something."

"Indeed, and I am sorry for it, but you'd best hurry back, just in case."

Barnaby huffed and swung open the carriage door, jumping out without bothering to put down the steps. Glancing back in, he noticed Evie biting her lip as if trying not to laugh. He wondered what the devil was funny about the situation, but he was too annoyed to consider it. Instead, he closed the carriage door and strode down the long driveway that led back to Heart's Folly.

Chapter 5

Dearest Rex,

I am bored and desire company. That wretched brother of mine is no doubt making your life unbearable, so I want you to come and stay with me for Christmas, and your sister, Delia, naturally. After your last visit, I instructed the staff not to move so much as a candlestick out of place, so it will be just as you remember it. We shall have such a jolly time without the duke to spoil it.

I am depending on you, my boy, or I shall be piteously alone for the season of goodwill.

—Excerpt of a letter to Leander Steyning, The Most Hon'ble Marquess of Wrexham from his aunt, The Lady Lucinda Steyning.

18th December 1844, Heart's Folly, East Sussex.

"Ouch!" Torie muttered a curse and tugged off her glove, sucking at the sore pad of her finger where she had accidentally stabbed herself with a bramble thorn.

She sighed, staring around her despondently. Exploring by herself was not as much fun as she'd hoped. One really needed a partner in crime for such an adventure. Perhaps she ought to have asked Emmeline to stay, but her friend had been looking forward to her day out and Torie did not want to spoil it for her. Emmeline did not share her fascination with Gothic tales, ghosts and hidden treasure. Indeed, the mere mention of phantoms was enough to turn the girl quite green. Torie smiled at the thought. She was a dear creature and a good friend, but not one for exploring the woods in the freezing cold. So, Torie owed it to her to have something to report, or the poor thing would feel guilty for leaving her by herself... and that wouldn't do at all.

Pulling her glove back on, she strode resolutely through the thickening trees and undergrowth, doing her best to avoid getting snagged on twigs and brambles. Layers of skirts and petticoats were not ideal for such a venture, but she would not let the stupid fashions of the day hinder her any more than need be. Mama was always cursing the new fashions. In her day, women had been much less restricted, but the new corsets made bending impossible, and the tight dropped shoulders hindered the ability to even lift your arms. Mama said the men of society were trying to restrain women in all aspects of their lives and that these new fashions were nothing more than a cage hidden behind layers of pretty silk and lace. Torie was inclined to agree, but society would also judge you harshly for doing away with corsets or not dressing appropriately. Much as it made her mother wild, there was little choice other than to conform, though Mama rebelled in other ways, supporting many women's charities that promoted education and opportunities for women in all walks of life, and by raising her daughters to be independent thinkers.

Torie knew that was why she could not stomach the idea of marrying most any of the men who would be considered eligible for a woman of her station. Nearly all of them would think of her as property, would take her dowry and spend it as they saw fit. She would be nothing more than another possession, the mother of the next generation, expected to turn a blind eye to infidelity and to be the perfect hostess whenever her husband needed to curry favour, whether politically or socially. No. That was not enough. Thank heavens her parents agreed wholeheartedly and would never force a match, but it was still a dismal state of affairs. For there was Barnaby, so good and honourable, and quite able to appreciate the fact that she had a brain in her head, even if he was a tad overprotective. She sighed.

"Stop it. Stop thinking about Barnaby dratted Godwin," she scolded herself, and then paused as she recognised the overgrown shape before her. "Oh! I found it," she said with relief.

Hurrying closer, she surveyed the thick tangle of ivy and bramble. It was definitely a building, a small one and in a poor state of repair beneath the undergrowth... was that a tree growing out of the roof? Torie made her way around the building, peering through the tangle to what lay beneath. It was built from the same flint and stone as the house, though it was a tiny building in comparison, and she wondered what use it had served. Digging into her pocket, she drew out the secateurs she had borrowed from one of the gardeners and began clipping away at what she suspected might be the entrance. Some twenty minutes later, she gave a little yip of triumph as she saw she had been quite correct. Behind the wall of ivy was a solid oak door.

Doggedly, she returned to her work, snipping away until her fingers ached, but finally there was enough space to stand before the door and reach the handle. Torie turned it, her heart pounding with excitement, but although the handle turned, the door was stuck.

"Oh, bother," she muttered, but it was too tantalising to come this far. She needed to get inside. Determined now, she set her shoulder to the door and pushed. Nothing. Torie took a deep breath and tried again. The door did not budge. She glared at it in frustration. "Now you listen here. If you think I'm leaving before I've looked inside, you've another think coming. I do not need some big, strong man to open the door for me. I don't!" she repeated crossly, and slammed her shoulder against the door, putting all her weight behind it. It moved. Only a tiny bit, but it had definitely moved.

"Ha!" she exclaimed, so delighted she did not care that the arm of her gown was thick with dust.

Instead, she did it again, and again, and with each push the door protested and creaked, but opened a little farther. By the time there was enough space for Torie to push through, she was sweaty and breathless, but triumphant. She'd done it.

Squeezing her skirts through the narrow opening was tricky and left her covered with dirt and cobwebs. Torie could only imagine the look on her maid's face when she saw the damage she'd done to her gown. She would have to give the poor woman an extra afternoon off or buy her something nice to make up for the work she was creating.

But, once she was inside, everything else was forgotten.

It was a chapel. A tiny forgotten chapel in the woods. Miraculously, the windows were mostly intact, and a strange green light filtered through the ivy leaves, bathing the intimate space in dusty shades of emerald, and giving Torie the oddest notions about fairies and mythical creatures. She was so lost in rapturous wonder, her imagination running wild, that she did not notice the scratching of tiny rodent feet, nor the scurrying sound, until something skittered across her toes. She screamed.

Barnaby was in a mood. What kind of mood, he was not entirely certain, as there were too many emotions seething inside him to pinpoint one. As a rule, he was an even-tempered sort of fellow who preferred to look on the bright side of life. Though as susceptible to melancholy as anyone else, he had decided long ago that there was little point in worrying about things he could not change, and his life was a deal jollier if he concentrated on things that made him happy.

For example, his parents did not approve of him. They thought him a dimwit and predicted he would never amount to anything. Family events tended towards the torturous, with stilted conversations and pointed questions about his future, and his unmarried status, that made him feel every bit the failure they expected him to be. So, three years ago, he had decided to save himself the misery, and simply stopped going. He was not entirely certain anyone had noticed. Certainly they'd not come after him, wondering where he was. Now and then he saw his brothers about town, but further than a nod and a how do, they did not speak.

Once, that would have bothered him, for surely brothers ought to look out for one another, but he had come to accept that his brothers would never be that way. Instead, he had focused his attentions on people who appeared to appreciate his company, and especially Louis, who had seemed in desperate need of a confidant, and he had been well rewarded by a friendship of the like he had not expected. Through Louis he had also met several new friends—even Lord Latimer, who seemed to have mellowed towards him, despite their shaky start.

Leo had been right, though: Barnaby had excelled at sports at school. This had been partly self-defence. He'd never been clever academically. Latin and Greek never made the least bit of sense to him, anything requiring numbers made his head ache, and studying anything in a book gave him an unwelcome sense of drowning whilst sitting down, which seemed rather ridiculous but was nonetheless accurate. Naturally, boys being boys, he'd been made an object of scorn. But then he'd discovered—out of necessity— that he could run much faster than anyone else, he had an unerring sense of balance and sharp reflexes, and a desire to win that made him quite ruthless when the opportunity arose.

This, finally, had made him popular when there was a game at stake, but he had never quite got the knack of making close friends, or of being one of the boys. When they started singing bawdy songs and speaking coarsely about this girl or that, and what they had or had not done with her, or wished to do, he always felt uncomfortable. It seemed wrong to him to talk so about a young lady, no matter if she had been as willing and enthusiastic as the fellows made out. Not that he had been entirely innocent. He'd had his share of willing partners too, but he'd always been discreet, and no one had ever known or had cause to speculate about his affairs... one of which had been the headmaster's daughter.

Now she *had* been a willing partner, he recalled with a wry smile. Mary was used to the boys trailing after her, sending her love poems and professing their ardent admiration. As one of the few females within miles of the school, it was inevitable, but she had chosen Barnaby. She was married now, with three children, and doing very nicely for herself. They had bumped into each other last year and Mary had smiled with delight at seeing him, teasing him for not being wed and telling him to hurry up and get a move on. It had been good to see her again, especially looking so well and happy. He sighed. It seemed so simple for some people: find a partner, settle down, have children. But it was not simple at all. Not if he wanted to avoid the kind of marriage his parents had. Barnaby shuddered at the thought.

Yet his stupid heart kept getting stuck upon people he had no business falling in love with. Not that he had been in love with Millicent. Nor was he in love with Lady Victoria, nor going to be. She was just so... so... aggravating! The wretched woman had got under his skin and now he did not know what he was feeling, hence his odd mood. He was irritable, impatient and... and plain frustrated, and why not? Lady Victoria was without a doubt the most beautiful woman he had ever set eyes on. She made his heart race and his breath catch, his palms sweaty. In short, she turned him into a blithering idiot, and the addled creature still seemed to want him. Why, though? Whilst Barnaby was not one for blowing his own trumpet, he was not so lacking in self-worth that he indulged in false modesty. He knew his strengths, but a duke's daughter... well, he wasn't a halfwit, no matter what his parents believed.

Despite it all, he was drawn to her, forever turning in her direction like he was following the sun as she dazzled him from the heady heights of her position, so far above him. Wanting her when he knew it was pointless rankled. Nonetheless, here he was, searching for her because the lady could not resist the temptation of a treasure hunt, for which Barnaby could cheerfully strangle Louis. He spent half an hour fruitlessly searching the house, before realising she must have gone directly into the woods.

Immediately, he set off, retracing the path they'd taken.

As he walked, the first fat flakes of snow fell from an increasingly sombre looking sky. Barnaby muttered a curse and walked faster, the snow falling quicker with each step he took. Finally, he saw the overgrown shape the lady had been so fascinated by and was about to sigh with relief when a scream came from inside the building. His heart, already overwrought by the events of the past days, panicked. He ran.

Barnaby saw the door. The overgrowth had been trimmed to allow entry. There was a thin gap, too narrow for him to fit through with ease. Without another thought, he slammed against the door with all his might. It gave way immediately, and he barrelled inside.

Another scream rent the air, this one louder and more terrified than the last.

Barnaby ran to Victoria, grasping her forearms.

"What?" he demanded, his heart thudding too hard, too fast. "What is it? Are you hurt? What happened?"

"Oh!" she exclaimed, shoving at his chest. "You frightened me half to death!"

"I frightened *you?"* he exclaimed, perceiving she was not, as he had feared, grievously injured or being attacked by unknown assailants.

"Yes! What on earth do you mean by exploding in upon me in such a fashion?"

"You screamed!" he retorted, wishing for the first time in his entire life to shake a woman out of sheer frustration, such was his discomposure. He resisted the urge, but discovered he was unable to let go of her. "I thought you were being attacked! I thought you were hurt!"

"Oh, don't be ridiculous," she said impatiently. "It was only a rat. I was startled, that's all."

Barnaby grit his teeth. "Well, I did not know that."

"Well, there's no need to be testy!" she flung back at him. "I didn't ask you to come."

"No, more's the pity! If you had, I would have had the good sense to get your father to lock you in your room, you dreadful girl! What the devil were you thinking, coming out here alone on such a day? Does anyone even know you're here?"

"Well, you do, apparently," she snapped back, her green eyes flashing. They were brighter than ever in the dim, verdant light of the strange building they stood in. "Why are you here? I thought you were gone with the others."

"I did go, but we were halfway up the drive when I broke out in a cold sweat worrying that you would break your pretty neck!"

She coloured, sending him a volcanic look that in usual circumstances he would have heeded, but he was too far gone.

"I'm not an imbecile, nor am I a child," she said, her tone icy despite the fire in her eyes. "I am a grown woman, quite capable of making my own decisions, thank you very much."

"Yes, idiotic ones," he remarked savagely, making her gasp with shock.

He didn't even mean it… well, not entirely at least. He knew she was an intelligent woman, even if she was a bit rash, but his blood was up, frustration seethed beneath his skin, and it was all *her* fault.

"Oh! How on earth I could ever have believed myself in love with you is beyond me! You're as beastly as all the rest of them," she cried, and then fell silent, the blush of pink intensifying across her beautiful face as she realised what she'd said.

"In… In love?" Barnaby asked, utterly dumbfounded.

"No." She pressed her lips into a tight little line and shook her head, but her chest rose and fell too fast, the scarlet of her cheeks blazing, and Barnaby… snapped.

He hauled her into his arms and kissed her, and not gently either. He couldn't help himself, could hardly remember how to breathe, let alone behave like anything but a caveman. Yet he had never in his life been the kind of brute who forced his attentions on a woman, and he wasn't about to start now. Though he was overwrought and not quite in his right mind, he would have stopped instantly had the lady made the least protest, but she did not. In fact, the moment their lips touched, she became pliant and acquiescent in his arms, melting into him with an immediacy that was at once gratifying and had alarm bells screaming in his head.

But, even as the carillon din exploded in his ears, her arms were sliding around his neck, pulling him closer, and he was deaf to anything but the pounding of his own heart. He could feel it thudding in his chest, and… and in hers, too, for her soft body was pressed close to his and her heart was keeping time, matching his for speed and urgency. With one hand settled upon the small of her back, keeping her close, Barnaby cupped her face, tilting her head back as he encouraged her to let him in. He sensed her hesitancy and knew in that instant that she had not been kissed before, at least not like this. Gently, he encouraged her to trust him, to open to him, feeling a surge of sheer triumph as she did as he wanted, her tongue shy and tentative as it met his. She gasped at the intimate slide and caress, her entire body jolting, and Barnaby could not help but smile at her shock, except that then he remembered why she was so innocent, why she had been so closely guarded that she had never even been kissed.

Duke's daughter, duke's daughter, out of bounds, retreat, retreat.

Barnaby broke the kiss and stepped away from her, breathing hard. Confound it all, was he out of his bloody mind? Staring at Lady Victoria, her bonnet awry, hair all this way and that, and her lips swollen from the fervour of his kisses, it was not a difficult question to answer. Yes. Yes, he damned well was.

"That…" he began hoarsely. "That was a mistake."

As was what he'd just said, judging by the lady's expression.

She looked as if she wanted to throttle him, not that he could blame her after a kiss like that. Barnaby was still reeling himself, his blood surging through his veins, his nerves skittering about beneath his skin like demented ants. He felt giddy and disorientated and… and *good Lord!* Was there opium in her lip balm? It seemed the only reasonable explanation for the way desire thrummed through him, the sense of instant addiction to the taste of her leaving him taut as a bowstring.

"I see," she said, putting up her chin, and though her eyes glittered rather too brightly, generations of breeding confronted Barnaby in her cool green stare, reminding him of the futility of letting this go any further.

"I'm glad you do," he said, suddenly weary and sick at heart.

This was why they must stay away from one another. He'd never been so overwhelmed by temptation before. Even now, knowing it was the road to disaster, he wanted nothing more than to pull her back into his arms, but he had already hurt her feelings and, if he allowed this madness to continue, things could be a great deal worse.

"It's for the best, Victoria, you know it is."

"Do I indeed? How very wise of you to know what I am thinking."

"That's not what I meant, and you know it," he said, fighting to remain calm.

"Oh, so now this ability to read minds is mutual. How fascinating."

Barnaby snapped his mouth shut, a muscle ticking in his jaw as he fought not to reply and make the situation worse. Instead, he took a deep breath and gathered the shreds of his composure. "I apologise, my lady. The truth is, kissing you was the greatest honour of my life, but I shall not let temptation lead us both to ruin. One of us must keep our heads, and since you show no inclination for the task, I must try for both our sakes to—"

"Oh, go boil your head, Barnaby!"

Barnaby jolted in shock at the angry and none too polite words, watching as the lady turned on her heel and stalked away, heading farther into… into… what was this place, anyway? A church, he realised, staring about himself and then looking up as he saw daylight coming from the far end of the building. A small tree had grown through the floor, the flagstones uneven where the roots had levered them up. The trunk poked out through an opening in the roof. It looked as if the timbers had rotten, and the roof had collapsed in on itself.

"Victoria, don't go down there, it might not be safe," he called, hurrying after and realising before he'd finished speaking it had been the wrong thing to say. In the mood she was in, the chances of her doing anything he suggested were slim to none.

"Oh, just go back to the house and leave me be. I promise, I shall not throw myself at you again."

"Victoria," he said with a sigh. "Be reasonable."

"Why? To make your life easier? No, I don't think I shall be reasonable. I am heartily sick of being reasonable, well-behaved, biddable, and polite. I think, just for this morning, I shall be unreasonable, unmanageable, and downright bloody-minded. So there."

At least she had restrained herself from sticking her tongue out at him, Barnaby thought ruefully.

"Fair enough," he said, for he supposed it was.

He had often thought strong-willed, capable women like Victoria and Evie must be constantly biting their tongues or simmering with frustration when men talked to them as if they were simpletons, or gave them advice they had neither solicited nor required. He had seen it happen repeatedly, and seen the way their eyes glazed over, the frozen, polite masks sitting on their faces as they no doubt ground their teeth to dust. So, if Victoria wished to take her bad mood out upon him, he supposed it was the least he could do to endure it.

"It is rather charming, in an abandoned, rat-infested way," he offered, trying to smooth down a few of her ruffled feathers. "You did well to find it."

She shot him a sceptical glance. "Don't mention rats," she muttered. "I was trying to convince myself it had been a mouse."

"Oh, yes, probably," he agreed at once.

"I think it must be of an age with the house. It's built from the same materials."

Barnaby nodded. "A private chapel, I suppose. It's rather sweet, isn't it?"

Victoria nodded. "It's lovely. Such a shame it's been abandoned, but perhaps Evie and Louis will restore it, now I've found it."

"Yes, it's a shame to let it fall further into ruin, but there's a lot of work here to put it right. Victoria, I wish you would come away from that end of the building. It's clearly not safe."

The lady rolled her eyes at him. "It's obviously been this way for years. I don't see why it should fall down now. Besides, I want to see the altar. It's at a funny angle."

Barnaby sighed and went after her, stepping over thick ropes of ivy that crisscrossed the floor and wound over the abandoned pews. She was right, the altar looked to have been pushed to an odd angle.

"Oh, there's an opening, and stairs going down!" Victoria exclaimed, staring down at the floor, the excitement in her voice audible. "Look, the tree roots have pushed through and shifted the altar. Do you think it's a crypt?"

Barnaby shuddered at the idea but said nothing, not wanting for her to think him fainthearted. "I don't know, but I do know you're not going down there."

"Oh, Barnaby!" she said in frustration.

"No, hear me out." He raised a hand. "It's pitch black down there and we've no way of lighting it. If you must investigate, at least let's come prepared. We'll go back to the house and fetch a lamp, and—"

Silently, Victoria raised a dust covered lamp in one hand. "And there's a tinderbox and tapers over there," she added, looking appallingly smug.

Barnaby sighed inwardly but held his tongue.

"Oh, don't look so Friday-faced, you know as well as I do you were hoping to talk me out of coming back again, and there's no time like the present."

"Fine," he said, resigned. "If you can get the lamp lit, I'll go with you. If you can't, we'll return to the house and come back when we're better prepared."

With a bit of luck, the daughter of a duke didn't have the first clue about the workings of a tinderbox. Not when there was always an army of staff to do things for her.

"Fine," she replied, a determined glint in her eyes.

Victoria retrieved the tinderbox, an ancient looking brass affair Barnaby guessed was from the previous century. Sadly, the box was full and perfectly dry, and Barnaby watched as Victoria took out a small length of jute twine and unravelled it. Next, she took the striker and flint and a piece of char cloth, and began striking the flint, leaning over with her elbows on the altar to keep her arms steady. She was clumsy at first and it took her a few goes to produce a spark, though to be fair, she was making a better go of it than he'd expected. She must have watched it being done a thousand times, he supposed.

"My father taught me," she said tersely, making him jump, for he'd not spoken aloud.

"Oh," he said.

"I know what you're thinking," she carried on. "You think I'm a spoiled little princess who has never lifted a finger in her life. Well, perhaps I am spoiled, but I'm not useless, nor do I wish to be. Papa insisted on all of us learning basic skills in case we ever had need of them. So I know how to make a fire, and light a lamp. I know how to untack and groom my own horse. I can cook—not with a great deal of skill, admittedly, but I can—and I know how to clean a fireplace, and—"

"I don't think you're a spoiled princess," Barnaby cut in, before she could list all the practical things she had learned to do in order not to be thought pampered. "I just think you're used to getting your own way."

She snorted at that. "Oh, do you? There speaks a man."

"What's that supposed to mean?" he asked indignantly.

"Ask any woman when the last time was they got their own way," she retorted. "Society does not allow us to have our own way. I'd like to go out riding by myself, astride, not side-saddle. I'd like to drink brandy and port, and to stay at the table when the men discuss more interesting topics. I'd like to have a conversation about something important, something that matters, without being told I ought not to worry my pretty little head about such things, and I am so sick of this blasted corset!" she added, straightening with a gasp, a hand to her midriff.

Barnaby looked askance. "I cannot imagine your father would ever—"

"Oh, of course not! Papa is different. Mama is the most different woman of all, but she's a duchess and can afford to be. I want to find a man who lets me speak my mind without getting cross or telling me to hush, or that I'm getting overwrought. Someone who is kind and understanding and patient and not overbearing, but strong enough to hold his own with me. I thought that might be you. I thought you liked me," she added sadly, before giving a little crow of triumph as the char cloth caught a shower of sparks and a tiny orange glow appeared.

Barnaby started, surprised both by her words and her exclamation. He could not help but smile, however, as her eyes glittered with delight, and she wrapped the fluffy pile of unravelled jute carefully around the char cloth. Victoria pursed her lips and blew gently until a thin stream of smoke curled out from the tiny bundle. She shot him a grin, her victory in this little conquest provoking a rush of tenderness towards her, even if it meant he was honour-bound to poke around in a blasted crypt, of all things. Though that was an odd thing, now he thought about it.

"Why did they hide it?" he asked.

Victoria glanced up before turning her attention back to the smoky bundle she was coaxing into flame.

"Hide what?"

"The crypt. Why hide it beneath the altar?"

She frowned with concentration. "Body snatchers?"

"On a private estate?"

"Oh, that's a point. Well, I don't know, then, unless…."

Her eyes grew big and round. She stared at him, and then gave a shout of pain as the smoky bundle burst into flames. She dropped it into the lid of the tinderbox and snatched up a taper, lighting it and transferring the flame to the waiting lamp. To Barnaby's dismay, it lit at once, but rather than gloating about her success as he'd assumed, she turned back to him.

"The treasure! Mrs Payne hid the treasure, and no one ever found it. What if that's what's hidden down there?"

Before he could answer, she slid the glass cover back into place, reached for the lamp, and then dropped the handle with a hiss of pain.

"What is it?" Barnaby asked, stepping closer.

"Nothing, I… I burnt my hand a little, is all," she admitted sheepishly. "I'm not so good with a tinderbox as I made out, I suppose."

"Yes, you are, but I distracted you," Barnaby said, reaching for her hand. "Show me."

Victoria raised her palm, and Barnaby took it in his. It was not a severe burn, but there was a small angry red patch on her fair skin.

"Here," he said, reaching for his handkerchief and wrapping it around her hand. "Do you think you can go five minutes without hurting yourself? You're going to clean me out of handkerchiefs if you keep this up," he added, tying a neat knot with the ends. Then he made the mistake of turning his attention from her hand to her eyes.

"Thank you, Barnaby," she said softly, and oh, it sounded wonderful, the way she said his given name, the intimate way she spoke it, just the two of them together in this hidden place, lost in the woods. His heart kicked behind his ribs.

"You're welcome," he replied, disconcerted to discover he felt breathless, and sounded it too.

Barnaby swallowed, but found he could not look away from her, nor let go of her hand. The moment stretched out and everything they could be together, how it would feel to call her his own, became a weight, bearing down on him, making his lungs tighter and tighter. He could love her so easily, he realised, and with such a depth and breadth of feeling it felt like standing on the edge of a cliff. Beneath him lay a sheer drop, and falling would be disastrous. If she came to her senses and changed her mind, he would never recover. No, far safer to take a step back, to keep away from the edge, from danger, and yet he could not make himself move.

"Perhaps we ought to investigate before the oil runs out," she suggested.

"Oh, er… yes. Yes, best had." Barnaby shook himself out of his stupor and nodded, reaching for the lamp, though he could feel the blasted thing was at least half full. Plenty of time for poking around dead bodies, he thought with a grimace. "Here, hold it for a moment and let me see if I can push the altar back farther," he said, passing the lamp into her unbandaged hand.

Victoria held it aloft, illuminating the dark hole in the stone floor with steps leading down into the ground as Barnaby shoved at the heavy wooden altar. The damn thing weighed a ton and screeched against the stone flags as he put his shoulder to it and heaved. Finally, it gave way, leaving a gap wide enough for them to get through.

"There," he said, breathing hard. He turned to see Victoria staring at him.

"You're very strong," she said, and then bit her lip, her cheeks turning a becoming shade of pink in the lamplight.

"Oh. Um. I suppose," he said, feeling the back of his neck grow hot. "Best let me go first and check it's safe," he added, taking the lamp from her again.

He turned back to the hole, repressing a shudder of distaste as he held the lamp up and made his way down the rough stone steps. It was not far to go; the lamplight illuminating not a crypt, but a passageway. It was well made, if crude, not quite high enough for Barnaby to stand upright, and only wide enough to walk single file.

"Barnaby?" Victoria called.

"It's a tunnel," he shouted back up, more than relieved that there were no dead bodies to contend with, though the dark damp of the tunnel was quite horrifying enough in his opinion.

"Oh! See? I told you!" she exclaimed and, before he could say another word, he saw a dainty foot and slender ankle appear above him.

"Dash it all, Victoria, wait until… oh, here…" he said, as it became obvious she would not wait for him to help her down. Instead, he reached up to grasp her hand, keeping the lamp held high for her as she made her way down.

"This is so exciting! Let's see where it goes."

Barnaby was so close to denying her, to telling her it wasn't safe—and that it was foolish beyond measure to go poking about in tunnels as old as this one—but… but she was alight with pleasure, vibrating with anticipation, and he did not want to keep telling her no, did not want to be the man who kept her from doing all the things she wanted. So, he smothered a sigh and nodded.

"But you stay behind me, you hear?" he ordered her.

"Yes, Barnaby," she said meekly, clearly too delighted to do anything but agree with him. He still held her hand in his, and so he firmed his grip, holding the lantern aloft, and set out along the tunnel.

Chapter 6

My Lord Wrexham,

You are in grave danger.

Come to Lewes Railway station <u>alone</u> at two in the afternoon of the eighteenth, and I will reveal more.

—Excerpt of a letter to Leander Steyning, The Most Hon'ble Marquess of Wrexham from an anonymous correspondent.

18th December 1844, Lewes, East Sussex.

Leander Steyning, Marquess of Wrexham, or Rex to his intimates, was an idiot. A dim-witted, pigheaded idiot, because once again, his father had bested him, using his suspicions to lure him out of the safety of the small world he had created for himself and plunging him into the kind of nightmare that woke him in the middle of the night, sweating and breathless.

Humboldt had begged Rex to allow him to accompany him, but Rex had been adamant that only his coachman and two footmen come along. He had instructed the footmen, who were new to his aunt's employ, to return for him in an hour's time, which he deemed long enough for the mystery letter writer to hand over whatever information they had and depart. Only now, three hours later, and still with no concerned correspondent, nor returning footman having approached him, he could no longer deny the reality of his position. He had been duped.

His father, the duke, had employed those footmen, and no doubt bribed the coachman too. He had also written that letter—or more likely, paid someone else to write the letter—luring Rex outside of the safety of the small world he inhabited, knowing he would be helpless once he was sitting here alone, in a busy public space. Rex did not know why exactly his father loathed him as deeply as he did—though the feeling was certainly mutual by now—but he always had. Even when he'd been a boy, before Rex had realised the futility of his efforts, he had tried so damn hard to please him, to be the best, to study hard, be good at everything, to be popular… but the harder he tried, the more his father hated him. Once Rex had accepted that, they had mostly avoided each other. It was fine. It was just the way things were. But then he had lost his sight, and now his father not only loathed him, but Rex very much feared he wanted him dead. If he were dead, his half-brother, Cecil, would be next in line for the title, and the duke and Cecil were as thick as bloody thieves.

Still, murdering the heir to a dukedom was not a simple thing to do. Getting a blind man committed to a lunatic asylum and taking control of his assets and every aspect of his life, however… oh, not hard. Not hard at all. Especially when that blind man was idiot enough to walk into a trap. Yet he had, and here he was, sitting on a bench outside the railway station in a public place, with no idea of how he was going to get home.

The outside world pressed down upon him, the open space that gaped cavernously all around him growing teeth and claws, littered with mantraps and so much noise and bustle that his head spun. The sound of hurrying footsteps, the swish of skirts and snatches of conversation boiled around him, making his heart race as panic invaded his blood.

Stop it, stay calm. Breathe, you damned fool, he told himself severely. Panic was not his friend, that much he had learned in the years since he had lost his sight. He would simply have to ask someone to arrange a hackney for him, though in a small town like Lewes on a busy weekend he might be waiting awhile. Well, he could wait. Patience was another thing he'd had to learn in recent years. He'd never had much of it before, always wanting everything now, in the moment, but now his life had slowed to a crawl, and he'd had to make peace with that too.

Taking a deep breath, Rex calmed his racing heart and reminded himself that he was not utterly helpless. He was the Marquess of Wrexham, goddamn it, and that title commanded respect. Concentrating on the sound of the passers-by, he listened carefully, picking out the different steps moving past him. That one was a man; the sound of the footsteps was heavier, flatter, and he was in a hurry too. No, he was no good. The next was a couple, a man and a woman. He could hear the way the heel of her shoe rang out, a lighter sound on the paving slabs, but these two were moving slowly, their voices soft, perfume drifting on the air between them. Ah, lovers, and they would not be pleased to have their time together interrupted. He waited until they had gone, and another set of footsteps followed. A man's step, quick, but not hurried. Perhaps this one, then.

"Excuse me," Rex said, timing his question at the precise moment the man walked in front of him. The footsteps faltered.

"Are you addressing me, sir?"

"Yes. Forgive me for importuning you, but might I request your assistance?"

"What assistance do you require?" the man asked, his voice full of suspicion.

"There seems to have been some mix-up in the time of my arrival here, and my carriage has not come for me. Might I call upon you to find the nearest coaching inn and—"

"Sir, you might be well above my station and used to having your every need met with a snap of your fingers, but I'm no lackey. The nearest coaching inn is half a mile in that direction and your legs as able as mine, I don't doubt. Good day to you."

"No, wait, you don't understand…!" Rex called after him, before cursing under his breath.

The problem with his condition was that no one would know he was blind to look at him. Sometimes he tried to give people clues, with a walking stick, and dark glasses, which he did not really need, but riled his father—a bonus not to be ignored—but more often pride and anxiety made him prefer that people not know if they did not need to. Hubris would be the death of him, or at the very least, the reason he got locked away in an asylum. He could just hear his father talking about this little adventure, his voice troubled and apparently full of concern.

The poor boy was in the middle of the town all alone, what he was doing there I cannot fathom, some foolish nonsense about meeting someone giving him secret news. He thinks someone is trying to kill him, of all things. Paranoia is an increasing problem for him. A troubled mind, just like his uncle. He went blind too, swiftly followed by paranoia and madness, and though I hate to admit it… poor Leander is following the same path. Such a pity.

A shiver of panic ran down Rex's spine and his fingers tightened on the arm of the bench. Something cold and wet touched his face, and he started in surprise, reaching up to touch the spot, which was swiftly followed by another, and another. For a moment he could not think what it was and then he realised. It was snowing. Well, wasn't that just perfect? He was already frozen to the marrow from sitting here the past three hours without moving, and now it was snowing. His father might just kill him after all, and no one could ever blame him for it if Rex died of bloody pneumonia.

Panic rolled over him again, all his fears of being lost and alone, helpless in the great outdoors, pressing down on him with a smothering weight that made it hard to breathe. If only he knew the town a little better, he might not have been so helpless, but his aunt had only moved here recently. If he'd stopped to think for a moment that would have rung alarm bells, for why would someone with information about a plot to kill him contact him here, of all places? But it was too late for hindsight now. He needed to get back to his aunt's house before he damn well froze to death.

Determined, he tried to rein his terror back in, to think rationally, but then he jumped as a cacophony of barking erupted close to him. Rex gasped as he heard the scratch of claws and at least three dogs ran past, barking furiously. They were gone a moment later, but his nerves were shot, and it was becoming hard to think. His chest heaved as he attempted to calm himself once more.

"My lord?"

Wrexham leapt again at the soft voice, turning towards it like a drowning man clutching at a lifeline.

"Yes?" he said at once, hope blooming in his chest. "Yes, who is that?"

"My Lord Wrexham, it is Miss Knight. Miss Emmeline Knight. We met at the Duchess of Bedwin's dinner. I pray you will forgive me for approaching you, I do not wish to be intrusive, but... is everything...? Are you well, my lord?"

"Miss Knight," he said, the relief he felt so overwhelming he was uncertain if he wanted to laugh or cry. "Miss Knight, I am so very, very pleased to hear your voice."

There was too much emotion audible, he knew at once, too much obvious relief, but he could not help it.

"Lord Wrexham?" she said, and he heard the anxiety in the way she said his name now, heard the rustle of her skirts as she took a step closer and lowered her voice. "May I be of assistance to you?"

"You may, Miss Knight. Indeed, you may be the answer to my prayers, and I thank God for you."

Torie did not think there had been such a perfect moment in her life since she was a little girl, when things had been so much simpler. Here she was, exploring a long-forgotten tunnel, searching for treasure, and holding Barnaby Godwin's hand. Even though the wretched man was as exasperating as ever, he *had* kissed her, and had liked it too, if she knew anything. Not that she knew much about men and kissing. Her father had become rather overprotective where his daughters were concerned after what had happened with her two older sisters. Not that they had come to any harm, and they were both blissfully happy in their marriages. It was more that Papa hadn't had an inkling of what was going on under his nose, even though both Lottie and Eliza had been well chaperoned. So now, *well chaperoned* might as well be synonymous with living under house arrest, and the chances of Torie ever being alone with a man were slim to none.

Yet, here she was, alone in the dark with the man of her dreams, and Mama and Papa away shopping in Lewes. The thought had Torie suppressing a grin. It was certainly an opportunity not to be missed, especially not if she could persuade Barnaby to kiss her again. Oh, and what a kiss it had been. So much more than she could have imagined, so intimate and so… stirring. Even now, thinking about it, her cheeks heated, and her blood seemed to move faster through her veins. Something hot and liquid bloomed in her core, making her restless and… she let out a sigh.

Barnaby turned, holding the lamp up to look at her. "Is anything the matter?"

"N-No," she stammered, mortified, wondering if he could discern the route her thoughts had taken just by looking at her and her blazing cheeks.

He frowned a little, but turned back to concentrate on the tunnel as it changed direction, angling sharply to the right. Barnaby hesitated and Victoria squeezed his hand, knowing he was worrying on her account.

"Please," she pleaded.

His expression told her in no uncertain terms that he thought this was the height of stupidity, but he held his tongue and they walked on. They had been walking for almost five more minutes, easing past tree roots and brushing aside cobwebs, when Barnaby stopped again.

"This is ridiculous," he said. "We have no idea where we are going, no one knows we are here, if the tunnel gives way, if one of us has an accident—"

"Oh, but Barnaby," Victoria said, excitement bursting in her chest.

"No, Victoria, I must put my foot down. This is far enough—"

"Yes, it is," she said, almost laughing at the consternation on his face.

"It is?"

"Yes, look!" Victoria pointed to the edge of the spill of lamplight where she could just make out the end of the tunnel and the shadowy indication of a crude wooden door.

Barnaby followed her gaze, his expression one of astonishment. "Well, bless me."

"Did you really think it was a tunnel to nowhere?" Victoria asked, shaking her head at him.

"I was beginning to think it was leading us down to Hades. I'm still not convinced it isn't," he added darkly.

"Such a worrywart," Victoria said with a sigh.

"Well, one of us must try to use some sense when the other is a blessed hoyden."

Victoria stared at him in shock. *"Am I?"*

"Well, you needn't look so dashed pleased about it," he replied with a huff.

But Victoria was delighted with this news, viewing herself suddenly in a new light. Though she had always been fascinated by ghosts and Gothic novels, the idea of adventure and lost treasure and derring-do, she had never believed herself to be especially courageous. Not like her older sisters had been when pursuing their own happy-ever-afters, but if Barnaby thought her a hoyden... well, anything was possible. Filled with a sudden burst of confidence, she could not wait another moment for the next part of this adventure.

"Come along," she said, pushing past him in the narrow confines of the tunnel and heading directly for the door.

"Victoria, I told you to stay behind... oh, what's the use." Barnaby hurried after her, watching as she reached for the door handle and turned it.

There was a rusty sound, metallic creaking and protesting, but it turned, and Victoria pushed but the door only budged an inch and then stuck.

"Oh, bother," she said in frustration. "It's jammed."

"Here, let me try. Hold this."

Victoria watched in fascination as Barnaby set down the lantern and stripped off his coat, handing it to her. She did not know what he saw in her face as she took it from him, but he did not read her correctly, as usual.

"I'm not the Comte de Villen," he said, sounding irked. "I can't afford to mess up a good coat because I have three dozen more to choose from."

"I... I wasn't...." Victoria said helplessly, and then held her tongue, unable to tell him she had been gazing at him with admiration, for she had never seen him in shirtsleeves before.

She had never seen him anything but immaculately turned out. Now, after their time in the tunnel, he had dirt on his cheek and his hair was dishevelled, and watching him standing there rolling up his sleeves to expose strong forearms… it was a rougher, rumpled version of Barnaby that was intriguing and rather wonderful.

Barnaby turned back to the door and gave it an experimental push. Victoria held his coat against her as she watched. She could still feel the heat of his body in the material and, though she knew it was silly, she could not resist the temptation to lift the coat to her nose and inhale. Something warm and spicy, like ginger and clove, teased her senses, and a woodsy, mossy note of cedar. It made her imagine cosy nights in front of a fire, wrapped up in that scent, with Barnaby's arms around her. Victoria closed her eyes and sighed blissfully, and then gasped as she heard a thud, her eyes flying open to see Barnaby shoving at the door. It groaned but did not budge. Dust fell from the ceiling and Victoria coughed, rubbing it off her face as Barnaby stared suspiciously at the ceiling.

"This might not be safe," he said, concern in his voice. "Perhaps—"

"Oh, no. Please, Barnaby, we've come this far."

He looked back at her and sighed before returning his attention to the door. Victoria held her breath as she admired the breadth of his shoulders, wondering anew at how much strength the fine tailoring of his coat had hidden. Muttering under his breath, Barnaby stepped back and then threw his weight at the door again, hitting it hard with his shoulder. It gave, opening a bit more with a screech of protest, the ancient wood scraping painfully over the stone floor beneath it.

"I think the lintel has dropped, that's why it's so tight," he said, sounding a little breathless. "One more push should do it, though, I think."

Victoria watched in awe as he put his shoulder to the door again and pushed hard. Suddenly, the door gave way and Barnaby righted himself at the last moment before he fell headfirst into the darkness beyond. More dust fell, and he choked, moving out of the way and running a hand through his hair, messing it up even more than it had been. He was sweating a little from his efforts, and breathing hard. Victoria clutched his coat tighter. The desire to press herself against him, to revel in all that masculine heat and strength, was tantalising.

"Well, there you go, then," he said, picking the lantern up again and gesturing to the open door. "My lady wanted a Gothic adventure with tunnels and hidden rooms, and who am I to deny her?"

Victoria bit back a smile, delighted to hear the triumph in his voice, to see the satisfied amusement glittering in his eyes. No matter if he thought her fascination with ghosts and blood-curdling tales silly, he was pleased with himself for having provided a way in.

"Thank you, Barnaby," she said, moving closer. Victoria hesitated before him, dying to see what lay behind the door but unable to resist. She reached up and pushed his dusty hair back from his forehead, and then rubbed the streak of dirt from his cheek. "There, good as new," she said softly.

Barnaby's eyes darkened, his gaze falling to her mouth, and then he straightened, holding the lantern up. "Come along then," he said, and all trace of amusement was gone from his voice now, the words no nonsense and crisp.

Victoria sighed and followed him in.

Chapter 7

Dear Hester,

I am writing this as my carriage is loaded. Why I am stirring myself to leave the warmth and comfort of my home for a jolting, uncomfortable journey is beyond me. Oh, that's a fat lie, and we both know it. I am beside myself with joy. There, I said it. Happiness is something I view with the utmost suspicion after so many years of disappointment and sorrow, but to be spending Christmas with my grandson and his wife, and to know that they look forward to my presence, well, that is an unexpected gift at my time of life. I only hope they have that wretched dog under control now. I've had to leave Regina behind, and I know she'll sulk for days on my return.

I hope you have a lovely Christmas too, Hester, and if I might give you a piece of advice, don't let the past drag you down, don't turn your back on a chance of happiness. It's never too late. I know it seems unbelievable that I, the greatest cynic on earth, should say such a thing, but that is exactly why you ought to heed me. I had given up, and yet life gave me another chance, it gave me Wulfric and Cara, and, God willing, I will live to see the next generation before I shuffle off at last. Even though there is little time left for me, I am excited for the future, and you ought to be too. Grab hold of happiness with both hands, my dear, and never believe it is too late.

—Excerpt of a letter to Hester Henley, Lady Balderston, from Lady Lydia De Vere, The Right Hon'ble, The Dowager Viscountess Latimer.

18th December 1844, Lewes, East Sussex.

"Ah-ha, this is where you are hiding yourself," said a deep male voice.

The familiar, smug tones of the Duke of Axton had Hester jumping with such force she almost flung her knitting into the fire.

"Oh!" she exclaimed, putting one hand to her heaving chest. "Oh, you devil, Axton. Are you trying to kill me? What are you doing here, anyway? I thought you had gone with the others."

He smirked, looking appallingly pleased with himself. "That is what I wanted you to think, my dear," he said serenely. "For I knew that if I went, you'd stay, and if I stayed, you'd go. So... a little subterfuge, and now here we are, alone at last, and I think you might call me Alfred, or Alfie, if you prefer. You used to like that."

"Firstly, I am not your 'dear,'" Hester retorted, gathering up her knitting and shoving it haphazardly back into the tapestry bag she carried it about in. "Secondly, I don't have the least desire to be alone with you. I'm no green girl, dazzled by a fancy title, I'm afraid, *Axton*. Go bark up another tree, this one is full of crows."

He grinned at her, not looking the least bit discomposed by her set down.

"Firstly," he said, moving further into the room. "You have never in your life been dazzled by my title and, secondly, you have always been *my dear.*"

Though his eyes twinkled with mischief, she heard the way his voice softened, heard the sincerity there... but Axton always had been a charming blighter when the mood took him. The rest of the time, he was irascible, impossible, and downright imperious. Reminding herself firmly of these facts and, more pertinently, that he was not to be relied upon, she stood, smoothed down her skirts and, tapestry bag in hand, went to stalk past him.

The duke's hand shot out, grasping her wrist. It was only for a moment, his clasp releasing at once, but the touch was electric, jolting her back decades, making her remember what it had felt like all those years ago to be held in his arms, to be the focus of his attention. It had been intoxicating that he, of all people—handsome, arrogant, and so far above her—had professed himself in love with her, and she'd believed him. More fool her. Furious with him for raking up the past, for disturbing feelings she had buried so many decades ago and believed long dead, she turned to glare at him.

"What do you want, Axton?" The ghost of a smile hovered at his mouth, though somehow his expression remained grave. His gaze held hers and though she tried to stop it, she could not help but get drawn back into the past, into the stormy grey of his eyes. They could be as cold as the northern sea, but now they were soft with regret and... Hester looked away.

"Well?" she demanded.

He let out a huff of laughter. "I want so many things, Hester, but then you always said I was spoiled."

"You are."

The duke laughed and nodded. "My son's lovely wife, Bella, would agree, I don't doubt, but I'm not such a monster as all that, either. I was, I think, for a long time, but I— Christ, Hester, I was miserable. I've been miserable for bloody years, decades, and I don't want that anymore. Bainbridge taught me a lesson when he married for love. I never believed that mad boy would amount to anything, but God knows I'm proud of him. He's a better man than I ever was, but… but he's made me believe it might not be too late. Hester, I want to be happy. Since I walked away from you, I have had no peace, no contentment, nothing that came close to happiness. I want you. I want you back. I ought never to have let you go, I know that. I knew it then, but I was too bloody blind to see that duty was not reason enough to give you up. I was young and stupid, and I have paid the price for that. I don't want to pay it anymore."

"That's enough!" Hester said, startled to hear her voice tremble. What was the madman doing, stirring all this up again? "I am sorry you were unhappy, Axton. I truly am, but I was not. I married well, and I was content."

"I know," he said, nodding. "And I am grateful for that at least, grateful it was only my own heart I broke."

"Oh, pish," Hester said, hugging her knitting bag to her chest and glaring at him. "Are you losing your marbles? You never broke your heart over me. You're getting sentimental in your old age, that's all."

"Perhaps I am sentimental," he admitted. "But the rest is still true."

Hester gave an exasperated sigh. "The past is dead and gone, Axton. Our time is over. I'll not have you raking things up after… good heavens, it's fifty years since we were—"

"And yet I love you still."

Hester stared at him, feeling as though the ground had shifted beneath her feet, her carefully ordered world dismantling itself piece by piece as those words sank into her heart.

"Stop it," she said, her voice choked, and then she turned and ran from the room.

Barnaby held the lamp up, illuminating the space they had revealed. It was a small room, perhaps only ten feet wide by fifteen long and lined with shelves which appeared to be full of supplies. The bottles and jars were old and thick with dust, but obviously full. What looked like a bed frame and several moth-eaten chairs were ghostly shapes beneath holland covers. Barnaby wondered what on earth this place was. A priest hole, perhaps?

A chill breeze drifted past his neck, and he frowned, looking around until he saw a small opening at eye level, only a narrow slit an inch high. He moved closer, discovering ivy blocking the hole, and he tugged it aside, squinting out at a world turned white. The snow must have been falling thick and fast whilst they were underground. The view was far from expansive and did not help to orient him, for he could see nothing he recognised. There was only trees and undergrowth, and an expanse of snow.

"We can't stay here long," he said, gesturing outside. "The snow is already thick, the last thing we need—"

An ominous rumble overhead cut his words off and Barnaby did not think, only reacted. Grabbing Victoria, he pulled her to the far end of the room, pushing her down and covering her body with his own. Dust and debris showered down over them, making them cough. There was a groaning sound outside the door, then the splintering of wood followed by the dull thud of tons of earth and stone falling. Everything became eerily quiet.

"W-What was that?" Victoria asked as he sat back. She raised her head, her green eyes wide. "What just happened?"

"Are you hurt?" he asked, grasping her by her shoulders, his heart thudding. For all he knew, he'd led her into a death-trap. Perhaps the rest of the ceiling would fall in next, not that he was about to mention that to her. He let go of her and cupped her face, sliding down her shoulders and back down her arms, reassuring himself she was in one piece.

"I'm fine," she said, though Barnaby felt sick as he wondered what might have happened if the tunnel had given way a few seconds earlier.

Hell and damnation, she could have been killed, buried alive! It still might only be a matter of time. What the hell had he been thinking to allow this, to let her poke about in something so obviously dangerous?

Her cool hand cupped his cheek, her thumb stroking his skin. "I'm fine, Barnaby. You kept me safe. No harm done."

"No harm done," he said, forcefully suppressing the emotion simmering beneath his skin. He ran a hand through his hair, finding it gritty with dust, and eyed the ceiling above them. For now, all was still, but for how long?

Pull yourself together, Godwin.

The little opening he'd found to the outside meant this room was not entirely below ground, even if it were hidden from view. The roof was not going to fall in. That did not mean they were any better off, however, as no one had the faintest idea where they were. He took a breath before turning back to her, torn between needing to keep her calm and disbelief that she could not see how bad this was.

"You realise we are trapped? That was the sound of the tunnel collapsing outside the door. It might only be the section immediately outside the door, or it might be the entire tunnel. No one knows we are here, Victoria."

"Well, perhaps there's another way out," she suggested hopefully, far too calm for his equilibrium to cope with. "And if there's not, we'll wait for them to come and find us. They *will* come looking," she added, still far too reasonably for his nerves to stand. But then she was used to getting what she wanted with a snap of her fingers, why not a rescue party too?

He tried to keep his temper in check, to let her keep her illusion of all being well for the time being, but....

"Ah yes, once they return from shopping and we don't appear for dinner this evening, they will realise. How long will it take to discover us, I wonder? Even with a search party, it will be quite the challenge. No one knows we went to the woods, and the snow will have covered any trace of our tracks by now. No one knows about the chapel, or the tunnel, or this hidden room. So perhaps they'll find us, eventually, but not before we've spent at least a day, and likely the entire night, alone together. Perhaps several nights. Perhaps a week. Do you see where I am going with this?" he demanded, though he restrained himself from telling her he had some uncomfortable doubts about them being found at all.

She blanched at his words.

"Oh," she said, her voice flat, understanding dawning.

"Oh," he repeated, stung by the way she'd turned alabaster white.

Well, good. It was about time she was faced with reality. Perhaps now she'd stop harbouring foolish romantic notions about a man who couldn't afford to buy her preferred perfume, never mind all the gowns, slippers, hats, gloves, jewels and gewgaws a young woman of her breeding would expect as her due. Barnaby regarded her as she glared back at him. With sharp, angry movements, she tugged at the ribbons on her bonnet and flung the thing to the floor beside her.

"You must forgive me, Mr Godwin. In the excitement of our predicament, I had forgotten that marrying me was a fate worse than death," she said, sarcasm dripping from every word.

Barnaby had to admit, she really was single-minded. Wrongheaded, but single-minded. He opened his mouth to speak, to make her understand, but she beat him to it.

"Look, there's a spoon there, perhaps you can dig your way out? You've incentive enough to make it in time."

She turned her face away from him, but not before he saw the wounded look in her eyes. Barnaby groaned and rubbed a hand over his face. No matter her hurt feelings, he had to get them out of here before anyone discovered them missing. She might think marrying him was something she wanted, but the reality of it would be another matter when she did not have a new gown for every ball she attended, when her friends laughed behind her back, perhaps even shunned her for lowering herself by marrying him. Not that he believed her shallow, not in the least, but there were elements of her life she must surely take for granted, and she would resent losing them when they were gone.

He went to the door, which they had left half open, and was confronted with a solid wall of stone and soil. Barnaby glared at it furiously. The devil take it. He didn't even know if it was safe to clear the opening, or if that would make the already unstable tunnel collapse entirely. Yet it had looked so sturdy and well made. Confound him for a bloody fool. It would serve him right if they were trapped here for days, and he was forced to marry her.

The idea made his stomach flip with an odd combination of anticipation and horror. He wondered if Bedwin would castrate him for this. Perhaps he would think Barnaby had engineered the situation, but… no. That was ridiculous. There were easier ways of compromising a young woman than collapsing tunnels and hunts for hidden treasure. How absurd this was! All they needed now was the ghost of a mad monk and Victoria would be in alt, as Jules had suggested. Except, now that he turned to study her, all traces of her earlier excitement had vanished. Even the collapsing tunnel had not seemed to diminish her enjoyment of this mad adventure, but now she looked sad and lost. His heart clenched.

She was huddled in the corner where he had left her sitting on the cold stone floor. It was only then he realised she still had his coat. Her knees were drawn up, her cheek resting upon them, upon his coat. The sight of her soft cheek against the fabric he wore so often made an odd sensation stir in his chest. Guilt, probably. Her expression was pinched, her dark eyebrows drawn down, and he knew she was still smarting over his words, which could have been more diplomatic. Barnaby sighed. They were likely to be here for a good long while, and whilst he did not wish to encourage her foolish dreams, he did not want to make her unhappy, either.

Reluctantly, for he sensed danger in her nearness, Barnaby returned and sat down beside her, his back to the wall.

Victoria gave him a wary glance and sat up, offering him his coat. Barnaby took it and settled it around her shoulders. "You're cold."

She frowned at him. "I expect you are, too. You're only in your shirtsleeves now."

She glanced at his bare forearms and her cheeks went a bit pink before she looked hurriedly away again. Despite himself, Barnaby could not help but smile.

"I'm fine. I've never felt the cold much. Too many freezing holidays with my aunt in her draughty castle in Scotland, and once you've swum in a Scottish loch a time or two, nothing else will ever seem cold again."

She gave him a sceptical glance, and he smiled at her.

"It's true. Here," he pressed his hand to her cheek, his warm palm registering the chill of her skin. She really was cold.

"Oh," she said, closing her eyes and shivering beneath his touch. "You *are* warm."

Barnaby did not know if it was her words, or the shiver, but despite their unprepossessing surroundings, he felt a thrill of desire and snatched his hand back. The sensible thing to do would be to get up and concentrate on finding a way out of here but her nose was pink with the cold, and he could see her breath clouding on the air in the lamplight. The last thing he needed was for her to take ill, he reasoned. It would only be gentlemanly to keep her warm.

"Come here, I'll warm you up for a minute before I try to find us a way out of here."

He put his arm around her, and she nestled into him without the slightest hesitation. Barnaby did his best to ignore how good it felt to hold her close, how perfectly her soft curves snuggled against him, as if made precisely to fit there. Her head rested upon his chest, one hand splayed out on his waistcoat. It was a warm, serviceable wool waistcoat with a subdued design in shades of brown that he'd liked because it made him think of autumn and falling leaves. He could not shake the idea that her hand ought to rest upon some lavishly embroidered silk affair of the kind Louis César would wear, and which would consume Barnaby's carefully arranged budget for the entire month in one fell swoop. Not that he was penniless, far from it, and he had plans, not that anyone knew about those. Not even Louis. He'd told no one about it, because gentlemen did not work—even if the alternative was starving, apparently—and if his father found out about it, there would be the almightiest scene. Though, now he came to think about it, he didn't much care what his father thought.

"Huh," he said, so surprised by this epiphany that the sound emerged without him considering it.

Victoria's head came up, regarding him with interest.

"Er… nothing. Just thinking," he said awkwardly, before returning to the idea.

In his youth, he would have bent over backwards to please his family, but since he'd cut them from his life for the sake of his own sanity, he had not reconsidered what that meant. He was free of them. Free of their expectations. He did not care if his father did not like that he was running his own business. It was none of his affair, not any longer. They had disowned Barnaby long before he had them, so now… they could go to the devil. His father did not support him, had not done so since he came of age, for the family coffers could not stretch that far, though his older brothers had always seemed to have the best of everything. Barnaby shoved that thought aside. He was not prone to envy and resentment, but that did not mean it was comfortable to remember how often he'd been left out in the cold.

"I'm sorry."

Barnaby turned to find Victoria staring at him, her eyes swimming with tears.

"I'm so sorry, Barnaby. You're right, this is all my fault. We might be trapped here for days, if they find us at all. I ought never to have teased you into coming with me. I ought to have waited. You must think me horribly spoiled, and I'm sorry for the spoon comment. You ought not be forced to marry someone you don't love, just because they were st-stupid enough to—"

Barnaby's heart lurched at the misery in her eyes, at the way her voice trembled, and he could not stand it, could not stand for her to think he did not care, that he did not think her the most wonderful, beautiful creature in the entire world, so he kissed her.

Her words became a gasp as he slid his hand around the back of her neck and pulled her in, kissing her until he felt her trembling ease, until he felt her relax in his embrace. He drew back then, staring down at her and wiping away a tear that had fallen, leaving a wet track through the dust upon her beautiful face.

"Don't be sorry," he said, realising he meant it. "You're brave and adventurous and that's a wonderful thing. Who else could have found this place but you? And it must be connected to the hidden treasure, I'm certain of it. Perhaps we'll find it yet. I'm glad I came, Victoria, and yes, I am worried, but we'll be fine. We'll find a way out together because we are resourceful people who don't give up. Yes?"

"Yes," she whispered, staring at him, a look of such adoration in her eyes that his chest ached.

Did she really care for him? Could it be real, not just some young woman's fancy?

Barnaby hesitated, uncertain he should say the words circling his brain.

"I'd marry you in a heartbeat, Victoria, if I was certain it was what you wanted, that you wouldn't come to regret it, but I'm not certain. Not at all. I do not think you realise how profoundly your life would change, and I do not want to see the look in your eyes when reality dawns."

She returned an imperious look of such irritation he almost laughed. There was the duke's daughter. "Barnaby, I'm not a fool, and I'm not so spoiled as all that. Besides which, I have a dowry. Papa was very generous and—"

"Don't tell me!" he said, holding up a hand. "Please. I don't want to know. I don't doubt it's a sum large enough that I would consider myself wealthy, but it's still a drop in the ocean compared to your father's wealth, compared to the status you have now as his daughter, or the many grand estates you can call home."

"But those things are Papa and Mama's, Barnaby, not mine, and we do not live like royalty. Papa despises ostentation, and Mama keeps our feet on the ground."

Barnaby sighed. This conversation was getting them nowhere. "It's of no matter, Victoria. We really don't know each other very well in any case. Just... let us concentrate on getting out of here for now. We can discuss the rest later."

He got to his feet and Victoria stared up at him, her expression considering before she took the hand he held out to her.

"Very well. For now," she said easily, but the look in her eyes told him she was not done with him yet.

Chapter 8

Dearest Bella,

Well, I did as you told me to. I gave her the truth, laid my heart before her, and got it soundly stomped on. She ran away and I fear I'll not see hide nor hair of her for the rest of my stay here. I know, I know... what did I expect? I can hear your voice in my head, and I know you're right, but I'd hoped all the same. Yes, I know, I'm an arrogant devil to believe a strong-willed woman like Hester would fall into my arms without a murmur of protest after what I did. Such conceit. It comes with the dukedom, you know.

I shall not give up, though if you have any advice for this poor old fool, you'd best despatch it at once. It has been a long time since I set my mind to wooing a lady and I'm uncertain I remember how to go on.

I hope that great lummox of a son of mine is looking after you and the next addition to our growing brood. Oh, and when I was in town, I found those sweetmeats you were so fond of the last time you were breeding. You should expect a half dozen boxes to arrive any day, I should think.

Yrs affectionately.

A x

—Excerpt of a letter to The Most Hon'ble Arabella Grenville, Marchioness of Bainbridge, (daughter of Mr and Mrs Alice and Nathanial Hunt) from her father-in-law Alfred Grenville, His Grace, The Duke of Axton.

18th December 1844, Lewes, East Sussex.

Emmeline started as Wrexham stood up, the discovery of how much larger he was than her provoking a rush of feeling she was unprepared for. She had forgotten just how handsome he was, too, and he was as beautifully dressed as before. His company at the dinner party had been both fascinating and challenging, disturbing in ways she could not quite put her finger on. He had made an impression on her, and she had found her thoughts returned to him often since that night. He was so unlike anyone else she had ever met before, that she had hoped she would see him again. She had not expected it to be so soon, however, or in such circumstances.

"My lord, how long have you been here? You look frozen to the marrow."

"That good?" he replied dryly. "My, you are a tonic to a fellow's self-esteem, Miss Milly."

"That's Miss Knight, to you, my lord," she replied.

He grinned, and she shook her head, amused despite his teasing.

"I think I had best take you to the nearest inn to warm up before I see about your carriage," she said, fighting the urge to reach out and brush the snow from his shoulders. She suspected he would not like her touching him without invitation.

"I'd not say no to a brandy or three to thaw me out. I feel a kinship to an icicle that is most disconcerting. So lead on, Miss Milly. I would offer you my arm, but the fact is that I need yours to guide me," he said, an edge to his voice.

She wondered what it must cost his pride to ask it of her. He was a strong, beautiful man who'd been born to one of the most powerful titles in the land, and yet he must ask for her assistance. She knew enough of men and their pride to believe it must sting, at least a little.

"I should be honoured, my lord," she said, and reached out to take his hand so she could place it on her sleeve. Before she could, his fingers tightened on hers.

"Thank you," he said, his voice low. "Of all the people who might have come to my aid, I'm glad it was you."

"So am I," she said, before she could think better of it, and then blushed furiously at the impropriety of what she was doing, holding this man's hand in public.

He chuckled, a warm, rich sound that was so delicious she could not help but stare at him.

"Are you blushing, pet?"

"Never you mind," she retorted, placing his hand on her arm.

He huffed out a laugh and moved his hand until it lightly clasped her elbow. "Lead on, sweet, and I shall follow like a lamb."

Emmeline snorted at that. "Lamb, my eye," she muttered under her breath, praying that no one saw them together, or the gossip mill would have a field day.

The snow was falling thick and fast now, the soft crunch of it underfoot quietening the world around them. The streets were all but empty, most people having sought shelter. Indeed, Emmeline was supposed to have done the same and returned to her sister and Louis by now. They would wonder where she had got to when she had only been popping into the stationery shop next door to buy ink. But then she had seen Wrexham sitting alone, and she had known at once that there was something wrong, though she could not say how. Perhaps it had been the rigid set of his shoulders, or the fierce expression he wore, daring the world to test him further.

"There's a step coming up," she warned him. "In three steps. Two. Now."

"You're good at this," he observed, but Emmeline was already staring up at him, rather astonished by the ease with which he moved, and the trust he put in her.

It was rather humbling and… and strangely intimate. His strong profile caught her gaze, and she could not help but admire this handsome, intriguing man. Not for the first time, however, she ought not to have been daydreaming. Emmeline gasped as her foot slipped on a patch of ice, going out from beneath her until a tumble seemed inevitable, but then Wrexham's arms firmed around her, hauling her against him.

"Steady there, Miss Milly," he said, amusement behind the words, his deep voice resonating through her body.

He held her tight against him, his chest hard against her softer form, his arms a cage around her, yet she had no thoughts of trying to escape. Her breath caught, and she froze, too startled and befuddled by this man to know how to react. He was far stronger than she could have anticipated, and his head was angled down towards her. Did he know how close their faces were? His warm breath fluttered over her, eliciting a ripple of shivers over her skin. She need only reach up a fraction of an inch and their lips would touch. Emmeline felt giddy with the realisation that she wanted to close that gap.

"If you're going to kiss me, you'd best do it before anyone sees," he whispered.

She gave a squeak of alarm, pushing out of his hold. "Lord Wrexham!" she admonished, though she was uncertain if she was more shocked by his words or her own wayward thoughts. "I am risking my reputation quite far enough in aiding you, without… without…."

Emmeline faltered, knowing she was more irritated with herself than with him. After all, his reputation before he lost his sight had been that of a rake and a libertine. There was no reason to suppose anything had changed.

"Without being importuned by a cripple," he finished for her, his tone clipped now, touched by something that sounded like shame. "Forgive me. I did not mean to… I am sorry. I forgot myself."

His demeanour had changed entirely, a tinge of colour cresting his high cheekbones, his usually expressive features fixed, unreadable. She was immediately contrite, and not a little angry that he should feel embarrassed for all the wrong reasons. She suspected he believed she had pushed him away more out of disgust than propriety, and that was so far from the truth. Though she knew it was dreadfully inappropriate to continue this conversation, she could not let him believe that of her, or of himself.

"That is not at all what I meant," she said crossly.

He tilted his head, as if trying to gauge what she did mean, listening intently.

"Oh, Wrexham!" she said in frustration. "You are the most disconcerting fellow I have ever met, but if you believe I see you as a cripple, well, you need your blasted head examined."

"Ah, another person believing I am not in my right mind," he said, and she was uncertain if he was funning with her or being serious.

113

"Well, you're not. Not if you think I trust you anymore than I do any other handsome fellow given the opportunity to get me alone."

He seemed to brighten a little at that, one eyebrow quirking. "You think me handsome?"

"Oh, really," she said in disgust. "Come along. We must not be seen conversing like this in the middle of the street. Drat you for being the most provoking man, for I shall be in so much trouble for this!" Emmeline walked on, as fast as she dared in the snow, until she reached the inn. They stopped just outside, and she turned to Wrexham.

"We're here," she said.

His lips quirked. "I know, I can hear the chatter and smell beer and roast dinner. Everyone has gone inside, out of the weather."

"They have," she agreed. "Come here, out of sight," she added, guiding him to a dark corner where they were less likely to be noticed by any passers-by.

"I cannot be seen in there, especially not with you. So, I will find you a seat, and then I must go at once, but I promise, I will ensure a carriage is sent to collect you as soon as possible. I promise, Wrexham."

"I believe you," he said, and something in the way he said it made her cheeks heat again.

She stared up at him, more puzzled and intrigued by this beautiful man than ever. "What happened today? I know something did. Why were you there for so long by yourself?"

He hesitated, and she knew instinctively that he was wondering how far he could trust her.

"I would never betray your confidence, my lord. *Never*," she added forcefully, rather startling herself with her vehemence.

He let out a breath, and she was uncertain if it was laughter or frustration. "My God, you're too sweet, so…." She watched as he took his hat off with one hand and ran the other through his blonde hair. "Miss Knight, may I call upon you?"

In that moment Emmeline was glad he could not see her, could not see the way her mouth opened and closed, for she was certain it was most unbecoming.

"C-Call? Upon *me*?" she all but squeaked.

His lips twitched. "Yes, pet. Upon you."

"Well, I… I… Yes," she said, breathlessly.

He nodded, looking pleased. "Then perhaps I shall trust you with the story, if you are certain you wish to hear it?"

"I am," she said at once, almost reaching out to touch his hand but stopping herself at the last moment, wanting him to put his trust in her so fiercely she could only wonder at it. "I am sure. Though at present I am staying at Heart's Folly."

"Ah, yes. Your sister married the Comte de Villen. Tell me, is he as beautiful as everyone says?"

"Yes, certainly he is," Emmeline answered at once and then bit her lip, wishing she hadn't spoken with such alacrity, but it was rather an empirical fact, and not one worth disputing.

"Ah, you certainly think so," he said, his voice darkly amused. His head dipped, and he turned his hat between his hands. "I was considered so, once. But I expect that is hard to believe. It was a long time ago now."

He smiled, but the expression was bitter and mocking, more of a sneer, and Emmeline could not bear to see it.

"I promise you, nothing has changed, my lord," she said, before she could think better of it.

He stilled, his attention riveted upon her, as though he could hear her thoughts.

"You think me as handsome as the beautiful comte?" he pressed, but that was too far, and Emmeline knew better than to answer.

"I think you a conceited coxcomb fishing for compliments," she said tartly, though she rather wished she hadn't sounded quite so flustered.

He grinned, the devil, looking very pleased with himself.

"Miss Milly?"

"It's Miss Knight," she corrected him, striving to sound cross and not utterly charmed by the wicked man.

"Is there anyone around, watching us?" he asked.

Emmeline looked about them, peering around the corner of the inn. "No, I don't think—"

Before she could finish the sentence, his hand moved to her face. She started in shock; he had removed his glove and his fingers were icy as he traced the curve of her cheek, then touched an errant curl of hair that had escaped the pins, and followed the path of her jaw.

"So soft, pet, like satin."

Emmeline could not move, her nerves jittering wildly beneath the touch of his cold hand. He held her in place and ducked his head, pressing his mouth softly to her cheek, so close to the corner of her mouth she was sorely tempted to turn her head towards him.

"Thank you," he whispered.

Emmeline snapped out of her stupor, taking a step back and shaking herself back to reality.

"Yes, well... I... I think we had best get you inside," she said, sounding dazed.

Somehow, though she was shocked and utterly befuddled, she guided him around to the front door, sought out the landlord, who took him to a private parlour, and then ran away like a terrified little girl with barely another word. Emmeline found sense enough in her scattered brain to arrange a carriage to fetch him, and then gave herself a very stern talking to about spending time alone with wicked men, before she found her way back to her sister.

Barnaby and Victoria had searched every inch of the walls, floor, and ceiling, to no avail. There was no secret entrance.

"Do you think we could dig our way out?" Victoria asked, staring anxiously at the mountain of earth and rubble blocking the doorway.

"Yes, possibly. If all that's fallen is what is blocking the door, but I'm worried what might happen if we do," he said.

"You think the rest of the tunnel might collapse," she said with a sigh.

He shrugged. "If it hasn't already. We don't know how far that pile goes. It might be more extensive than we realise. Besides which, we're not done here yet," he added.

"What do you mean? We've looked everywhere."

Barnaby shook his head. "We've looked everywhere we can see."

"But you looked under the bed," she protested.

"Yes, but not behind the shelving."

Victoria frowned. The shelves were a simple affair, just sturdy wooden planks on a frame, the wall clearly visible behind them. She didn't see how they were hiding anything, but set to helping Barnaby, who was moving all the jars of ancient preserves out of the way. Curious, she rubbed at a dusty label.

"Quince gelee," she read, before looking at another. "Oh, this is cherry gelee. Must be jam, I suppose."

Barnaby peered at the label. "Shouldn't try it if I were you," he said, deadpan.

Victoria snorted. "I wasn't about to."

Once they had removed all the jars, they lifted the shelves to one side. Victoria stared at the wall with a sigh.

"Nothing."

Barnaby ran a hand through his hair, his frustration apparent. Oh Lord, this was all her fault. If she'd not been so eager to have an adventure, they could have returned to the house for the lantern, as Barnaby had suggested, and actually told someone what they were up to. But she'd wanted to find something first. It had been *their* discovery, not something she wanted everyone else involved in, and she'd wanted to keep it that way, just for a little while, but now look. She sighed and glared at the wall as if it was the fault of the thick stone and... That was odd.

"What's... Oh, Barnaby look." She hurried over and slid her hand over the flat surface at the base of the wall. "It's fake!" she exclaimed.

Barnaby stared at her hand, laid on the smooth insert, not on the rough, uneven texture of a stone wall. He shook his head. "How?"

"It's a trompe l'oeil painting. An optical illusion," she said, so excited now she could hardly speak. "Look, it's just a section of wood fitted into the wall. They painted it to look like the rest of the stone wall, and behind the shelves it was perfect, but from the side you can see it's flat, not bumpy like the wall."

"Well, would you look at that," Barnaby said, astonished as he turned to Victoria, and they both burst out laughing. "This really is turning into a Gothic adventure. Are you happy?"

"So, so happy!" she said, clapping her hands together with glee.

Barnaby snorted. "Come on then, let's see if we can pry it off. Because people don't go to all that trouble to hide nothing."

It took a good hour to prise the painted section of wood from the wall, but finally the fixings loosened. Barnaby got his fingers around the back, having eased it forward just enough to get hold of it, and tugged. It shifted another inch and Barnaby took a breath and tugged again. The wood came free with a shower of debris, and they scrambled back, coughing, until the dust had settled enough to investigate.

"Oh. Oh, no it... it can't be," Victoria said in dismay.

"More jam," Barnaby said, staring at the wax sealed glass jars with confusion. He picked one up and stared at the label. "Strawberry this time. I mean, I enjoy strawberry jam as much as the next fellow, but why on earth go to so much trouble to hide it?"

"Is there anything behind the jars?" Victoria asked hopefully.

Barnaby took each jar out until there were twenty assorted shapes and designs, some glass, some earthenware, on the floor beside them. "There's a wooden back," he said, tapping the back of the square hole they'd uncovered, which was only two feet wide by two high. "But the sides and the floor are solid, no hidden panels."

Victoria gave a huff of disappointment. "Well, that's so frustrating."

"Hold on." Barnaby's muffled voice came from inside the hole. "Because if I just...."

She heard a solid thudding sound and guessed he was hitting the wooden back of the opening. A moment later, he crawled out again, turning himself around.

"It's solidly fixed and there's no room to move. But I think perhaps I can kick it out."

Victoria watched, an odd fluttery feeling in her stomach as she observed him turn onto his back, laying on the floor with his feet in the hole. He was dirty and thoroughly dishevelled now, his white shirt smudged and grubby, his hair all awry and thick with dust, and… and she had never wanted him more. How odd, to feel this desperate desire to put her hands on him when he was sweaty and dirty. Victoria jumped as Barnaby's boot slammed against the wooden back and she fought to concentrate on what he was doing, instead of the lewd imaginings of what might lie beneath his clothes.

"There!" he said, grinning at her a moment later as he scrambled to his knees and peered into the hole. "Bring the lamp."

He paused a moment, undoing his cravat with deft fingers and wiping his sweaty, dust coated face with it. Victoria froze, lamp in hand, staring at the triangle of skin exposed at the base of his throat. She could hear her own heart beating.

"Victoria, illuminate the opening, please, not me," he said, giving her an odd look.

She jumped, blushing. "Oh, yes, of course. Silly of me. Here." Mortified, she got to her knees and pushed the lamp into the opening, peering through. "There's another room, a big one," she said, excitement coursing through her again.

Barnaby knelt beside her and looked. "So it is."

They turned their heads at the same time, grinning madly, to discover their faces so close they almost touched.

"I'm so glad you're here, Barnaby," she whispered, hoping he felt at least a little the same way.

He looked at her for a long moment before his mouth quirked, the corner twitching upwards. "I'm glad too, Victoria."

She let out a breath, relieved and happy at the admission.

"My friends call me Torie," she added shyly, wondering if he would relax enough to allow such familiarity.

"Well, shall we go on to the next part of our adventure, Torie?" he asked, his eyes alight with amusement.

Emma V Leech

"Yes, please!"

Barnaby laughed and pushed the lamp farther into the hole before crawling in after it.

"What can you see?" she demanded, beside herself with excitement.

"Er… saucepans," he replied, which was rather deflating.

"Saucepans? Oh, bother! What is wrong with these people? Why are they hoarding saucepans and jam like it's treasure? Whoever heard of such a thing?"

Barnaby pushed farther into the hole, and she heard the metallic crash of pots and pans before his feet disappeared entirely.

"Barnaby?"

She peered through the hole to see his face appear on the other side. "Come through. It's quite safe," he said, gesturing for her to follow.

Fascinated, despite her dreams of treasure chests and long buried jewels turning into centuries-old jam and frying pans, Victoria lay down on her belly and wriggled into the hole. Her skirts and corset made movement nigh on impossible, but after a lot of squirming and cursing, she finally got her head out the other side.

"Here, let me help," Barnaby said, reaching into the hole and grasping her under the arms. He pulled, his grip firm but….

"Oh, it's no use!" she cried in annoyance, when several minutes of twisting and tugging left her hot and annoyed, but no further through the hole. "I'm stuck."

"Your skirts," Barnaby guessed.

She nodded, rather mortified. "Gothic adventures were easier in my mother's days without all these dratted skirts and petticoats," she said crossly.

Barnaby rubbed a hand over his face, and she rather suspected he was trying not to laugh.

"It's not funny," she retorted, irritated.

"N-No," he said, a little unsteadily, struggling to keep a straight face if she was any judge. "Barnaby. Stop laughing at me!"

"I'm n-not laughing," he said, trying so hard not to that he ended up scowling at her.

"Well, see if you find this funny," she said tartly, and crawled back into the room in which they'd been trapped.

"What are you doing?" Barnaby called through the hole. "Victoria? Don't go back in there. We can't be certain it's safe. Victoria, come back here."

But Victoria didn't answer. She folded up Barnaby's coat before stripping off her wool cloak and dress, and then undoing her petticoats. Shivering, she stared down at the pile of clothing once she was done. How strange to be so cold when her cheeks were burning, but she wore only her stockings and shift, and she was about to give the man on the other side of that wall quite an eyeful. Well, there was no other way out and no way of getting through that gap with all her clothes on. Barnaby would just have to deal with it.

"Here," she called through to him, before bundling all her clothes and Barnaby's coat into the cloak and stuffing them into the hole.

"What's this... *oh.*"

Barnaby's voice sounded faint and a little strained from the other side of the wall, but Victoria did not hang around to hear if he had anything else to say. It was far too cold to stand about barely dressed, so she got back to her knees and crawled through the hole.

Chapter 9

Dear Thorn,

I am well, thank you brother for your concern, and little Tilly is growing fast, sometimes I think before my very eyes. She's as imperious as a duchess and has more of our father about her than I like to admit. 'No,' is her favourite word, I'm certain, and she has us all dancing to her tune. The devil of it is that we don't care. She's a delight and a joy to me.

Yes, I shall be at Dern for Christmas, though only for a few days, as it pains me to leave Tilly behind. I comfort myself with the idea that she does not yet know what Christmas is, but it breaks my heart all the same. I swear it will be the last we spend apart. Yet she is beloved by all. For, once fortune has smiled on me, for the nurse who has taken my daughter in her care is as affectionate as any mother, and fiercely protective. The woman holds me in utter contempt, I might add, but I can hardly blame her for that as I do too, but Tilly adores her, and that is all that matters.

Some days I believe I am being punished for my years of indulgence and then I look at

Tilly's sweet face and wonder how I can think so. She is a gift I am not – can never be – worthy of. But I shall try.

Inheriting Aunt Marguerite's property <u>was</u> a poisoned chalice, though, of that I've no doubt. The place is a beautiful wreck, falling down around my ears, and yet I am determined to put it to rights, to make a home here, for me, for Tilly.

I know this little idyll cannot last. Father will discover my secret. We both know he is giving me this time. He knows I've got myself in a mess and he's just waiting until I have courage enough to face him. How hurt Mama will be too. Christ, could I hate myself anymore? But I shall rebuild this blasted house if I must do it with my bare hands, I will be everything my daughter needs, and I will prove to our parents I can be a good father, a responsible human being and perhaps then their disappointment might be bearable.

I beg your forgiveness for the hundredth time, Thorn, for making you keep this secret for me.

I shall see you soon, brother.

Pip x

—Excerpt of a letter to The Right Hon'ble Mr Thomas Barrington, (younger son of The Most Hon'ble Lucian and Matilda Barrington, The Marquess, and Marchioness of Montagu) from his older brother, The Right Hon'ble Philip Barrington, The Earl of Ashburton.

18th December 1844, Heart's Folly, East Sussex.

Barnaby stared down at the bundle of clothes Victoria had just shoved through the gap. Dimly, he registered the colour of the walking dress she'd been wearing, but his brain did not seem to comprehend what that meant, and then he saw Victoria's head emerge from the hole.

"Here, let me help you," he said, reaching for her as she crawled free.

Barnaby lifted her to her feet, his hands at her waist to steady her and then… and then his brain melted.

He stared, and stared, and then… he stared a bit more because, well, frankly, what else was a fellow supposed to do?

"Victoria," he said, or at least he thought he said it.

There was every chance he only thought it and he'd been entirely struck dumb. But he was electrified, vibrating with a pulsing energy that seemed to begin at the place where his hands rested on her waist and thrummed into him, a slow simmering sensation beneath his skin that grew hotter and hotter. His breath caught as he registered the softness of the body beneath the thin cotton of her shift, saw the swell of her breasts above the low neckline, the dark outline of her nipples in the glow of the lamplight and the hard tips that pushed against the soft fabric. *She's cold,* said an urgent voice in his head. *You ought to warm her up.*

Barnaby swallowed, a faint voice in his head was pleading for sanity, but he could not quite make out the words. He was caught in a dream, watching as if from afar as his hand slid up from her waist and cupped her breast. His breath hitched at the same moment Victoria gasped in shock.

He looked up then, expecting a slap, or at least angry words… hardly surprising, he was acting like a complete cad. Honestly, he hoped she did slap him, because he was very afraid of what he might do next if she didn't.

But Victoria was staring at him, eyes wide and dark. Her lips parted and her tongue swept out, pink and wet, leaving her mouth the same way.

Step away, he told himself.

Step away now.

Barnaby, move, for the love of God.

And then she arched into his touch, a soft sound leaving her as her hard little nipple pressed into his palm.

"Bad idea," he managed, his voice strangely hoarse.

"Sorry," she replied, but didn't move.

So they just stood there, staring at each other, his hand cupping her breast, his brain running frantically between, *kiss her, move away, kiss her, move away,* over and over again until he thought he'd run mad.

"Barnaby!" Victoria cried in frustration and pressed her mouth to his.

Heat, desire, and the kind of insanity inducing need he had only ever read about in poems surged through him and he hauled her against him, kissing her hard, almost savagely, until she gave a little squeak of alarm and pushed him away.

Barnaby let her go at once, stumbling back, his brain clearing now he no longer had his hands on her.

"Christ!" he said, breathing hard. "Bloody hell. I mean… Victoria, I'm… I'm so sorry, I…."

Victoria clapped a hand to her mouth to smother a slightly hysterical laugh.

Barnaby blinked. She was *laughing?*

"It's not funny!" he exclaimed crossly.

"W-Well, it is a bit funny," she stammered apologetically.

"Victoria, if you hadn't stopped me, I would likely have despoiled you on the floor of... of whatever this place is!"

"No, you wouldn't. Besides, I wouldn't let you. That's why I pushed you away. I'm no prude, Barnaby, but I do think our first time ought to be in a bed."

"Our first—" He stared at her, too startled to say the words out loud. He turned his back on her before he could do something there would be no coming back from. "Get dressed," he ordered, his voice taut.

Barnaby crossed his arms, tormenting himself with imagining what was going on from the rustling of feminine garments behind him. Closing his eyes, he tried to shut out the sound and the images, but he could not chase the memory of how it felt to touch her from his mind. The lush softness of her breast beneath his palm was indelibly imprinted upon his brain and he would remember every detail of that moment until the day he died. Which would be soon if Bedwin ever discovered what had just happened. He only prayed she did not need help with her corset, or he was a dead man.

"You can turn around now."

Barnaby did, letting out a breath of relief as he discovered her fully clothed, if rather haphazardly.

"What is this place?" Victoria asked, staring around the room with curiosity.

"A kitchen—the original kitchen, if I guess correctly," Barnaby said, striving to get his mind to concentrate on something other than breasts and the proximity of a woman who was driving him to distraction with remarkable speed. "They used to build them separate from the main house because of the risk of fire, but that still means we're close to the house now, if I'm right. So... So we had best get back before we're missed."

Barnaby did not miss the disappointment that flashed in her eyes.

"Not yet," she said, her voice soft and cajoling. "Couldn't we just have a little look around? Please?"

Barnaby sighed and wondered at what point he'd thrown away what remained of his senses. Likely the moment he touched her breast, he thought ruefully, but it didn't much matter now, because there was no way on God's green earth he could refuse her.

"Fine. Come on then. We'll look around."

Hester opened her bedroom door and peered down the corridor. All was quiet, thank heavens. The skies outside were almost fully dark now, and the house too quiet. Lifting the lamp she had lit, Hester made her way down the corridor towards Victoria's room. Other than Axton, she knew Victoria was the only one not to have gone on the shopping trip and, judging from the thick flurries of snow still falling outside, Louis and Evie and their guests had decided it was prudent to spend the night in Lewes rather than travel in a snowstorm. That meant Hester was alone in the house with blasted Axton, and there was no power on earth that would make her dine with the wicked creature alone. Hopefully, Victoria would be amenable to eating together in Hester's room tonight, which would avoid any awkwardness.

The scent of pine and spices perfumed the house, and Hester trailed her hand over the greenery decorating the elegant banisters as she made her way to Victoria's room. With a sharp knock, Hester called out to the young woman.

"Victoria? It's Hester, dear. *Victoria*?" Hester knocked again and waited for a long moment before turning the door handle quietly, in case the young woman was sleeping, but the room was in darkness. Only the dim glow of firelight cast any light about a room that was obviously empty.

Hester frowned. Well, perhaps she was in the library. If she remembered rightly, the girl was a prodigious reader. Making her way down the stairs, Hester saw a footman heading towards the dining room with a full coal scuttle.

"Young man. Can you tell me where Lady Victoria is?"

The footman turned and inclined his head thoughtfully. "No, my lady. Would you like me to make enquiries?"

"Yes. I think I would," Hester said, the first stirrings of unease tiptoeing down her back. "I suppose there is no sign of the comte and comtesse?"

"No, my lady. We assume they have decided to spend the night in Lewes. The snow is almost a foot deep in places already and shows no signs of stopping."

Hester nodded and made a shooing motion. "No doubt, now run along and find what has become of Lady Victoria and make haste. I shall be in the library."

The footman nodded and hurried away, returning ten minutes later with the disconcerting news that no one had seen Lady Victoria since early that morning.

"No one? And no one thought to look for her?" Hester demanded.

"We thought she was in her room, my lady," the footman said, his expression pained.

Hester let out an impatient breath. "Well, she's not."

"Perhaps Mr Godwin has seen her?" the man suggested hopefully.

"Barnaby?" Hester said, staring at the man in surprise. "He went with the others."

"Beg pardon, my lady, but he didn't. He came back. He were looking for the lady too, as it happens."

The fellow coloured, and now Hester realised why none of the staff had set about looking for her. They believed a tryst was afoot.

For a moment Hester entertained fond imaginings of the set down she would give her young nephew for endangering the reputation of the Duke of Bedwin's daughter. And then she reconsidered. Barnaby was the only good thing her wretched prig of a brother had ever produced, though in Hester's opinion that was only because she'd spent a good deal more time with him than she had the other horrid boys. Perhaps it was arrogant of her, but she thought it was largely her doing that he had turned out so well. He was a good man, honourable, decent and kind. He'd make an excellent husband. It would be quite a comedown for Lady Victoria, of course. With her breeding, her beauty—and not to mention her dowry—she could expect to make a splendid match. But splendid matches were not always happy ones. Now she came to think on it, she had noticed the way Victoria looked at Barnaby and had wondered if the girl had a tendre for him.

She did not, for one moment, entertain the notion that there was a tryst going on. Her nephew was far too decent for such behaviour. However, if they were alone together….

Hester pursed her lips, considering. Yes, that might be a very good thing for Barnaby. Just what he needed. However, there was always the possibility that they were not together, and that one, or both, were in difficulties. After all, if they were not in the house, with the weather as it was… Barnaby would never keep a young lady out in the cold, but if he'd realised she was missing, he would have gone looking for her. Oh, blast and bother. There was nothing else for it.

Hurrying back up the stairs, Hester made her way to the duke's rooms and knocked.

The door opened a moment later, a snotty looking valet regarding her with such condescension her already frayed nerves sparked, lighting her temper.

"Out of the way," she said, with the *obey or die* tone she used when she was dealing with men who thought they could speak to her like a foolish old lady. The valet's eyes widened, and he took a hasty step back.

Hester strode into the duke's rooms, entering an elegant living room that showed no sign of the man. Setting down the lamp, she stalked to the adjoining door.

"Axton, I really must... *oh!*"

Hester froze, realising too late she really ought not to have marched into the duke's bedroom unannounced, at an hour when he was bound to be dressing for dinner. Thankfully, he was not naked, but that was, in Hester's opinion, a small mercy. He stood in his stockinged feet, trousers in place—thank the lord—but his shirt hung open and.... For a few years she had heard reports that Axton was becoming a fat old man, bitter and angry and too keen on keeping company with his wine cellar to be a good companion. Yet, since his appalling mother had died and his daughter-in-law had taken on the running of the vast mausoleum he called home, things had changed. For the better. Here was the man she remembered from so very long ago: older, without a doubt, his hair steel grey, matching the hair on his chest, but that chest was strong still, broad and powerful and made her feel things that....

Hester turned her back on him.

"Really, Axton, can you not at least make yourself presentable when a lady comes into the room?"

"I would have done, love, only you didn't seem to have done looking," he replied mildly.

"Arrogant man. You took me by surprise, is all."

"Ah, yes. Surprising of me to be dressing in my bedroom at such an hour. Forgive me. Now, you dreadful creature, what has ruffled your feathers to such a pitch that you must come barging in on me to stare at my magnificence?"

"I was not staring at… oh, never mind that, you old goat. Lady Victoria is missing, and so is Barnaby."

The duke let out a low chuckle, and Hester tutted with annoyance.

"It's not like that!" she protested. "At least, I don't think it is. The thing is, they are not in the house, and Barnaby would never keep a young woman out on a night like this. He's far too considerate. I'm worried, Axton. I think something has happened to them."

"Are you quite certain they are not in the house, love? It's a big place. Plenty of empty rooms available to, er… find a bit of privacy."

"I am not your 'love!'" Hester snapped, annoyed with the arrogant devil for speaking to her with such familiarity when they were strangers now. "And no, no I am not certain, but the staff haven't seen them and… and I'm worried," she admitted, wrapping her arms about herself.

Oh, why must Axton be such a thorn in her side, even after all this time? She had made peace with herself when he had walked away. She had even forgiven him for it once she had met her husband and discovered there was still happiness to be found in the world. But now he was here, stirring everything up when she had been quite content with the way things were. Damn and blast Louis César for inviting him.

Hester jolted as large, warm hands settled on her shoulders. "I'm sure they're fine, Hester. Give me a moment and I shall help you look for them."

"Thank you," she said, letting out a breath.

Just for a moment, she wondered what it might be like to allow herself to lean into him, to feel that warmth and strength at her back. It had been such a very long time since she'd had anyone to lean on, over twenty years since her husband had died. She was a strong woman, capable and disinclined to suffer fools, but that did not mean that she didn't want someone to share her troubles with, someone to….

"I'll wait in the other room," she said, annoyed with herself for even thinking about it.

She stalked away from him without another word.

Chapter 10

Dear Alana,

Thank you so much for coming to visit me at Dern yesterday. Do you think anyone ever talked as much as our mothers did? I don't think either of them stopped to breathe, they chattered so hard. It was lovely to see Mama happy, though; she has been a little dispirited of late with Pip being away so much and I haven't helped matters with my dreadful escapades. I don't know if you know why but I am rather in disgrace. I was too mortified to admit it to you during your visit, but I have not been out much of late, and the weather has been so dismal I have been quite blue devilled too, so your company was exactly what I needed.

I was disappointed to hear you would not be staying in the area for long, so your letter, inviting me to stay with you and your family at Holbrook House next year, was a lovely surprise. I so want to come, only I am still in rather a lot of trouble so I shall have to wait and see. I shall keep everything crossed that I am out of the doghouse by then.

—Excerpt of a letter to Miss Alana Cadogan (daughter of Mr Jerome and Mrs Bonnie Cadogan) from The Lady Catherine 'Cat' Barrington (daughter of Lucian and Matilda Barrington, The Most Hon'ble Marquess and Marchioness of Montagu).

18th December 1844, Heart's Folly, East Sussex.

Victoria sighed with frustration. "It's just an old kitchen," she said, scowling, and looking rather like a grumpy kitten. Barnaby wanted to kiss her again. He cleared his throat.

"I think so, yes."

"But it makes no sense!" she exclaimed, throwing up her hands. "Why go to all that bother, the tunnel and the hidden room?"

"Well," Barnaby said slowly. "Perhaps it was used as a priest hole, or at least a place to hide someone who needed to remain out of sight. It makes sense, doesn't it? Then the only real access is via the chapel, but you could still get food and drink to whoever was in there from the kitchens without raising suspicion. There was a bed in there, so we know they were expecting whoever was there to stay for some time."

"Yes. I suppose that does make sense," Victoria agreed, though she sounded reluctant. "Except for the fact that panel was hidden from inside the room."

Barnaby frowned. "That is a bit odd," he agreed. "Then I don't know."

Victoria sighed, looking so dejected Barnaby had to fold his arms to stop himself from drawing her to him and hugging her.

"I suppose we ought to go back to the house before everyone comes home," she said with a sigh.

Barnaby moved to the window and rubbed at the dirty glass, peering out. "Unless they came back a long while ago, I don't think we'll be seeing anyone tonight."

Victoria moved to stand beside him and looked out. "Oh! Oh, my, Barnaby. Isn't it beautiful?"

Before Barnaby could object, she had hurried to the door. She tugged at it several times before it would open for her and allow her to run outside. He followed her, watching with the strangest sensation in his chest as she laughed and turned in a circle, her face tilted up to the sky. It was dark now, the velvety sky studded with stars that sparkled as brightly as the moonlit snow, but nothing shone as bright as she did. He grinned as she held out her tongue and laughed as she caught a falling snowflake upon it. She turned to look at him then, her eyes alight with the joy she took in the moment and he... he was lost. This beautiful, vivacious woman was breathtaking. She was brave and funny and not the least bit spoiled as he had accused her of being, and... she wanted *him*. Why, he could not fathom, when she could have snapped her fingers and found an earl or perhaps even a duke kneeling before her, but she said it was true. Could he really walk away from her if it was? What if she didn't resent the change in her circumstances? What if she was the one he had dreamed of and he turned his back on her because he was afraid of getting hurt again, or being labelled a fortune hunter? Was he really such a coward? Did he care so very much what people thought of him that he would not even try?

"Victoria," he said, his voice barely above a whisper, but it was so very quiet, as though everyone and everything in the world had stopped for this moment, except the falling snow... and except for Victoria, for she had heard him speak.

She had heard and was moving towards him. Barnaby moved too, closing the gap between them until there was none and she was in his arms. He stared down at her, snowflakes spangled her sable lashes, settled in her dark hair like glittering diamonds.

"Victoria," he said again, uncertain of what it was he wanted to say, but then she smiled up at him and suddenly words did not matter.

Nothing mattered except this perfect moment, and so he kissed her.

"You're walking without a cane," Hester observed as they opened the door on yet another empty room.

Axton turned to look at her and nodded. "That's because I'm being good and following the blasted diet Bella made for me."

"You? Following a diet?" she said sceptically.

He chuckled, and it was still the deep, rumbling sound she remembered of old. "Yes. Hard to believe I would follow any rule made by someone else, I know, but there you are. Gout is damned painful and—"

He broke off and Hester looked at him with interest as he raised the lamp, investigating the empty space with apparent concentration.

"And?" she demanded.

It was hard to tell in the lamplight, but she thought perhaps he blushed. Axton never blushed. She couldn't believe he was capable of it. One had to be aware of one's shortcomings to be able to blush. He made a gruff sound and turned back to her.

"Bella said I had to be honest with you," he said, looking deeply unhappy about it.

"And so?" she said, staring at him curiously.

"And so... I didn't want to have to use my cane because I didn't want to look like an old man, I wanted... I hoped that you might still want me. I still want you, Hester. You're still a very beautiful woman. Honestly, I think perhaps you've grown more beautiful with age."

"Oh, stuff and poppycock," Hester said, not about to believe such nonsense, even if her stupid heart was banging about in her chest in the oddest way, and it was suddenly hard to breathe.

He laughed then, his grey eyes twinkling with mirth. "Ah, love. I always could rely upon you to knock sense into this thick head of mine, but in this instant, I'm serious, and I'm right, too."

"Axton—" Hester said severely, folding her arms.

"No, hear me out. I'm not comparing you to the girl you were. My God, you stole my breath back then. I think I fell in love with you the moment I set eyes on you, and no, it's not like that. Of course it isn't. We were both so young, and I was so damned stupid. But you are more beautiful to me, Hester, because you have lived and loved… and just look at you. You're proud as a queen, and with every right to be. You are magnificent, my lady. You're the woman I ought to have made my duchess all those years ago. I wish you would let me do it now."

Hester stared at him, utterly speechless for once. Had he just proposed to her? The foolish man

"What is *wrong* with you?" she cried, uncertain if she was furious with him or if she was about to weep. She didn't know anything anymore.

This dreadful, overbearing man had left her to marry a more suitable choice. From everything she had heard, he had become increasingly dreadful and overbearing with each year that had passed, and she had told herself she'd had a lucky escape. She had been happily married, and though she had always regretted that they'd never been blessed with children, it had been her only regret. And yes, perhaps in the years since her husband had been gone she had remembered her youth, remembered the beautiful, arrogant duke who had stolen her breath and made her feel so dreadfully alive. Oh, they had fought like cat and dog, but they had loved too, just as fiercely. Things had been different then, society not so buttoned up as it was now, the blasted hypocrites.

"You're the only thing that has ever been wrong with me, Hester," Axton said, his voice soft now. "If I'd known what I was giving up, if I'd had the slightest idea of the lonely years stretching before me without you, I'd never have let you go. Not for a moment, not for anything."

Hester turned away from him, unable to withstand the look in his eyes, or the sincerity blazing there. She had known his marriage had been a disaster. He and his wife had loathed each other, but... she had never realised, never considered, that he might have loved *her* all this time.

"We're supposed to be looking for Barnaby and Lady Victoria," she said weakly.

Axton turned her back to face him, his big hand cupping her face, and oh lord, it was so good to feel a man's touch after so many years alone. No. Not a man's touch. *His* touch.

"Axton," she protested, but it was half-hearted now.

"They're young, they can look after their own hearts. Let us think of our own. Let me begin to make amends for fifty years of idiocy and bad decisions. I have a great deal of making up to do, and there is no time to lose," he said, and there was amusement shining in his eyes, but that sincerity was still there too.

He meant it. For once in his life, the big lummox was being entirely honest and hiding nothing. He was putting his heart on the line and, if she chose, she could crush it. She could have her revenge for the humiliation and pain he had caused her so long ago... but, in the end, he had suffered for his decision, and she had not. At least, not for years and decades as he had, and she did not want to hurt him. This man was not the one she had known. Oh, he was still there, the charming rogue, the arrogant duke, but time had tempered those hard edges, experience had softened him, and perhaps he really had learned what love meant, after all this time.

"Give me a chance, Hester."

"Another chance," she said tartly.

His lips quirked. "A second chance."

"Why should I?" She stared at him, not quite ready to give.

"Because I love you, and I think, odiously conceited fellow that I am, that you do not hate me quite as much as you make out."

"Pfft," she said, but she did not object when he put his hands on her hips, drawing her a little closer. Heat, the warming thrill of desire, familiar yet so long forgotten, flared from the place he held her, his hands burning through the fabric of her gown.

"Stubborn female," he said, shaking his head. "Admit it. You adore me."

"I certainly do not," she retorted, but she still said nothing as he gently drew her nearer, instead laying her hands flat on his chest. His heartbeat thrummed, strong and a tad too fast beneath her palm.

"Little liar," he murmured in her ear.

Hester shivered, her breath catching as his lips pressed against her cheek.

"You adore me," he repeated.

"Oh, all right, you great, numbskull. I adore you! There," she said crossly. "What are you going to do about it?"

He gave her a look of such ducal indignation she could only laugh. "Why I shall make you my duchess, obviously. What else should I do?"

"You might ask me, I suppose," she retorted.

Axton, devil that he was, waved this away. "I'm a duke. Asking is for plebs."

"Oh, you—" she began, but the words died as he pulled her close and kissed her, and Hester sighed, giving in, because Alfie had always kissed like it was the end of the world and she was the last thing he ever wanted to see.

Besides which, she did adore him, and she could scold him to her heart's content once she was his duchess. So Hester did what any sensible woman would do, and held on tight.

Chapter 11

Madam,

I hope that you and your husband, the earl are in good health and spirits.

I am pleased to report the workmen have successfully carried out the repairs to the church roof. Happily, we were blessed with a week of sunshine and dry weather, and so it was not as complicated as we feared. However, on closer inspection, I am told that the roof is in rather worse condition than we hoped, and the repairs are only a temporary solution. I will of course be seeking several opinions and quotes, but the first I enclose for your information. Not a cheap undertaking, I fear. I will, of course, speak to the Parish Council concerning fund raisers, but as you know, they are already working diligently towards several goals, and I fear the roof might overstretch their energies and their goodwill.

As I know you will have been fretting on their behalf, I am also relieved to inform you that the boys are all well and back at school and have recovered from the influenza, which

Emma V Leech

afflicted so many. However, as we have begun third declension nouns and adjectives in Latin, I believe many of them are rather wishing they could suffer a relapse. I am universally despised.

I called upon Mrs Simmons yesterday who was in excellent spirits, and she asked me to scold the earl soundly for not visiting her this weekend. Believe me, I am not about to do so, but I pass on the sentiment. I explained you were in town until the week before Christmas, but this was apparently not sufficient an excuse for his absence. As I am certain you remember, she is partial to marzipan sweets. Perhaps a peace offering?

—Excerpt of a letter to The Right Hon'ble Harriet Cadogan, Countess St Clair from The Reverend Harry Martin.

18th December 1844, Heart's Folly, East Sussex.

Barnaby's lips left hers for the first time in what might have been a lifetime, or no time at all. Victoria blinked, staring up at him, giddy and happy and more alive that she had ever felt in her life before. She smiled, the rightness of this moment, this man, the feeling of being in his arms the only thing she could think about. His expression was more serious, though, and she knew he had not kissed her lightly, not without thinking it through. She reached up and touched his face.

He jolted at her touch. "Your hands are icy," he said, covering her hand with his own and turning his head to kiss her palm.

Victoria sighed with pleasure. Her feet were wet and frozen, the snow having soaked her boots, but she never wanted this moment to end. "I could never regret you, Barnaby," she said, remembering his fears for their future, hoping he would trust her on this, but knowing it was too soon. He *had* kissed her, though.

"You say that now," he replied, his eyes searching hers, studying her intently. "But it's no guarantee, is it? I want to believe you, though. I do."

"That's a good start."

"I want this, Victoria. I want you, but—"

She pressed a finger to his lips. "But you're cautious. I understand. Lady Millicent led you on, gave you reason to hope when there was none. I would not do that, Barnaby. I have admired you for a very long time, and I know I can trust you. I hope you will come to trust me. You are a good man, one I know will never let me down, and I shall be that for you too, I promise. I shall be someone you can rely on. Please, give me a chance to prove that to you."

He stared at her for a long moment before nodding.

"Yes," he said on a breath that clouded around them. Barnaby laughed, his mouth tipping up into a smile. "Yes, I shall, though you know your father is going to murder me?"

Victoria shrugged. "Oh, no. He'll make you *think* he's going to murder you, but Mama won't let him. You'll see."

A gust of wind swept up, tugging at her cloak, and Victoria shivered. She did not think she had ever been so cold in her life.

"Come along. Let's get back to the house before you catch pneumonia, or your mama will kill me before your father can get a look in."

She laughed, despite her wet feet and frozen toes, and took his proffered arm, and they hurried together back to the house.

As Barnaby had predicted, it was close by. The old, forgotten kitchens had been built next to the wing of the house that had yet to be renovated. They hurried around the side, trying to find a way in that would avoid the staff, for once the servants knew Victoria had been missing all day with Barnaby, no power on earth would stop their tongues wagging.

"Here," Barnaby said, finally finding an unlocked door.

Victoria hurried after him, closing the door behind her.

"Watch your step." Barnaby turned, holding out his hand to her.

Victoria looked around, seeing why he was concerned. The room was in near darkness, only dimly lit by the moonlight filtering through the window. The workmen were using this room as a store for materials and tools. They had seen this on their tour of the house.

"If I remember right, this leads back to the main corridor," Barnaby said, guiding her carefully around the building supplies until they were back in the main part of the house.

"I'm freezing," Victoria said, stamping her feet and then regretting it as pain radiated through her bones. "Let's find a fire, please."

"You'd best go to your room. Then you can call for a servant and order some dinner, have a hot bath. Come along."

Victoria wasn't about to argue, too keen to sit before a warm fire, and she knew the servants would have kept the one in her room burning. Louis César and Evie were generous hosts and devoted to ensuring their guests were comfortable.

They hurried to the entrance hall and up the main staircase, moving quickly in the hope no one would see them, but the house was quiet, with no one in sight and only a few lamps burning.

"This is me," Victoria said, opening her door and hurrying inside.

Barnaby hesitated on the threshold, but Victoria tugged at his hand, pulling him into the room.

"There's no one about," she said, grinning at him.

Reluctantly, he walked in, closing the door, and then went to the banked fire, building it up for her until it was blazing merrily.

Victoria stood before it, stripping off her gloves and her damp cloak. Her fingers were blue and painfully stiff.

"S-So cold," she said, teeth chattering.

When Barnaby had kissed her, she had not noticed her discomfort, had not even thought about it, but now she realised how chilled she was after so many hours in damp tunnels and the hidden room, not to mention the snow.

Barnaby tugged a heavy wingback chair close to the fire. "Sit down," he told her, crouching before her once she had, and untying the wet laces of her boots. He tugged off one boot, and then the next. "Victoria, your stockings are wet through, and your feet are icy."

"I k-know," she said, clutching her arms about herself.

Tutting, Barnaby got up and went to the bed, stripping off the counterpane and settling it around her shoulders.

"You must take your wet stockings off," he instructed before turning his back.

Victoria tugged her skirts up and tried to pull up the legs of her drawers to get to the garters, but the mass of her skirts got in the way, and it was too awkward. She glanced up at Barnaby, who faced determinedly away from her. With a sigh, she stood, reaching for the tie of her drawers and tugging until it gave way. She wriggled them down, leaving them in a heap on the floor before sitting again, her numb hands fumbling to undo her garters, but her fingers were blue and painful, and she gave up with a huff.

"I can't undo the garters," she said irritably. "My fingers are too cold."

Barnaby turned back to her. "You can't sit around with wet feet."

"They'll dry, eventually." Victoria shrugged.

"Yes, by which time you'll have pneumonia," he said darkly.

"Well, in that case, you undo them."

Barnaby stared at her. "What?"

"You undo them!" she said in frustration, tugging the counterpane closer around her shoulders. "Or they'll just have to dry by themselves. I'm too c-cold to move."

Barnaby's brain stalled at the idea of putting his hands under Victoria's skirts.

"Er...." he said, which was not helpful.

She looked up at him, huddling deeper into the chair and shivering harder. Hell, the poor girl was frozen to the marrow. He ought not to have let her linger in the snow. They'd had quite a day, what with hidden tunnels and getting trapped. It had been cold and damp, and then walking through a foot of snow back to the house as more fell around them had only made things worse.

Well, he was not about to let her fall ill after the day they'd had. He looked about the room, seeing the washbasin, and hurried over to take two of the fresh towels stacked neatly beside it. Determined to be all business, he went back to Victoria and knelt before her, moving a fancy piece of fabric out of the way. He lifted it and almost choked. Frilly, frivolous, lace-edged drawers. She'd taken her drawers off. God help him.

Unbidden, a memory returned to him from last summer. One evening, he'd sat out in the garden with a large candle lit so he could read and enjoy the lovely night. But he'd forgotten the candle and the next morning there was nothing but a puddle of wax in the blazing sunshine where the candle had been. He rather thought that was what his brain looked like now. It certainly felt that way, his good intentions slipping away, desire sliding through his veins like hot brandy, sweet and intoxicating. Feeling dazed and not entirely in his right mind, Barnaby tried to carry on, spreading one towel over his thighs and setting the other down. Then he took hold of her cold foot and placed in on his thigh, wincing at the icy sensation even through the layers of the towel and his trousers.

Barnaby cleared his throat. "I'll… I'll undo your, er, garters, then."

Victoria nodded, apparently too distracted by how cold she was to care.

"Right," he said, still staring at her foot. Lord, but it was dainty, so tiny, her pretty ankle slender and…. "Right," he repeated, and took hold of her skirts.

Carefully, he lifted the first layer and folded it back into her lap before reaching for the next, steeling his nerves for the struggle to come.

"You'll be there all d-day," she said through chattering teeth, before reaching down, grabbing a handful of material and tugging the lot up in one go, exposing her legs to mid-thigh. Barnaby almost groaned. He wasn't ready, had not prepared himself mentally for the onslaught. The fabric all billowed up in her lap, the excessively feminine froth of petticoats and lace rustling madly and wafting the scent of orange blossom and vanilla and woman in his direction. If this was a test of his fortitude, he had the strong suspicion he was going to fail. Badly. He was done for and going directly to hell.

Though he tried to keep calm, Barnaby's heart gave an excitable thud behind his ribs, and he told himself sternly to behave and keep his mind on the job. Except the job was the garter tied just above her knee, and she had exposed her slender legs in front of him. He would have to touch her thigh. His mouth went dry. If her skirts were pulled just a little higher, he'd see that secret, most feminine place, and—

"No."

"What?" Victoria asked him.

Barnaby jumped, fighting a blush, not having realised he'd spoken aloud, nor quite so vehemently.

"N-No trouble at all," he stammered, forcing his attention to the garter, which was pink and lacy, and... good God, how many frills and ruffles and brain-melting bows did a woman need?

He was going to die from an excess of flounces and furbelows. Gingerly, trying hard not to touch her skin, he tugged at the garter, undoing it with trembling fingers. He let out a sigh of relief as it came loose, except then he had to take her stocking off.

He set the garter aside and steeled himself to peel back the stocking, delicately trying to get hold of the lacy welt trim at the top, but his fingers were all thumbs, and he could not pick the fabric up without the risk of pinching her. Barnaby held his breath as he slid his fingers beneath the fine fabric, trying to ignore the feel of her skin, which was like trying to ignore a lightning bolt as desire shot directly to his groin.

Behave, behave, behave. You're a gentleman, Barnaby Godwin, damn your eyes.

Except his eyes were suffering too, riveted to the exquisitely shaped, naked leg that he revealed as he drew the stocking off.

Get on with it before she freezes to death, you blithering idiot!

Ah, yes. He was supposed to be warming her up. Working quickly, he stripped off the other garter and stocking as Victoria shivered, blithely unaware of the war being waged within the man kneeling before her. Barnaby took the towel and gently began rubbing her feet to restore the circulation. To begin with, Victoria winced, closing her eyes, but by degrees she relaxed, and Barnaby watched her face as her expression softened. Little by little, her trembling stopped, and she gave a deep sigh of pleasure.

"Oh, Barnaby, that feels so good," she said, the words followed by a sound he could only describe as a soft moan.

Barnaby wanted to moan too, with pain and baulked lust, because he was going to go bloody mad.

"I'm glad," he said, his voice sounding far deeper than usual. He stilled, wondering if he ought to stop now. If only he could get out of the room without doing anything he ought not, then there would be no harm done.

"Don't stop."

Barnaby's gaze snapped to Victoria's, for the words had been sultry and breathless and made his heart kick about in his chest and the rest of him get ideas that were very dangerous indeed.

"Victoria, I really ought to—"

"Not yet," she insisted. Her face was flushed now, and he supposed that was usual after being so cold, but her eyes were dark, fixed upon him with such a look, and then she licked her lips, leaning towards him, reaching for him.

"I really ought to—" he said desperately.

"I know," she whispered, her mouth so close to his that her breath fluttered over his skin, and he shivered. "In a minute."

She kissed him, and he did not know what his brain looked like now, but melted wax would have been an ambitious step up. His good intentions went up in smoke as she pulled him closer, winding her arms around his neck. Barnaby pressed closer, pushing her back into the chair, moving into the space between her legs. His hands gravitated to her knees without conscious thought, for he had no thoughts, he was nothing but feeling, and as he touched her skin, his breath hitched, and he moaned.

Victoria was not helping matters, or she was helping exceedingly, he wasn't sure which, for her hands had slid up the back of his neck, into his hair. She opened her mouth, welcoming him in, gliding her tongue over his as he had taught her to. Oh, he ought not to have taught her that, but it was too late now. She was using those sweet skills against him, and his hands were moving up her thighs, the feel of her silken flesh beneath his fingers so good that he wanted, *needed* more.

"Victoria," he gasped, burying his face in her neck, breathing in the delicious scent of her.

"Don't stop," she commanded, dragging his mouth back to hers.

Barnaby swallowed a groan, his hands slipping beneath the bunched-up skirts and petticoats to where she was warm. He stroked the generous curve of her hips before returning to her thighs, tracing that delicate skin at the juncture with his thumbs. She gasped, and he waited for her to say no, to push him away, but the dreadful girl did nothing of the sort, only kissed him harder. So he did it again, his thumbs dipping lower, finding the feathery soft curls nestled in that most female place, and any thoughts of leaving this room without touching her had dissolved like honey in hot water.

The sound of a door opening, and a soft burst of laughter was the only warning he had.

"Alfie, stop that, you wicked man, I told you, I already looked and they're not... *oh!*"

As though plunged into a nightmare of the sort that would haunt him for the rest of his days, Barnaby looked up, his hands still burrowed beneath Victoria's skirts, to see his Aunt Hester staring at them with an expression he suspected was the twin of his own. Complete, undiluted horror.

"Aunt!"

"Barnaby!"

Barnaby hurriedly helped Victoria rearrange her skirts and stood, shielding her from Axton's view.

"Well, I'm blowed, didn't think the boy had it in him," the duke said, because for reasons Barnaby could not even guess at, he was there too and… and holding his aunt's hand.

"Why is Axton holding your hand?" he demanded, partly because it gave him a moment to regroup, but mostly because the duke was known to be a wicked bastard, possibly mad, and he'd already hurt Aunt Hester enough for one lifetime. If the old goat was trying it on….

"I rather think what you were holding is more to the point, my fine fellow," Axton pointed out mildly, his eyes twinkling with mirth.

"Axton, that's enough of that," Aunt Hester said, sending the man a look that suggested he hold his tongue if he wanted to live through the night. She let go of the duke's hand but remained standing close to him. "Barnaby, I am surprised at you, truly I am. Well, you've done it now. You must marry the lady, of course."

"What?" Barnaby exclaimed, staring at his aunt, so shocked by her pronouncement he couldn't think straight. "Marry her… but… you're the only one that's seen, Aunt."

"And the duke," Aunt Hester reminded him.

"Yes, but… surely the duke would—"

"Oh, no." His aunt shook her head. "He can't be trusted. A terrible tattlemonger."

"Hester, that's coming it a bit strong, I—"

Hester sent the duke another *hold your tongue or die* look, and the fellow subsided.

"I can't be trusted," Axton confessed with apparent gravity. "Tongue enough for two sets of teeth, eh, my dear?"

He winked then and Aunt Hester blushed. *Blushed!* What the devil was going on?

"I see." Barnaby said.

He was caught securely and with no means of escape. He waited for panic to set in, for the sensation of a noose tightening about his neck... but it didn't come.

"Lady Balderston, really, I don't think Mr Godwin ought to be punished for— It was my doing entirely. He only came to help me because I was so cold and, and I kissed him, and if I hadn't... Well, it's all my fault—" Torie insisted miserably.

"Don't talk nonsense," Barnaby said, cutting her off, horrified that she should attempt to take the blame when her reputation hung in the balance. This was bad enough without her making herself look like a strumpet, which was so far from the truth, it was laughable. "This was entirely my doing. You're an innocent, I took advantage. That's all. Nothing to be done about it."

Somehow that had sounded rather cold and not quite as he'd wanted it to, but he was feeling befuddled and uncomfortable under his aunt and Axton's piercing gazes.

"B-But Mr Godwin doesn't want to m-marry me," Victoria said, tearful now.

"Oh, come now—" Barnaby began, for that was patently ridiculous. Surely she knew that much?

"Then what the devil was he doing in your room, taking liberties?" Aunt Hester demanded scathingly. "Barnaby, downstairs, at once. I wish to speak with you in private. Heaven alone knows what we shall tell Bedwin in the morning when he left his daughter in my care. I was never more astonished. You, of all men."

Barnaby wondered if he would wake up soon, because this could not be real. It simply couldn't be his life. He was not the sort of fellow who went about ruining young ladies. Except he had.

There was no getting away from it. Not that he particularly wanted to get away from it, but this had not been the way he had wanted things to proceed and now—Holy God. *Bedwin.* The thought of facing the duke and telling him....

"I need a drink," Barnaby said faintly.

"Good idea. Me too," Axton agreed at once. "Just a small one," he added, catching Aunt Hester's sharp look.

Barnaby ran a none-too-steady hand through his hair and then turned to look at Victoria. She was huddled beneath the counterpane still, her cheek blazing with humiliation, eyes too bright. The poor girl looked utterly miserable. He crouched down and took her hand.

"It will be all right, Victoria. I promise. Don't worry," he said, hoping he sounded reassuring.

"But you don't want to marry me. You said so," she replied dully.

"I'd need to be out of my mind not to want to marry you, foolish girl. I'm only sorry I'm not a better catch."

She shook her head, scowling. "You're the only one I ever wanted, but not like this. I did not mean for this to happen, please believe me. I did not mean to trap you," she said, her voice quavering now.

"Of course not. I know that. Now, stop fretting. I shall get some dinner sent up to you and a hot bath, and then you get some sleep, and we shall talk in the morning. Don't worry. I shall take care of everything. My word upon it."

Victoria looked as if she would say more, but Barnaby squeezed her fingers gently and she subsided with a nod. He didn't like to leave her alone, not when she looked so unhappy, but his aunt was going to have his hide, and he would much rather that happen in private.

"Until the morning," he promised her.

Victoria nodded, and so Barnaby stood and followed his aunt and the duke out of the room.

Chapter 12

Dear Reverend Martin,

I am well, as is St Clair, I thank you and hope this letter finds you likewise.

How tactful you are. I knew the moment St Clair gave you the living that we had made an excellent choice and you have done nothing but confirm that with each year that passes, but really, if you are to survive Holbrook and its environs, you must learn to be more forthcoming. I am not the least bit sensitive, and lack imagination, so unless you hit me over the head – metaphorically speaking – I can be quite obtuse.

In this instance, I understand perfectly, lucky for you. We shall, of course, pay for the repairs to the roof. I pray you will not be so fearful to ask such questions in the future. One thing I can promise you is that if I do not wish to do something, I shall tell you. I am never subtle. Best remember that. I do hope you are more ruthless with your parishioners, for I can well imagine all the old ladies bully you into tea and biscuits quite mercilessly, and I fear what the unwed ones may be driven to, having such a handsome young vicar on their doorstep, if you are too polite to say what you mean. I know certain young ladies have been causing you some difficulties. If I might suggest you nip that in the bud in no uncertain terms, before you get yourself caught in a tangle there's no getting out of. Speak up, Reverend, and not just to God.

If you wish to practise your skills, you might demand that I help you with whatever charitable fund raising you are organising in the New Year.

I am so pleased to hear the boys are well. I have purchased some books whilst in town, which I think they will enjoy and shall deliver them on my return. I am eager to see how they go on. How is Jeb? I hope he is not still gloating over that toad he put in my basket when I visited last? I assure you, I am not squeamish in usual circumstances, and I <u>never</u> scream. Only, reaching for my gloves and finding that poor creature instead was disconcerting to us both.

I could never despise you for third declension nouns and adjectives in Latin, but then most people consider me an odd duck.

Dearest Mrs Simmons, she does adore St Clair so. I shall send him to her the moment we return with marzipan in hand and a penitent expression. Thank you for both the warning and the suggestion.

—Excerpt of a letter to The Reverend Harry Martin from The Right Hon'ble Harriet Cadogan, Countess St Clair.

18th December 1844, Heart's Folly, East Sussex.

"Here," Axton said, handing Barnaby a generous measure of brandy. "Reckon you need it. Look like you've been hit in the head with a blunt object."

Barnaby silently took the glass and drank, too stunned to reply.

"I'll take one of those, Alfie, dear," Aunt Hester said, settling herself beside the fire in the parlour. Now really, that was too much.

"Alfie, dear?" he repeated, incredulous. "Since when has he been *Alfie, dear?*"

"You're the one in the dock, Barnaby," his aunt replied coolly, though there was a tinge of colour on her high cheekbones that was interesting.

A chink in the armour. Well, he'd never seen that before.

"Perhaps, but I don't reckon I'm the only one with some explaining to do." Barnaby studied her face, alarmed when she dropped his gaze and turned to look at the fire. His aunt could etch glass with some of her sharper expressions. This was very odd. "I saw you both holding hands. What the devil is going on? If that man has been taking advantage of you—"

"Oh, hush," Aunt Hester said with a huff. "Taking advantage indeed. As if anyone could."

"He could," Barnaby said darkly, glaring at the duke.

He might be an old man, but he was powerful, and he'd a reputation for being a devil with the ladies. Aunt Hester might be ancient too, but she was still a glamorous old stick, for all that, and the duke *had* broken her heart once before. Nothing saying he couldn't do it again if she still had a soft spot for him.

"Yes, well, that's as maybe," she replied with a smile. "But that's my affair and none of yours."

"It is too my affair. Whose else is it, I'd like to know?" Barnaby objected fiercely. "Uncle is no longer with us; you've no brothers nor sons. If the duke's intentions are honourable, he can dashed well say so to me."

He turned to glare at Axton, whose eyebrows rose.

"Well, you're full of surprises tonight, young man, and I must admit, I never liked you more," Axton remarked approvingly.

"That's hardly a recommendation in the circumstances," Barnaby shot back, glowering.

Axton merely returned a very toothy grin.

"Oh, Barnaby, really," Hester said, impatient now. "We're grownups and can manage our own affairs."

Barnaby snorted and his aunt threw up her hands. "Very well. If you must have it, Axton proposed, and I accepted."

Barnaby gaped in astonishment.

"Did you accept?" the duke asked, rather too innocently, his eyes sparkling. "Was *that* an acceptance?"

"Drat you, Axton, don't be a nuisance. You know very well it was," Hester said, looking flustered but not displeased.

Barnaby could hardly believe his eyes.

"Well," he said, shaking his head. "Well, I never did."

He sat down heavily, hardly knowing what to say. Axton silently took his empty glass, refilled it and handed it back to him. Perhaps the duke wasn't such a dreadful man.

"Now that's out of the way, we shall return to the matter at hand. What were you thinking, Barnaby?" Aunt Hester demanded.

"I know what he was thinking," the duke muttered, lips twitching.

"Mind your tongue, your grace." Barnaby growled.

"Barnaby!" His aunt exclaimed.

"I'll not have him speak ill of the lady," he said hotly.

To his surprise, his aunt looked pleased with him. "No, indeed. You are quite right, my boy, only… well, I have never seen you so—"

"The boy is in love, Hester. Brings out the best in us," the duke said. "Well, those who have a lick of sense anyway," he added wryly.

"I'm not—" Barnaby began and then sighed. "Or perhaps I am. It's all rather a muddle, to tell the truth. I've been avoiding her, avoiding thinking about her. Told myself it was pointless. Well, you know what happened with Lady Millicent, but then we found that blasted chapel and the underground tunnel, and getting trapped with the roof falling in makes a fellow think, and then she was so cold, and she couldn't get her stockings off and… well, you see how it is."

His aunt stared at him. "Indeed, I do not see! What *are* you prattling on about?"

To his surprise, the duke bent and patted his shoulder.

"I see," he said with a confiding nod. "I see very clearly."

"Don't be an ass, Axton. You've no more clue what he's on about than I have," Hester exclaimed.

"I see *very* clearly," Axton repeated, going all ducal and arrogant in the blink of an eye. "The poor fellow fell for Bedwin's daughter, but thought it was hopeless, so he didn't let himself think about her. Didn't stop him from loving her, though. Then, this weekend, they're thrown together, they've obviously had some kind of adventure and excitement, then the girl was out in the cold.

A gentleman is duty bound to see his lady warm and dry. He took her to her room, tried to look after her, one thing led to another. Perfectly clear."

"Oh," Hester said, eyebrows raising. "Well, I never. I suppose I do see when you put it like that."

The duke chuckled and pulled his chair up next to Aunt Hester's so he could sit and hold her hand. Barnaby didn't even object. "There, there, darling girl. You can't be right all the time, but take heart. I'll say something stupid shortly and order will be restored."

"Foolish man," Hester said, but with such affection it was obvious how happy she was.

The duke beamed at her. Barnaby sighed. Well, at least his aunt was content.

"Now, then, Barnaby. I understand how it happened, now Axton has explained," his aunt went on. "And the truth is, as wickedly as you've behaved with that young woman, I'm pleased with you."

"What?" Barnaby's head shot up. "Why?"

"Why?" Hester repeated with a laugh. "Good heavens, Barnaby. She's the catch of the season. Fortune hunters surround her on all sides, and you took the prize! You're made, my boy, and I'm so proud of you. She's a delightful girl and will suit you admirably. I think you'll be very happy together."

Barnaby could not help but stare, too incredulous for words. "Aunt Hester, when Bedwin comes home, he's going to hang me up from the nearest tree by my tender parts. He'll not let me wed his daughter. I'm so far beneath her I may as well have been buried in that blasted tunnel. If I'd done things properly, maybe— *maybe*—I'd have stood a chance, but to have ruined her?" He shook his head. "He'll kill me, hush up any scandal, and I'll never see her again."

"Stuff and nonsense!" his aunt said, and with such force that Barnaby could not help but pay attention. "Now, you listen to me. In the first place, you are the finest young man—barring perhaps that pretty comte of yours—"

"Hester!" Axton protested.

Hester waved this away.

"You are the finest, most honourable young man I have had the pleasure of knowing, and I *am* proud of you."

Barnaby gaped. His aunt had never said such a thing in her life before. Truthfully, he'd always believed she considered him rather a twit.

"Close your mouth, dear," she said, not unkindly.

"Yes, Aunt."

"Secondly, you are not so far beneath her as you may think."

Barnaby snorted.

Hester gave him *the look,* the one that could pierce a fellow to his innards, and Barnaby held his tongue.

"You, my boy, are *my* nephew, and I am soon to be the Duchess of Axton, you might remember."

Barnaby smiled at her and shook his head. "That's true, Aunt, and I'm very happy for you, but I don't think Bedwin—"

"Hold your tongue when I'm speaking."

Barnaby sighed.

"I've never discussed this with you, but when I came to London, I visited my solicitor here and changed my will. I've left you everything. I never did like your brothers. Dull, brutish fellows, and your father is an idiot. So, it's all yours. You are the only one with an ounce of sense, and you've always been very sweet to me. You wrote regularly and never forgot my birthday, and you even made that terrible journey to visit me now and then.

Such things mean a good deal to a lonely old widow. I'm afraid you'll inherit the castle, for which you may not thank me, but your uncle left me well provided for, and I am far from penniless. It's all yours when I'm gone, and not to be sneezed at."

Barnaby gaped at her. "Aunt Hester," he said, touched beyond words. "I... I don't know what to say. I never expected, never dreamed—"

"I know you did not, Barnaby, and that's why I shall give it to you. Your wretched brothers toady up to me when I'm in town, hoping I'll leave them my money, but never once did they write, never once did they do anything for me. You are a good man, a kind one, and I wish to see you happily settled and well provided for. You love the lady, and it looks to me like she's head over ears in love with you. So, perhaps you've not a great fortune, but you've a respectable living and an inheritance to look forward to. It's enough to satisfy Bedwin, I assure you. All he wants is for Victoria to be happy, that I can promise you."

Barnaby gave a choked laugh and got to his feet. He knelt before his aunt and took her hand, between his own. "I do not know how to thank you. Truly."

Hester reached out and patted his cheek, her expression fond. "Be happy and don't stop visiting. Especially when my great nephews and nieces arrive. I'd like to be a part of it, Barnaby. I never had children of my own, but you are the nearest thing I ever had to a son."

"My word upon it," Barnaby promised, feeling rather emotional. "You'll be sick of the sight of us."

Hester laughed, her eyes sparkling with delight and Barnaby got to his feet, rather dazed.

"There is one other thing," Axton said. The duke got to his feet, facing Barnaby, his expression serious.

"Yes?" Barnaby standing as he turned to look at him, hoping the old goat wasn't about to throw a spanner in the works.

"Well, Hester says you're like a son to her and, seeing as you are her only male relation—the only one she wishes to claim, at least—then it seems we must arrange the marriage settlements."

"Axton!" Hester exclaimed. "If you think you'll touch the boy for a dowry at our time of life, you old skinflint—"

"Hester! A little credit, please," the duke said, his expression reproachful.

Hester subsided. "I apologise, Alfie, dear. Go on."

Barnaby was so startled by his aunt apologising he nearly missed what the duke said next.

"The marriage settlement," the duke continued gravely. "I am not expecting a dowry, naturally. I lost any right to that for the way I mistreated the lady so many years ago, but bearing that in mind, I feel reparations ought to be made as they were not at the time. So, the amount that her dowry would have been—with interest, of course—assuming it had been properly invested over the past years, plus a generous amount gifted by me—which is only the smallest recompense for the trouble and pain I caused, I reckon—would come in around, shall we say, ten thousand pounds?"

Barnaby frowned at the duke. "Forgive me, your grace. I'm lost. Ten thousand pounds?"

"Yes, dear boy, and stuff all this 'your grace' nonsense. I'm to be your uncle by marriage. You may call me Alfred."

"Er… very well, Alfred, but I still don't understand," Barnaby replied, completely at a loss.

"Ten thousand pounds. Is it enough, do you think?" the duke asked.

Barnaby turned to stare at his aunt, but she was gazing at the duke with an expression of adoration, one hand pressed to her mouth, the other to her heart. "Oh, Alfie, you dear, dear man."

Barnaby looked back and forth between them, totally bewildered.

"Enough for what? What is going on?"

"For you, Barnaby," the duke said gently. "I did a terrible thing many years ago, and I walked away from the woman I loved because my parents believed she was beneath me. I thought I was doing the right thing for my station, for what was due the title, but I have regretted that decision, every moment of every hour of every day that followed. I can never get that time back, but I shall not waste a second of the time I have left, and it is very clear to me that Hester admires and loves you like a son. Hester does not give her heart to just anyone. It is a privilege reserved for a select few. So, let me ensure you do not feel you are beginning your life with the Lady Victoria by lowering her in society. I shall give you the ten thousand, and you are honour-bound to accept it, for I give it as amends to Hester for my idiocy, such paltry amends as it is. In return, all we ask is that you and Victoria and any children you have be a part of our lives. No one will turn their nose up at you, my boy. Close family of the Duke of Axton is no small thing, and money can make many in society close their interfering mouths."

Barnaby's knees gave out, and he sat down, not bothering to check there was a chair beneath him, and narrowly missed hitting the floor.

"Ten thousand," he repeated, bewildered by his good fortune. "I'm dreaming."

"Then that makes two of us," Aunt Hester said, her voice thick with emotion as she got to her feet and went to Axton, embracing him in full view of Barnaby and not appearing to care a jot. "Axton, you devil, I do love you so."

In that moment, dazed and happy as he was, it was a sentiment that Barnaby was not too far from echoing.

Chapter 13

Dear Miss Milly,

I am writing to express my gratitude for the help you provided yesterday. There I was, sitting in the snow like an idiot, wondering what on earth I could do and praying for a miracle, and lo, there you were. I imagine many fellows have flattered you and called you an angel, but you truly were mine.

Of course, when I say <u>I am writing</u>, that is obviously not true. My private secretary, Humboldt, has the dubious pleasure of writing and reading all my correspondence. I tell you this in case you felt inclined towards writing billet doux. Not that I could blame you for developing a tendre for me. You are clearly susceptible to my charms, but I am told Humboldt blushes prodigiously and I should hate to discompose him, the poor fellow. He's doing it now. I cannot see it, naturally, but I can feel the heat of his chagrin clear from the far side of the room.

I was hoping that I might call upon you before Christmas, but it appears I have taken a chill from so long in the cold and I vain creature *that I am, I refuse to appear in public with a red nose and sniffing. So, I will keep my vile ailments to myself and leave you with the image of the handsome fellow you rescued in your mind for the time being. <u>You did say I was handsome, Miss Milly, do not deny it.</u> I told Humboldt to underline that bit. I hope he did so.*

Once I am well again, or as close as this imperfect fellow can get, I shall call upon you. We have much to discuss, you and me.

Yr obt svt.

Wrexham

—Excerpt of a letter to Miss Emmeline Knight (daughter of Lady Helena and Mr Gabriel Knight) from The Most Hon'ble Leander Steyning, The Marquess of Wrexham

19th December 1844, Heart's Folly, East Sussex.

Torie stared out of her bedroom window at Heart's Folly with her own heart as weighted down as the boughs of the trees outside, laden with snow. She supposed she ought to be overjoyed. Her wish had come true. She was to marry Barnaby Godwin. Except she had not wished to trap him into it, and he had looked so shocked and horrified by the idea that she knew she could not hold him to it. No matter what Papa said. She would not marry a man who didn't want her.

Oh, she wasn't a fool. She knew Barnaby liked her. He certainly desired her. Perhaps he was even fond of her, but fondness and desire was not love and she did not wish to force herself upon an unwilling bridegroom. She wanted a marriage where both partners considered themselves equal, like her parents did. It was true Papa could have married far higher than Mama, but he had never, by word or deed, treated Mama as anything less than his equal. He loved and respected her, and Torie wanted that, too. If Barnaby would always feel he was beholden to her, it would put pressure upon their relationship and they would not flourish under such circumstances, no matter how much she wished for it, or how hard she tried.

With a sigh, Torie rested her forehead against the cold window glass. She closed her eyes, remembering those blissful moments last night, before everything had gone wrong. If only the duke and Barnaby's aunt hadn't arrived. Things had been going splendidly well, and she'd been certain, if they could only spend some time alone, that Barnaby would see how perfect they were together, how happy they could be. She had never felt so wonderful as when he had put his hands on her. Excitement and desire had surged through her with such heat and wonder she had not questioned it. How right it had felt for him to touch her so. There had been no doubt in her mind, no possibility that he was not the man with whom she should have been doing this.

It had been natural, so natural she rather thought she would have given him her maidenhead if they'd not been interrupted. Another wistful sigh escaped her, and Torie shook herself. Her parents could be home at any time. Though the roads must be thick with snow, the day was clear and bright, and she doubted it would be long before everyone returned and discovered what she'd done. Torie blushed at the thought of everyone knowing she'd ruined herself, but there was no help for it.

It was rather too early for breakfast yet. Torie had slept ill and risen earlier than usual. She was in no hurry to face Barnaby, either, for she knew he would be kind, just as he had been last night. Even though she had got him into this dreadful mess, not to mention into damp tunnels and almost getting buried alive, he had not reproached her. Instead, he had reassured her that he would make everything right, and told her not to worry. Torie blinked back tears as she remembered and then scolded herself for being a ninny. She would simply have to keep herself busy until her father got home, and then… and then she would tell Papa the whole truth, and he would see she was very much responsible for the fix they were in. He could not possibly blame Barnaby, nor hold him to this forced marriage.

Feeling wretched, Torie made her way downstairs and greeted the staff who were going about their day and setting out the breakfast things. She thought she observed two of the maids exchanging glances as she passed, but hurried on without comment. Not wanting to get in their way, she went to the library instead, relieved to discover a fire burning. Taking a moment to peruse the shelves, Torie considered trying to read a novel, for there were some interesting titles, but she knew she did not have the concentration for that. Instead, she looked for anything that might document the history of the house or the family who had lived in it for so long. She still could not understand where the treasure was buried, for surely the tunnel leading to a secret place was ideal? It made no sense. Though perhaps Heart's Folly was riddled with tunnels and hiding places.

Torie's heart gave an unexpected skip as something Louis César told her came to mind. He'd said there was a tunnel between the original kitchens and the library. Despite everything that had happened with Barnaby, the lure of finding the treasure lifted Torie's spirits just enough to make her want to look for it. Besides which, if she did not keep busy, she would end up moping about and looking pathetic, and that did not appeal either. Yet, the endeavour was rather a daunting one as she looked about the vast library and wondered where on earth she ought to begin. Not to be put off, Torie decided she'd best be methodical about it and began in the corner beside the window, determined to find the hidden tunnel if it took her all week.

Emmeline handed her cloak and bonnet to the footman before stripping off her gloves. The grand entrance hall was a flurry of activity as everyone shed their outdoor clothes and hurried to get upstairs and change. The impromptu overnight stay away had been pleasant enough, but everyone was feeling rumpled and wanted to tidy themselves up.

"How lovely to be back," she said to her sister Evie, who grinned at her.

"It's become home very quickly," Evie agreed, nodding. "And the inn was rather cramped."

"Noisy, too," Emmeline said, trying not to yawn. "I didn't sleep a wink."

"Neither did I," Evie replied, though from the way her lips twitched as she sent an accusing look towards her husband, Emmeline did not think it had been for the same reason, or that she minded.

Louis César merely quirked an elegant eyebrow and returned an expression of complete innocence. Smothering a grin, Emmeline was about to go to her room when the butler approached her with a silver salver.

"This came for you, Miss Emmeline."

"Oh, thank you," she said, taking the letter from the tray.

"Who is it from?" Evie asked, and Emmeline shook her head, not recognising the handwriting.

"I don't know."

As Emmeline turned the letter over, she noticed the seal and her heart gave an excited leap. Not wanting her sister or anyone else to notice how flustered she was, Emmeline slid away, hurrying to the library to get some privacy. Slipping inside, she closed the door behind her and turned, only to almost leap out of her skin.

"Oh, Torie!" she exclaimed, pressing a hand to her thudding heart. She stared in consternation at her friend, who was kneeling beside the door, peering at the floorboards. "Goodness, you startled me. Whatever are you doing down there?"

Torie clambered to her feet, giving Emmeline a rueful smile. "Looking for secret tunnels."

Emmeline burst out laughing. "Well, of course you are. I ought to have known."

"You really ought. What's that?" Torie asked, gesturing to the letter she was clutching. "And why have you run to the library to open it in private?"

Emmeline sighed. That was the trouble with Torie, she noticed things.

"Oh, you won't believe what happened to me yesterday," she said, fighting the urge to squeal like a lunatic. It had not only been the noisy inn that had kept her awake, as the scene with Wrexham played over and over in her mind, especially the part where he'd kissed her.

Rather to Emmeline's surprise, Torie snorted.

"Perhaps, but I rather suspect my day is going to trump yours," she said darkly.

"Oh, well, let's compare notes," Emmeline said, taking Torie's hand and dragging her to sit by the fire.

With growing surprise, Emmeline listened as Torie outlined what had happened in the hours since they'd been gone.

"Good heavens," she said, staring at Torie. "You did have an adventure."

Unable to help herself, Emmeline burst out laughing.

"It's not funny!" Torie exclaimed.

"Oh, no. No, of course not." Emmeline hurried to straighten her face. "Only, I keep imagining poor Mr Godwin's expression when his aunt and the duke walked in on you."

Torie gave a huff of laughter then, remembering. "Oh, it was the picture of horror, you may be certain, though not so bad as when he realised he must marry me," she added glumly.

"Oh, come now, Torie, I don't believe that. I'm certain it was just the shock of the moment. You know how funny men get about marriage. Once he's used to the idea, I'm certain he'll be delighted. He certainly ought to be," Emmeline said staunchly.

Torie shrugged. "Perhaps. We'll see. But now you're back, that means Mama and Papa are here, and no doubt speaking to Lady Balderston right now. Oh, I want to die. It's so embarrassing. Tell me what happened to you quickly. It might take my mind off it, and you'd best hurry because I'll likely be locked in my room from now until doomsday, and... oh no!"

"What?" Emmeline said in alarm.

Torie put her head in her hands. "I was just thinking about poor, darling Octavia. She's only five and I've already ruined her life. Papa has been impossible enough with me, never letting me out of his sight, and now look. He will have Octavia sent directly to a nunnery to avoid any further trouble."

Emmeline sniggered, shaking her head. "Don't be such a goose, Torie. It's more than ten years until she comes out. I'm certain your father will have relented by then."

"Hmph," Torie said, unconvinced. "Anyway, the letter, who's it from?"

Emmeline bit her lip, blushing. "Lord Wrexham."

"Wrexham? The one you sat next to at the dinner party? Are you sure?"

"Yes, why?"

"Well, you said he's blind, that's all. How does he write letters?"

Emmeline frowned and turned her attention to the letter, breaking the seal. "I expect he dictates to a secretary. Lots of men don't actually put pen to paper. Papa doesn't write all his letters, there's far too many."

Hurriedly, Emmeline unfolded the letter and read the contents.

"You're blushing," Torie observed.

"Hush," Emmeline said, chewing her lip as she read, hardly believing the wicked man could be so very forward. Oh, he was so… so…. She looked up to find Torie staring at her.

"Tell me everything," Torie said. "Because if the look on your face is anything to go on, you'll be joining me in ruination any day now."

Emmeline's blush deepened, but she told Torie about finding Wrexham out in the snow, about guiding him to the inn, and….

"He kissed you!" Torie exclaimed, shocked.

"Only on the cheek," Emmeline said, rather defensively.

"He's blind, he probably just missed."

"No, he didn't!" she retorted, irritated. "If he'd meant to kiss me properly, he would have. It was more—"

"If you say affectionate, I shall laugh in your face," Torie warned.

Emmeline huffed. "I know it wasn't affectionate. I was going to say it felt more like a promise."

"A promise of what?" Torie demanded. "Disaster?"

Emmeline laughed, handing over the letter to her friend. "Trouble, certainly, if his letter is anything to go by."

Torie read, laughing and exclaiming at Wrexham's audacity. "Trouble indeed. My word, Emmeline, promise me you'll never be alone with this man. Blind or not, he's a wicked seducer, any fool can see that."

"He *is not*," Emmeline said, annoyed by the comment. "He's a bit wicked, I grant you, and I do believe it is in his nature to flirt and tease. It's as natural to him as breathing, but Torie, I think he's in trouble. I think a lot of that teasing and bantering is a way of hiding the truth."

"And what is the truth?"

"I don't know, but he says in the letter we have much to discuss. He asked yesterday if he might call upon me, and I got the feeling he needed someone to confide in. I promised him he could trust me to keep his secrets, and so, if he confides in me, I shall do what I can to help him."

"Emmeline, you know his father is that awful man, the Duke of Sefton. Everyone knows he and Wrexham loathe each other, and don't you remember how vile the duke was to Cara? I should hate for you to get on the wrong side of him too. I can only imagine the trouble he could cause you if he thought you were taking his son's part in whatever war they're waging. Are you certain you know what you're doing?"

Emmeline laughed. "Oh, Torie, I don't have the least clue what I'm doing, and I certainly don't want to attract Sefton's notice, but I can't just leave Wrexham alone. He's all but disappeared from society, from what I gather, so perhaps he doesn't have anyone else. I know I ought not, but I can't stop worrying about him. He's on my mind all the time, and—"

"And you're smitten," Torie said with a heavy sigh.

"No. Nothing like that."

Torie pulled a face. "You can't stop thinking about him, but you're not smitten. Mm-hm!"

"I'm not! I'm only…." Emmeline looked at Torie's patently disbelieving expression and scowled, considering her words. Could it be more than concern she was feeling? Emmeline remembered the touch of Wrexham's lips on her cheek and her heart began an odd little dance in her chest. "Oh, drat and botheration. Torie, you're right. I *am* smitten! Oh, the wretched man."

"Yes, you are."

Emmeline put her head in her hands. Something told her this was not like her usual infatuations that came and went in a matter of weeks. Wrexham was nothing like the sort of men she usually got all dreamy and stupid over, for one. They were usually bookish, intellectual types who liked poetry and discussing art. She did not know if Wrexham liked books or art, let alone poetry, but from what she had gathered of him before he went blind and disappeared from society, he had been a very physical man. Riding, boxing, fencing... if there was a sport to excel at, he was the best. As for his reputation with women, the little she had learned had put her to the blush. This was not the kind of man she had ever been interested in. Libertines were dangerous and even if, by some miracle, they really loved you, a man like that would inevitably cause trouble. Evie had illustrated that truth in the boldest of colours. But despite knowing this to be the reality of the situation, there was something about the marquess that called to Emmeline. He was just so very intriguing and like no one she had ever met before and she... she was smitten. Oh, this was very bad.

"This is most inconvenient. How did it even happen?" she demanded of Torie, who simply shrugged, her expression one of sympathy.

"The same way it always does. With a man. And now we're both in the basket," Torie said with a groan, and handed Emmeline back her letter.

Emmeline sighed and then sat up, brightening as a thought occurred to her. "I know what we ought to do."

"Join the circus?" Torie suggested.

"No!"

"A nunnery?"

"Certainly not!"

"Then I'm all out of ideas."

"The hat!" Emmeline exclaimed, bouncing in her seat. "This is the perfect time for you to take a dare."

Torie sent a sceptical glance. "How so?"

"Do you think you can make things any worse?" Emmeline demanded.

Torie considered this. "A fair point. Where is it?"

"Aggie gave it to me. I put it in my room. Come along, Torie, let's do it now."

And with that, Emmeline leapt to her feet, tucking her letter securely away in her pocket, before grasping Torie's hand and towing her from the room.

Chapter 14

Dear Max,

I hear via the grapevine that congratulations are in order. A son, indeed. You might have told me. Have you named him in my honour? But I forget, we are not friends any longer, so you shall have to accept congratulations from – what? An enemy? Or merely someone you used to know? There's a lowering thought. Perhaps I'd best ensure your enmity. Rather that than be forgotten.

Nonetheless, I shall raise a glass in your heir's honour with the hope he become as fine a man as his father. Lud, I can almost hear you asking yourself if I'm foxed as I write, old boy. You're damned predictable. Yes, as it happens. I'm foxed and bored to death, and I don't know what to do about it.

I miss the days when neither of us gave a damn about anyone or anything. I fear I'm getting old and dull, and the thought appals me. I must do something wicked to calm my nerves before people forget they're supposed to revile me and merely dislike me instead. Perhaps I ought to sacrifice a virgin on some pagan altar, though there's gossip enough that says I've already enacted such nonsense so perhaps I'll not bother. Virgins are too tiresome.

Speaking of, I did a good deed. No, it's true, bear with me. I found that troublesome chit of Montagu's loose on the town, dressed as a boy, would you believe? I know you'll burn this letter and keep the information to yourself, but it's too delicious not to share and there's no one else I can tell. The temptation to cause mischief for Montagu was tantalising, but then I thought of Lady Montagu and how worried she would be. Ah, I am getting sentimental in my old age. So I returned the child to her parents, no harm done. I don't like the way the girl looks at me. I think the idiotic creature is infatuated. Can you credit it? She had the temerity to inform me that she's eighteen in February and will be out next year. I believe I repressed the shudder that ran down my spine, but it was a near thing. I dropped her at her parent's door and fled.

Well, this won't do, I have debauchery to indulge in or else my despicable reputation will fade, and the ton will forget to talk about how scandalous and depraved I am. Be happy, Max. One of us ought to try it.

—Excerpt of a letter to The Right Hon'ble Maxwell Drake, The Earl of Vane, from The Most Hon'ble Ciarán St Just, The Marquess of Kilbane.

19th December 1844, Heart's Folly, East Sussex.

Torie and Emmeline stood, staring down into the hatbox that contained the dog-eared top hat that had belonged to their mothers. They shared an uncertain glance and then both leapt a foot in the air at the sound of a sharp rap on the door.

"Oh, my word. I swear my nerves are all on end today," Torie said as Emmeline hurried to see who it was.

"Hardly surprising," Emmeline replied with a grin, before opening the door. "Cat!"

"Em!"

"I found her on the doorstep," Aggie said from beside the girl, grinning as Cat burst into the room like the force of nature she was. She hugged Emmeline before running to hug Torie, too.

"I'm free!" she exclaimed, laughing and jumping on the bed with a flurry of skirts. "You cannot know how wonderful it is to be allowed out of the house after so long and... Oh! *The hat!"*

She picked it up, taking it out of the box before anyone had time to blink, let alone say anything.

"Now you've done it," Aggie said, shaking her head. "Cat, you might let them take a breath, you know."

"Are you taking your dares? *Now?"* Cat demanded, her silver-grey eyes, so like her father's, glittering with delight. "What marvellous timing. Who's first?"

Torie laughed and shook her head. "Well, I'm in the most trouble, so I suppose it had better be me."

"Trouble? What trouble?" Aggie and Cat chorused in unison.

Torie sighed and sat on the bed beside Cat. "Give me the blasted hat, and then I'll tell you everything."

Barnaby tugged irritably at his cravat and then jolted as a large hand landed on his shoulder, squeezing.

"Good God, man, settle your feathers. You're as jumpy as a harlot attending Sunday service," Axton—no, *Alfred*—said, giving his shoulder a fatherly pat.

Which was surprisingly comforting, but then Barnaby's father had been disinterested in giving fatherly advice or comfort. He was of the opinion his sole contribution to his offspring had ended once he'd impregnated their mother... a tradition Barnaby's brothers were continuing, from what he'd seen to date.

"I'd offer you a drink, but it's barely ten a.m., and your aunt will have my hide if you face Bedwin half cut."

"I don't think a tot of brandy is going to turn my head," Barnaby grumbled, though his stomach had tied itself into a knot last night and showed no signs of disentangling itself, so it might just make him cast up his accounts.

"No, shouldn't think so. Here then, just a nip, steady your nerves."

Barnaby hesitated and then snatched the silver hip flask Alfred held out to him and took a large swallow. Warmth bloomed in his stomach and his tight muscles relaxed a degree. He handed the flask back before he was tempted to drain it, barely containing an exclamation as the door opened.

He let out a breath of relief as he saw not Bedwin, carving knife in hand, but Louis.

"Barnaby," Louis said, his blue eyes sparkling in a way that made Barnaby groan with mortification. *"Mon ami,* what *have* you been up to?"

"Louis, don't. I am truly not in the mood. Bedwin is speaking with my aunt. They've been in your study for over an hour. I swear he's making me sweat on purpose."

"I should too, in his position. I mean, you *did* compromise his daughter. Really, Barnaby. I had no idea how wicked you are," Louis tsked, giving a mournful shake of his head. "All this time we have been friends, and you never gave me the slightest clue about your true nature. When I think how you scolded me for the way I seduced my wife, and all the time I have been nurturing a viper. I have been sadly deceived."

"You can go off people, you know," Barnaby said hotly, folding his arms.

Axton snorted with amusement as Louis laughed and sat down beside Barnaby, slinging his arm about Barnaby's shoulders. "There, there. I am only teasing you, and you cannot blame me when, for so long, the shoe was on the other foot."

Barnaby made a sound of discontent but did not labour the point.

"Stop fretting," Louis chided him. "Hester adores you. She'll be telling Bedwin just how fortunate he is in gaining you for a son-in-law when Lady Victoria is already in love with you. I mean, have you seen some of the repulsive fortune hunters who gather about her? It's not to be borne. If I were Bedwin, I'd be hard pressed not to stand guard over her, pistol in hand."

"Not helping, Louis," Barnaby grumbled.

"I am helping, you're just missing the point. He might not like the circumstances, but he'll not be displeased with you marrying Victoria, you mark my words."

Barnaby sighed and ran a hand through his hair. "I've been telling myself the same thing, but—"

"But Bedwin is rather terrifying," Louis replied with sympathy. "I know. In your position, I would be in the same state. I *was* in the same state when I had to face Evie's father, if you recall. I've faced some daunting situations in my time, but Mr Knight ranks high in my memory for terror, because I knew I'd behaved badly. But faint heart, etcetera. Keep your head."

Barnaby nodded, though his stomach still dropped when the door opened again, and Aunt Hester appeared.

"Barnaby, come along. His grace will see you now."

"We'll pray for you," Louis said gravely, though his eyes were lit with amusement.

Barnaby sighed and got to his feet, muttering about unfeeling best friends, and followed his aunt to find the duke.

"Now it's your turn, Cat. Torie has confessed all, so now you must tell us. What *did* you do?" Aggie said, her eyes wide as she regarded her friend.

Cat buried her face in her hands and groaned. "You'll think me an idiot, I know you will."

"Probably," Aggie agreed. "But tell us anyway, you mad creature."

She tugged Cat's hands away from her face and Torie wondered if Cat realised quite how beautiful she was. She certainly did not seem to care. Unlike many girls of her age, she did not primp or fuss about her dress or her coiffure, and was often far quicker getting ready than anyone else when she stayed with friends. Though, looking like she did, little fuss was required. She could wear sackcloth and not bother to brush her hair and still turn the head of every male in a ten-mile radius. When she came out into society, she would cause a sensation.

"Do you promise not to scold me?" Cat asked Aggie gravely. "Because I swear, I've been scolded enough to last the next decade."

"Oh, Lord, Cat. This is going to be bad, isn't it?" she said with a pained sigh. "Well, I promise to try. I can do no more."

Cat pulled a face, but nodded. "Very well, then, but try hard. If you must have it, I dressed up in boy's clothes and sneaked out to go to the Egyptian Museum in Piccadilly."

Torie and Emmeline gasped, staring at her in shock, but Aggie waved this away.

"Well, I knew you were going to do that! Don't fob us off, Cat, that's not why you're in such trouble."

Cat blushed a little, possibly the first time Torie had ever seen an expression of such chagrin on the girl's face. "I... er... Well, there was a bit of an argument. This stupid boy tried to pick my pocket, and I stopped him, but then he tried to hit me, so I hit him back. Drew his cork, too," she said, looking pleased with herself, though the expression faded quickly. "But the idiot boy wouldn't concede I'd won, and he called his friends over and it got really nasty and then, well, someone recognised me."

"Oh, *Cat!*" the girls said in unison, gaping at her in horror.

For anyone to have seen her acting in such a way, in public, and dressed as a boy...! The enormity of the trouble she could be in was staggering. So terrible even Torie's problems faded in comparison.

"Who recognised you, Cat?" Aggie demanded, her face pale with concern.

Cat cleared her throat, looking shifty. "The Marquess of Kilbane."

An appalled silence fell over them as they gazed at Cat in disbelief.

Without saying a word, Aggie got to her feet, calmly smoothed down her skirts and walked to the door, closing it quietly behind her.

Torie watched her go before turning back to Cat, a question in her eyes.

"She's gone somewhere private so she can swear and shout without shocking you. Aggie has the most marvellously vulgar vocabulary. You should ask her sometime. It's fascinating," Cat said, looking at them nervously. "Though I don't think she ought to have bothered. From the looks on your faces, nothing she could have said would have shocked you more than I have."

"Probably not," Emmeline agreed. "Oh, Cat, whatever happened?"

Cat gave an impish grin and then paused as her best friend marched back into the room. Aggie went directly to Cat and smacked her around the back of the head.

"Ow!" Cat complained, rubbing the spot.

"Well, someone had to. Are you completely insane?" Aggie demanded furiously, her hands on her hips. "You could have been murdered on the street. Kilbane could have abducted you, forced you to marry him, or… or done far worse and not married you! My God, Cat, you'll give me a nervous collapse before either of us are eighteen if you keep this up!"

"I'm fine!" Cat retorted. "And you didn't try at all not to scold me, you wretched girl. For your information, Kilbane was a perfect gentleman. Well, apart from telling me I was an outrageous chit, and he ought to throw me in the Thames and save my parents any more trouble. I keep telling you he's not so awful as everyone makes out, but the gossip about him is so much more entertaining than the truth, so nobody gives him a chance!"

Aggie snorted and folded her arms, looking mutinous but saying nothing.

Cat sighed. "Do you want to know what happened, or don't you?"

Aggie sat back down on the bed, still glowering. "I suppose so," she said grudgingly.

With a grin, Cat leaned in towards them. "Well, then…."

🎩 🎩 🎩

"What happened, what did he say?" Barnaby demanded as he followed his aunt, feeling very much like a schoolboy about get his hide tanned by the headmaster.

"That's a private conversation, Barnaby," Hester replied reprovingly.

"A private conversation about me!" he retorted. "And I think you might give me an inkling of what was said. Should I run for France, or is he being reasonable?"

Hester paused, turning to face him. "Barnaby, I have spent the past hour calming his grace down. He was *not* pleased."

"Oh, Christ," Barnaby said, running a hand through his hair.

"Stop sweating," Hester said, shaking her head. She took Barnaby's arm, walking him inexorably towards Bedwin. "He is still not pleased, by any means, but he is calm and ready to listen to you. It's not pistols at dawn, my boy. So just tell him the truth and look him in the eye. You've not acted well, but your character and your past speak for you. If you love the lady and sincerely wish to marry her, I believe you can bring him around."

"Right," Barnaby said, nodding. "Right. Will do."

He took a deep breath and held still as Hester tweaked his cravat into place and reached up, smoothing his hair back down.

"You're a good boy, Barnaby, and I'm proud of you, remember that. Now go into that room and make Bedwin see why you are the best man to marry his daughter, because it's true."

Barnaby huffed out a breath and then nodded.

"Thank you," he said sincerely.

"It's my pleasure," Hester said, patting his cheek fondly. "Now, in you go, and good luck."

Barnaby turned and knocked on the study door.

"Come," called a deep voice from inside.

Steeling himself, Barnaby entered the lion's den.

The duke was standing by the fireplace as Barnaby entered, and his expression gave little away. Though he must be close to sixty years of age, the man was still powerfully built and looked full of strength and vigour. His dark hair was tinged with grey, his green eyes cool and piercing, and his presence exuded authority in a way few men could.

Barnaby gathered his nerve and closed the door, walking into the room. "Your grace."

"Sit," Bedwin said.

"I'd rather stand, sir," Barnaby replied, not wanting to be in a position where the duke could loom over him.

"And I'd rather you hadn't compromised my daughter, but it seems none of us shall have what we want this day," the duke replied coolly.

Barnaby sat.

Bedwin observed him for a long, silent moment as Barnaby fought not to fidget. Then he turned and walked to a crystal decanter on a tray with glasses arranged on a side table.

"Drink?"

Barnaby's eyebrows went up and he looked at the clock. It was barely ten thirty in the morning.

The duke followed his gaze. "It's that sort of day. Do you want one or not?"

"God, yes," Barnaby said with feeling.

Bedwin poured two glasses and handed one to him before taking his own and returning to his position by the fireplace. He stared down into the flames and sipped his drink before returning his attention to Barnaby.

"Well? Explain yourself."

Barnaby took a large swallow of his brandy. "I tried to stay away from your daughter, sir, I swear that I did. She's beautiful, and funny and clever and… and she takes my breath away. I knew the first moment I met her that she was a danger to me."

"A danger to *you*?" he repeated, incredulous.

"Yes," Barnaby said simply. "I expect you know I had hopes of Lady Millicent."

"I am aware of the gossip," Bedwin replied. "She had several young men dangling after her the past two years, but you were her clear favourite."

Barnaby nodded. "Then you know I made a complete twit of myself." He coloured, frowning. "I don't think I ought to say more about that."

Bedwin regarded him over the rim of his glass. "Much as it pains me to say so in the circumstances, I disagree. The lady led you on. She was secretly engaged to another the entire time. A humiliating experience for any man. I can well imagine your feelings."

Barnaby clenched his jaw.

"Quite," he said tersely. "Which is why I was in no hurry to repeat the experience. I swore never to look above my station again. I certainly had no intention of turning my attention to a duke's daughter of all things. When Lady Victoria wrote to me and made me aware of her feelings, I knew I must keep my distance. I believed I had replied to her in a way that made it plain there could be nothing between us. That was not the end as I had hoped, however, but then I told her to her face that despite my deep admiration of her, there could be nothing between us, and I swear to you I meant every word. At least, I meant it when I said it."

Bedwin glared at him but said nothing, so Barnaby ploughed on.

"But I could not keep the promises I made to myself. Each time I saw her, my admiration for her grew and… Sir, you must know she's a force of nature. A whirlwind of life and adventure that sweeps you up and before you know what you've done, you're somewhere you ought not be. Please, understand, I am not suggesting this is in the least her fault, she did nothing wrong. She was simply beguiling and such an unearthly temptation I could not make myself stay away from her."

"She wrote to you to tell you of her feelings?" Bedwin said after a long moment, interest glinting in his green eyes as he completely disregarded everything else Barnaby had said.

"Er…" Belatedly, Barnaby realised he probably ought not to have mentioned that. "N-Not exactly that, no. I mean, it wasn't a love letter, more a—"

Bedwin sighed and motioned for him to stop talking. "Never mind. I am not a fool, young man. My daughters are single-minded, and I have been aware of Victoria's interest in you for some time."

"You have?" Barnaby stared at the man in surprise.

Bedwin returned a scathing look. "A father with a daughter makes it his business to know who her friends are, and upon which men her gaze lingers. A duke with daughters would be a bloody fool not to know every detail of every person she ever interacts with. Not that the knowledge has helped me. I seem incapable of keeping my girls out of trouble. I blame their mother," he added, though with such a wry smile Barnaby did not think it was really a complaint.

"Victoria did nothing wrong," Barnaby said earnestly. "She's entirely innocent."

Bedwin snorted, eyeing Barnaby with interest before moving from his position, propping up the fireplace, and sitting down. "I know my daughter, Mr Godwin, and I do not doubt she has earned her fair share of blame in this little debacle. She wanted you and she set out to have you. Well, by God, my girls get what they want, no matter my feelings or my efforts to stop them. What I want to know is how you feel about that, and what you're going to do about it? You clearly did not want an unequal marriage, which we both know this would be. So, tell me, how will this work? Will you spend your days making Victoria unhappy because you've lowered her social standing and feel guilty for it?"

Rather stunned by this, Barnaby took a moment to reply. "No! No, never that. I only ever feared she would regret me. I could not stand the idea that in a year or two she might look at me and regret not having married a duke or a marquess, someone of her own kind who could keep her in the manner she is accustomed to."

"You feared? Past tense?" Bedwin said.

Barnaby nodded. "I'll never be more than I am, sir. There would need to be a catastrophic amount of tragedy in the family before I got close to a title, however, my financial situation is rather better than I had reason to hope for, and… and I believe Victoria is sincere. At first I thought it was merely an ill-advised infatuation, a young woman's fancy, but for all her imagination and love of adventure, your daughter is not flighty, nor silly. She's an intelligent woman who knows her own mind, and I would be a fool to think she cannot judge her own heart. I believe she cares for me, and I— Despite my best efforts, I have fallen in love with her. I think we could be happy together if you will allow us to try."

Bedwin seemed to consider this, taking another drink before he answered.

"Tell me of your financial situation. Lady Balderston informs me she is leaving everything to you, and that you've recently had a rather large bequest. Ten thousand, is it?"

Barnaby nodded. "That's right."

"I'll admit that is far better than I hoped for from you, and my daughter is far from mercenary. If you ask her to live within a certain income, she will do it, but if you were to keep her as befits her station, that money will not last indefinitely and Lady Balderston strikes me as a lady with a deal more living to do. Of course, Victoria has a generous dowry, but you have hopes of being independent of that, if I have read you correctly. So, what else is there?"

Barnaby hesitated. "I have a small business."

"Go on," the duke said, narrowing his eyes.

"It's doing rather well but, until recently, I have lacked the investment necessary to grow. With my recent, er, windfall, that will change."

"I do hope this is not some get rich quick scheme," Bedwin said darkly.

"Oh, no, sir. I own a small stud. Always loved horses, you see, since I was a lad. Spent all my holidays in the stables, avoiding my father and brothers," he added with a wry grin. "We had the most marvellous horseman there. He's old as Methuselah's grandfather now, but he still knows more about horseflesh than any man I know. He's taught me so much, and… so, about ten years ago, with his help, I began breeding horses. I had some success, and so, two years ago, I decided I could make a go of it professionally, and… it's been doing quite well."

Bedwin sat up, obviously interested now. "What's the name of this budding enterprise?"

"Chevening Stud, sir."

"Chevening!" The duke stared at him. "Are you quite serious?"

"Yes, sir," Barnaby said, resisting the urge to tug at his cravat.

"Then I bought a horse from you early this year. A hunter," the duke accused him.

"Yes, sir. Trooper. A very fine animal, if I might say so." Barnaby felt his stomach drop, praying the duke was pleased with the animal.

"He's the best horse I ever owned, drat you, but why the devil did I not see you or hear mention of your name if the place is yours?"

Barnaby held out his hands. "Well, as I said, sir, I had hopes of Lady Millicent and a gentleman does not work for a living. Also, my father would have had an apoplexy if he'd found out. It's one thing for a fellow to breed a few horses, but this is very much a commercial undertaking and... well, I thought it best to keep my distance. So, my manager, Mr Granger, deals with sales and I occupy myself with the bloodstock."

"And this little business is doing 'quite well,' is it?" the duke demanded wryly. "Good God, I should think it ought to be. I've sent St Clair and Cavendish your way in the past couple of months alone, never mind all the fellows who demand to know where I bought Trooper. For heaven's sake, man, you ought to have begun with that. It's a fine establishment, something to be proud of, and I, for one, don't hold with the idea of not working. Idleness is fertile ground for discontent, and it's a short path into the kind of trouble no young man needs."

"Yes, sir," Barnaby said, a bit winded by the idea the duke might actually have found something to approve of.

They sat in silence for a few moments as the duke ruminated over all that had been said. Barnaby judged it best to hold his tongue and let the fellow think in peace.

Finally, the duke spoke. "Whilst I am an admirer of your stud's breeding program and quite agree the finest bloodstock is paramount in producing the best horses, it may surprise you to discover I do not feel that way about people. I have observed over the years that the great families of England who intermarry entirely with their own kind are peopled by a far greater percentage of beetle-headed nincompoops and outright lunatics than those who take a more moderate view. My Eliza's Mr Demarteau is hardly the kind of son-in-law that a man in my position would seek, but Nic has two things that no other man in England has: the ability and the desire to make Eliza happy. This he has done, without fail, and I have discovered a man I both admire and like very much."

Barnaby held his breath.

"I have seen you around, Mr Godwin, and I have heard much about you, and never once has anyone spoken ill of you. Furthermore, the way you followed Villen to France when you believed he was in trouble, and the care you took of Miss Smith whilst there, speaks of the kind of man who takes his responsibilities to others seriously and puts their feelings and safety ahead of his own. So, if Victoria will have you, I'll give you my blessing."

For a moment Barnaby could do nothing but stare at him, so touched and relieved by everything the duke had said he hardly knew which way was up.

Bedwin laughed and got to his feet, moving towards Barnaby, who stood hurriedly as the duke held out his hand to him.

"Don't look so shocked. I know a decent fellow when I meet one, and I think you'll do, Mr Godwin. I think you'll do very nicely. Welcome to the family, presuming you've not messed things up with Victoria, at least?"

"I certainly hope I haven't, and thank you," Barnaby said, dazed and overwhelmed. "I'm honoured that you should say so, and you may depend on me, sir. I shan't let you down, and I'll do everything in my power to make Victoria happy. I swear I shall."

"I believe you, Barnaby, and I think, under the circumstances, you may call me Robert. Now then, let us have another drink to settle our nerves and you can tell me more about this business of yours. As it happens, I'm in the market for a pair of carriage horses...."

Chapter 15

My Lord Marquess,

I also address this to the estimable Mr Humboldt, for whom I have the most profound and sincere admiration for putting up with his employer's unreasonable and outrageous demands.

Wrexham, what the devil were you thinking writing such a letter to me? I know you have been out of society for some time, but the rules have not changed in your absence. <u>You do not write to unmarried ladies</u>. I feel certain the much put-upon Mr Humboldt pointed this out to you, and you wilfully ignored him. Not that I am surprised. From what I have discovered of your character to date, I only wonder that he has not gone away and found a more restful employer to work for. The Zoological Society of London springs to mind.

And do not go supposing this in any way resembles a billet doux, you dreadful man. Your charms, indeed. I do not wonder that poor Humboldt blushes, no doubt with embarrassment for your hubris.

As for any aid rendered, it was my sincere pleasure to do so. Though I am certain anyone would have acted likewise, I was glad to render my service to you and would do so again, should you require it.

Much as it pains me to admit it, you are handsome, Wrexham, but never fear, your dubious charms are tempered by your over-inflated ego and appalling sense of humour. Still, I am sorry to hear you are poorly, and wish you a speedy recovery.

I cannot imagine what we have to discuss, but I look forward to you enlightening me.

Yrs etc,

—Excerpt of a letter to The Most Hon'ble Leander Steyning, The Marquess of Wrexham from Miss Emmeline Knight (daughter of Lady Helena and Mr Gabriel Knight).

19th December 1844, Heart's Folly, East Sussex.

"Oh, do come on!" Cat exclaimed, shaking her head. "You've been rooting about in there for ages."

Torie scowled at her. "I must find the exact right one," she said with a huff, before snatching up a small slip of paper and pulling it from the hat. She held the dare aloft and squeezed her eyes shut. "Oh, I can't look!"

"Come on! Read it," Aggie urged her, as Cat leaned across the bed and plucked it from Torie's hand.

"I'll read it, then," Cat said, carefully unfolding the paper.

"What does it say? What does it say?" Torie demanded, covering her stomach with her hand as butterflies erupted.

Cat shook her head. "I can't quite make it out. It's an old one and very blurry."

They all watched as Cat squinted, turning the paper this way and that and poking out her tongue as she concentrated on making out the words.

"Find your heart's... demise? Oh, surely not! Oh, *desire*! Find your heart's desire and... I can't read the rest."

"Give it here," Torie said, snatching the paper back, her heart thudding. Surely it couldn't say *heart's desire* when she had been searching for the treasure of Heart's Folly? But it did! The rest of the dare was impossible to make out, but it had to be an omen. "I must go!" she squealed, leaping from the bed so fast she upset the hat and all the dares spilled out.

"Torie!" Cat exclaimed. "Wherever are you going?"

"To do her dare, obviously," Emmeline said, laughing.

"Now? But how? Where? I don't understand what's happening," Cat complained.

"Good luck, Torie!" Emmeline called after her as Torie ran from the room, determined that finding the treasure would somehow make everything come right.

After all, the hat had all but spelled it out for her, and it hadn't guided any of them wrong yet. Uncertain of where she ought to start, Torie ran back to the library, flinging the door open and bursting into the room with such a flurry that Evie gave a little shriek of alarm.

"Torie! Whatever is wrong?"

"Oh, nothing," Torie said, offering a sheepish grin. "I was just in a hurry. I don't suppose you have a history of the house, or anything of the sort?"

Evie laughed and held up a small book. "As it happens, I do. Your interest in Mrs Payne got me thinking, and I remembered I'd seen a series of diaries that belonged to her. They were given to Louis with the estate ledgers when he bought the place. It's fascinating reading, though the tiny writing is making my eyes cross."

"Have you found anything about the treasure?" Torie asked.

"Just listen!" Evie said, her eyes alight with excitement. "There's an interesting bit here. Apparently, there used to be a chapel, with a secret tunnel that led to a hidden room. It was a last resort for Mrs Payne to hide her daughters if they failed to keep the soldiers out. They stocked the place with food and blankets, books and paints, and candles enough to last a couple of weeks."

Torie's eyes widened. "She hid her most precious possessions. Her daughters."

Evie nodded. "Yes! Exactly. Though it couldn't only mean her daughters, could it, for she promised God never to retrieve them if he kept them all safe? I don't think she meant to leave her daughters hidden away forever. It seems like she did well to prepare for the worst, though. They had a near miss. Ten soldiers broke into the property. Mrs Payne and her staff fought them off, but her daughters were only young, and she feared what the soldiers would do to them. It says here that she bade them run to their hiding place, and gave the eldest, who was seventeen, 'the treasure and the care of her little sisters,' and told her to take them and not come out until someone came to find them."

"Really?" Torie exclaimed, wide-eyed. "And so they went to the hidden room, with the treasure, and the paints... *oh.*"

"Isn't it wonderful? Imagine if we could find the remains of the chapel! Louis has gone to look for the plans of the property, because it must be marked, mustn't it?"

"Yes," Torie said, biting her lip. She knew she ought to tell Evie she had found the chapel, but... but it was still *her* adventure, and she only wanted to find the treasure. She'd give it straight to Evie, but it would be nice to have proven something to herself. Perhaps her father would not think her such a ninny for the mess she was in, too, if he saw she'd had reason for going off on her quest, however ill-advised he might think it. And perhaps Barnaby might be proud of her for finding it. Perhaps he might see that she was not a silly girl with a head full of romantic nonsense, but someone who could see past the obvious, and discover something truly wonderful hidden behind what some people might see as an ordinary façade.

She could only hope so.

By the time Barnaby left the duke's company, he was pleasantly mellow. Two generous glasses of brandy had soothed his nerves enough to comprehend that Bedwin had not only given his blessing for Barnaby to marry Victoria, but astonishingly, the man seemed to like him! And he even wanted to buy more horses. This was so beyond anything that he'd expected that he had the oddest sense of unreality, as if he was walking in a dream and might wake at any moment. He hoped not, though, for he could not wait to see Victoria and tell her the good news.

Twenty minutes later, however, he still had not tracked her down. So, he hurried to Miss Knight's room, wondering if Victoria was with Emmeline, as the two of them were close friends.

"No, though she was here," Emmeline said when she answered his knock. "But she left about forty minutes ago. Have you tried the library? I suspect that was where she was going."

"No, but I'll do so now. Thank you," he said, and hastened back down the stairs.

On reaching the library, he found Louis and Evie poring over an ancient-looking map.

"Barnaby!" Louis said, straightening at once and crossing the room towards him. "How did it go? Do you need a second?"

Barnaby laughed, shaking his head. "No. Nothing of the sort. It was just as you said, Louis. He put the fear of God in me to begin with, but then… he just wants Victoria to be happy, and he likes me. Can you believe it?" he said, still finding the whole thing incredible.

"Of course I can believe it!" Louis exclaimed with an impatient tsk. "I have been telling you this entire time, the lady is lucky to have you. So, he gave you his blessing?"

"He did," Barnaby admitted and then yelped as Louis hauled him into a hug, kissed him on both cheeks and stood beaming at him. *"C'est merveilleux!* Truly, Barnaby, I could not be happier. Congratulations, *mon ami."*

"Thank you," Barnaby said, unable to keep the ridiculous grin from his face. "Only I would like to actually *ask* Victoria to marry me before anyone else finds out, but I can't find her anywhere."

"Oh, she was here," Evie said. "About half an hour ago. We were talking about the treasure. I found Mrs Payne's diaries, you see, and we discovered she sent her daughters to some hidden room. There's an underground tunnel from the chapel, apparently, only we've never seen the chapel. I suppose it's a ruin now, but we were trying to find it on the map. Isn't it marvellous?"

"And, er, what did Victoria say about that?" Barnaby asked nonchalantly, because his beloved clearly hadn't told them she'd already discovered it.

Evie frowned. "Nothing much, actually, which is surprising as I thought she'd love such information, though she flew out of here like—"

"Excuse me, must dash," Barnaby said, and ran from the room, much to his friends' consternation.

Victoria sat on the freezing floor of the hidden room behind the old, deserted kitchens, and stared at the jam jars, wondering if she'd lost her mind, but this was the only hiding place she could think of. When Mrs Payne had sent her daughters down here, they must have feared that someone might discover them, despite the cleverly hidden room. Perhaps they feared that, if their house was taken, one of the servants might confess their whereabouts to save their own skin. If that happened, they would wish to hide the treasure somewhere safe, somewhere they could retrieve it if and when things quietened down. But Mrs Payne, her family, and the house she loved so much had all survived and, in thanks to God, she had left the treasure where it was. Why on earth would anyone hide jam behind a secret panel, unless it was not jam at all?

In her diary, Mrs Payne said they had supplied the hidden room with food, books, and paints. The eldest Miss Payne had both the time and supplies to paint a disguise on the panel between the room and the kitchens. Even if the hiding place was discovered, there was a chance the jam would be dismissed as an oddity as she and Barnaby had done, and if the soldiers had discovered the daughters via the kitchens, they could always still escape through the tunnel or vice versa.

Carefully, using the knife and the spoon she had brought for the job, Victoria peeled off the wax seal and peered inside. The jam was very dark, almost black, and when she poked it with a spoon, she discovered a dense, almost rubbery texture. Wrinkling her nose, she spooned the contents into the bucket she'd carried with her. Evie's staff obviously believed she was eccentric for asking for such things, but had supplied the items she'd needed without comment. No doubt they were used to odd requests from the nobility and nothing much surprised them. The jam dropped into the bucket with a heavy thud, but to Victoria's disappointment, there was nothing in it, only rubbery ancient jam. Well, it would have been too easy to discover something in the first jar, she supposed, and it made sense that they would hide the treasure in amongst other ordinary jars of jam to give an extra chance of evading discovery. So, undaunted, she kept opening jars.

Eighteen jars later, however, the bucket was almost full, and she only had two of the earthenware jars left. These had seemed the most likely to her, for they were impossible to see through, and so she'd instinctively left them until last. With her heart beating very fast, she peeled off the wax seal, spooning through the dark, sticky mixture. Nothing.

"Drat," she muttered, before turning her attention to the remaining jar. "Well, then. It must be you."

"Victoria! Torie, love? Are you here?"

Victoria jumped at the sound of Barnaby's voice. For a moment she considered keeping quiet and pretending she hadn't heard him, but that was cowardly, and he *had* helped her find this place, and the jam. No matter what happened between them now, he deserved to be a part of her discovery, assuming there really was anything to discover and she wasn't completely addled.

"I'm here," she called, just as his wonderfully familiar face appeared through the opening.

"I knew it!" He laughed before crawling through on his hands and knees, no doubt ruining another pair of trousers. "What on earth are you doing?"

Victoria looked around at the empty jars and the bucket brimming with centuries-old jam.

"Looking for treasure," she said, feeling a bit silly… but no, she had every reason to believe the treasure was here. Still, she wondered if he would laugh at her.

"In the jam?" he asked, surprised but not mocking.

"Well, they must have hidden it for a reason, Barnaby. Nobody hides jam, no matter how good it is, and Evie said Mrs Payne sent her daughters here when soldiers broke into the house, and that among their supplies of food and provisions they stored here for emergencies, there were books and *paints."*

"The daughters hid the treasure in the jam and painted the panel to keep it secure!" Barnaby exclaimed. "And you figured it out. Well, by Jove! That's dashed clever, Victoria."

Torie brightened, smiling at him. "Well, I thought so, but now there's only one jar left. Here, do you want to open it? Maybe you'll have better luck."

Barnaby moved closer, sitting on the floor of the room, cross-legged beside her. He shook his head. "No, love. This is your adventure, your discovery. If there's treasure to be found, you should be the one to find it. Besides," he added, his expression growing soft. "I already found my treasure."

Victoria's heart gave an uneven thud in her chest as she stared at him. Though it hurt her to do it, a sorrowful, deep ache began in her heart and radiated outwards, and she knew she must stop this. She shook her head. "It's all right, Barnaby. I know you don't want to marry me, not really. I won't hold you to it. I couldn't bear to make you unhappy, and I know you would—"

The words she had steeled herself to say to him were cut short as Barnaby pressed his mouth to hers. Victoria sighed, longing and regret surging through her like a winter tide.

"I'm not such a bad bargain as I thought I was, Torie, love," he whispered, breaking the kiss. "There's so much that's happened since yesterday. In fact, since the moment I arrived here, my life has been turned upside down and inside out."

"I'm sorry," she said at once, only for Barnaby to silence her with another kiss.

"I'm not. I'm not the least bit sorry. I'm only sorry that I underestimated you. I ought not to have done that. To have compared you with Lady Millicent and what happened with her was wrong and foolish, and I need to apologise to you for that."

"You do?" Victoria said, a little dazed and not entirely sure what was happening.

"I do," Barnaby agreed. "And there's something else I need to do. In usual circumstances I would think this is the worst possible time for me to do such a thing, but this is not the usual circumstances, for you are a very unusual woman, Lady Victoria Adolphus, and somehow, I think you'll enjoy this more than a moonlit night and roses."

"I-I don't understand," Torie said, and then gasped as Barnaby shifted, kneeling before her and taking one hand.

"You really ought to be standing, but we'll make our own rules, won't we, love? Because you are *my love*, my dearest Victoria, and I was a fool to fight it when the truth of it was staring me in the face."

"Oh." Victoria pressed her sticky hand to her madly beating heart. "Barnaby, are you quite certain? You're not just saying that because you think you ought to, because you're being kind?"

"I'm certain," he said, his dear face filled with sincerity, his eyes shining with an expression that made her throat tight with emotion. "I'm certain that I love you, that I want to be with you. And, as your father was so very kind as to give me his blessing, I'd like to ask you, dearest Torie, if you would do me the very great honour of becoming my wife?"

Victoria gave a little yip of joy and threw herself at Barnaby, kissing him soundly and overbalancing him so thoroughly that they both fell, sprawled over the dusty floor. When she finally let him up for air, Barnaby gave a breathless laugh.

"Might I take that as a yes?"

"Yes! Yes, please! Oh, most definitely, yes!"

Barnaby pushed back her hair, which was falling around her face as she stared down at him. "Can we marry quickly, love? Do you mind?"

She shook her head. "The sooner the better."

He grinned at her. "Just as well, as I think Louis' staff are gossiping about us. I believe our, er, little indiscretion has become the talk of the servants' hall."

"Oh." Victoria blushed, making him laugh again.

"Don't fret, Torie. Once they hear we're engaged, it will all be smoothed over. A Christmas wedding might be nice, don't you think?"

"I think it would be perfect, Barnaby," Torie replied, so happy she was on the verge of tears.

"It would, and how about finding that treasure, too? I'd love to see everyone's faces when you go back to the house, having solved the mystery."

"It doesn't seem so important now," she admitted. "Not when I have everything I've ever dreamed of. We've come this far, though."

"We have," Barnaby said, reaching over and picking up the spoon. "Go on, one last jar."

Torie beamed at him and took the spoon, scrambling off him to reach for the heavy earthenware pot.

"Here I go," she said, carefully peeling off the wax seal. "Wish me luck."

Barnaby grinned, leaning in to kiss her. "You don't need luck, you're marvellous."

Torie blushed and bit her lip, too overwhelmed to know what to say. So, she turned her attention back to the pot, and dug the spoon into the thick, rubbery jam. It struck something hard. She gasped, staring at Barnaby with wide eyes. "There's something in here!"

"Good heavens! You did it," Barnaby said, laughing as Torie began carefully spooning out the contents.

"Oh, my!" she exclaimed. "Oh, my, Barnaby, just look."

With shaking fingers, she put her fingers in the sticky mess to grasp a thick gold chain and pulled. Out came a necklace, covered in ancient jam, but glinting as bright as the day Mrs Payne's daughters had sealed it up.

"Bloody hell!" Barnaby said, his eyes almost on stalks and his expression so stunned Victoria could only give a hysterical hiccough of laughter.

She couldn't blame him, though. At the end of the chain was an enormous ruby, the biggest she had ever seen, surrounded by diamonds and set in gold.

"The heart of Heart's Folly," Victoria said, shaking and laughing and crying all at once.

"What a little beauty," Barnaby said in wonder.

"It *is* a beauty," Victoria agreed, carefully wiping the jam from the magnificent jewel.

"I wasn't talking about the ruby, love," Barnaby said gently.

Victoria paused, looking up and smiling. "I love you, Barnaby."

Barnaby grinned at her. "Well, I should dashed well think so! Bit much after all this if you turned round and changed your mind."

"I never shall," Victoria said solemnly. "Never, never, not ever."

"Well, that's all right, then. Shall we go back and show them what we've found?"

Victoria nodded. "Can we tell them we're engaged?"

"If you don't, I shall," he said, looking so pleased with himself she could not help but kiss him again.

One kiss inevitably led to another, and so it was sometime later that they emerged, dirty, sticky and exceedingly happy, to discover all the guests gathering on the steps of Heart's Folly. Everyone was warmly dressed in cloaks and scarves, for the snow was falling again.

"They look like they're ready for a treasure hunt," Barnaby whispered, taking her hand in his.

Victoria snorted. "Too late," she said, knowing she looked horribly smug and not caring a jot.

"What the devil happened to you?" Jules demanded, staring at his sister with revulsion. "You look... ugh, what is that black stuff all over you?"

"Jam," Torie said happily.

Jules glowered at their joined hands and then at Barnaby. "Godwin, I always thought you a decent sort, so I'll give you precisely two minutes to explain why you and Victoria look so dishevelled, and where the hell you've been, before I pound an answer out of you."

"Stand down, Jules," came a wryly amused voice as the duke placed a hand on his eldest son's shoulder. "They're engaged. Though, I admit, Barnaby, I would like an explanation as to why you both look so disreputable."

"We found the treasure, that's why," Victoria said, quite unable to keep the triumphant grin from her face. She didn't think she'd be able to stop smiling for weeks, perhaps months, such was her delight and happiness in the events of the past hour.

Their friends crowded around them with an eruption of exclamations and questions.

It took the duchess to bring some order to things and herd everyone back into the house so that Victoria and Barnaby, who were feeling decidedly chilly now, could warm up and have a cup of tea.

"Engaged!" Emmeline shrieked, tugging at Victoria's arm and practically bouncing on the spot! "When? What happened? Was it terribly romantic?"

"Just now, just before we found the treasure," Torie said, hugging her friend. "And yes, it was perfect. The most perfect moment I could possibly have imagined. Oh, Em, I'm going to marry Barnaby. Isn't it marvellous?"

"Marvellous!" Emmeline agreed, hugging her back and laughing, tears in her eyes, sharing in Torie's joy in the way only a true and dear friend could.

"Yes, yes, marvellous, very romantic. Congratulations. Now, for heaven's sake, Torie, show us the blasted treasure!" Jules demanded.

Torie stuck her tongue out at her brother and marched past him, into the parlour as everyone else followed her in. She went directly to the chair beside the fireplace and sat down, with Barnaby standing beside her, such pride in his eyes as he did so that she felt a little giddy.

Once everyone was settled and she had their undivided attention, she began her story, starting with the first time they had found the chapel, but leaving out anything she deemed too personal.

"So that's why you ran out in such a flurry!" Evie said, when Torie explained the moment when she'd realised where the treasure was hidden.

Torie nodded, looking a little sheepish. "I'm sorry, Evie, I know I ought to have told you then, but...."

Evie waved this away. "Nonsense. I shouldn't have told me either, if I were you. It was your adventure, your discovery. Though, I have to say, Torie, I am dying of curiosity. What was the treasure? I shall burst if you don't tell us at once!"

Torie glanced up at Barnaby, who was staring at her adoringly and grinning like a bedlamite. "Go on then, love. Put them out of their misery."

With a laugh, Torie took the remarkably heavy weight from her cloak pocket and carefully unwrapped the necklace from the clean handkerchief Barnaby had supplied for the purpose. She held it aloft and the astonishing jewellery swung back and forth, the massive ruby and encircling diamonds glittering in the lamplight. The room erupted, their friends and family all eager to get a better look and exclaiming with excitement. Torie was congratulated and feted, though she tried to explain that Barnaby had been as much the discoverer as she had. Naturally, her modest fiancé waved this away as nonsense.

Once everyone had settled down again, Torie got to her feet and went to Evie. "This is yours now, Evie."

Evie gasped, staring at her. "Oh, no! But, Torie, you found it. We might never even have looked if not for your interest. I thought it was an old wives' tale, and—"

"No," Torie shook her head. "Barnaby and I have discussed this, and the jewel belongs here. The heart belongs with Heart's Folly. It must have been a gift from Mr Payne to his beloved wife. After all, if the man built her this wonderful home, it's just the sort of thing he would do. So it deserves to remain here, with you, with a woman who is as adored by her husband as Mrs Payne was."

"And with a bit of luck, you'll have as many daughters," Barnaby said, grinning slyly. "Six, was it, Torie?"

"Seven, I think," she replied, snorting as Evie's eyes grew round and even Louis looked a little startled.

"That is the most remarkable gift, Lady Victoria," Louis said, sliding an arm about Evie's waist and pulling her close. "And you may rely on the fact I could not adore the lady of the house more, no matter how many daughters she produces, though I am happy to try for seven. I think we ought to have at least a son or two in there as well, though, *mon amour,"* he added gravely."

Evie gave a bark of laughter. "You do, do you? Dreadful creature," she said fondly.

"It needs rather a good clean," Torie said, handing over the necklace. "It's still a bit sticky."

"It's wonderful," Evie said, sounding choked.

Louis handed her a handkerchief with an expression of tender amusement. "She's the most appalling watering pot these days," he said as Evie snatched it from him with a disapproving sniff.

"Well, I think I had better get cleaned up," Torie said ruefully.

"Me too," Barnaby said, looking down at his dusty trousers with dismay. "I'm afraid I shall run out of clothes soon. I had no idea this trip would be so hard on my wardrobe."

"You are looking thoroughly disreputable," Aunt Hester agreed, looking him up and down with a pained expression. "So run and change quickly, before your lovely fiancé goes off the idea of marrying such a ne'er-do-well."

"Oh, I shan't do that, no matter how he looks. And it's my fault, in any case," Torie said stoutly.

"We didn't doubt that, my lovely hoyden," the duke replied with a sigh.

"This is why one must always pack for every eventuality," Louis said gravely. "That will teach you to tease me over my luggage."

"Oh, no it won't," Barnaby retorted. "No man needs that much luggage."

"I do," Louis insisted. "And if you're thinking of borrowing something, I should be a deal more polite to your host if I were you. Come along with me at once. Elton will be overcome with joy to have the opportunity to get his hands on you."

"Oh, no, Louis, really. There's no need—"

"Hush, Barnaby. There's really no point in fighting it," Louis insisted, propelling him towards the door.

Torie could not help but laugh as Louis escorted Barnaby out of the room, her adorable fiancé grumbling all the way.

Chapter 16

Madame,

I was sorry to discover your absence upon my visiting you this morning, as I had hoped to address this to you in person. However, as this is the third time I have called with no response, I feel I must seize the day and put my feelings in writing in the strongest terms.

You __must not__ send your daughter, alone and unchaperoned to my home. Whilst I appreciate the generous gifts of biscuits and cakes, it is most inappropriate for a young woman to visit a bachelor establishment such as mine unescorted. Either you or another adult must accompany her, or she must not come at all. Though it pains me to be at all rude, if this happens again in the future, I shall not, under any circumstances, open the door to her. If any were to see her visiting me at the rectory in such a ramshackle way we both know the rumour mill would shred the young lady's reputation, and mine, into the bargain. As Vicar of this parish, I have a responsibility to set an example to my flock and I would beg your aid in this endeavour.

Please speak to Miss Steadman and ensure no further visits of this nature are forthcoming.

To make my position clear, I am a young man yet, and have <u>no intention</u> of marrying anytime soon.

Forgive me for speaking plainly, Madame, and I pray I have caused you no offense but in my experience, it is best to lay one's cards upon the table so there is no chance of misunderstanding.

Yr obt svt

—Excerpt of a letter to a parishioner from The Reverend Harry Martin, Parish of Holbrook, Sussex.

22nd December 1844, Heart's Folly, East Sussex.

"Are you quite certain about the waistcoat?" Barnaby demanded, staring at his own reflection with concern.

Elton had seemed to think it was just the thing and Barnaby could hardly pretend that Louis César wasn't the most elegant man he'd ever known. However, that was Louis César. The man looked like a young god. Barnaby was not a young god and had no desire nor expectation to be. He did not, however, wish to look a prize twit on his wedding day.

Louis gave a long-suffering sigh and rolled his eyes. "For the tenth time, *oui, mon ami*. The waistcoat is precisely *comme il faut* and, if you attempt to take it off, I shall strangle you with it. There, does that soothe your uncertainty?"

"Not really, but if you're going to take a pet over it, I'll keep it on."

"I shall indeed take a pet, so leave it alone, and do stop fussing with that wretched cravat! *Mon Dieu*, you try my patience this morning. It is a wonder you have not reduced poor Elton to tears. The man is an artist, and there you are quibbling and arguing over his every choice."

"I am not wearing pink, and that's an end to it," Barnaby said stubbornly, folding his arms.

Louis waved this away. "It was not pink, it was coral, but it is of no matter. That copper tone was an inspired choice. It brings out the colour of your eyes but is subtle and understated. Very elegant, Barnaby. I am proud of you."

Barnaby sighed, knowing when he was beaten. "Fine. I'll wear it."

"I should think so, too. Now, a little something for your nerves, perhaps?" Louis said with a smile, handing Barnaby an elegantly engraved silver hip flask.

"Oh, bless me, yes, please," Barnaby replied fervently, practically snatching the flask from Louis' hand.

"That is my best brandy, do not guzzle it so. It is to be appreciated and… oh, never mind. I give up. A man is entitled to be nervous on his wedding day."

Louis sighed and took Barnaby's place before his dressing room mirror, putting the final touches to his own appearance as Barnaby sat down, nursing the hip flask.

A knock at the door startled him so much he almost dropped the flask, but caught it at the last moment as Elton reappeared.

"I believe it is time to go down, *monsieur,*" he told Louis.

Louis nodded and turned to regard Barnaby. "Well, *mon ami,* you are fortunate in having a duke in the family who can procure a special licence with a snap of his fingers."

Barnaby nodded. "I suppose so, only right at this moment it all seems to have happened rather too fast, and—"

"Just nerves, Barnaby, deep breaths. You may keep the hip flask. Come along, your bride awaits."

With a firm hand gripping his arm, Louis escorted Barnaby from the room and down the stairs. As they passed a large window that overlooked the front of the house, Barnaby paused.

"It's snowing again," he said, smiling. "Torie will like that."

"Yes, though anyone wanting to leave ought to do so today, I'm afraid. One of the gardeners here is a true old countryman, and he tells me this weather is set in for the week at least. I don't think anyone will be going anywhere for a while if they dally. Not that we mind, the more the merrier. Which leads me to something else I was going to say. If you've no plans, why not stay with us for a while? It's a big place, and you know we'll not be the least put out if we don't see you while you're here. We're still rather in the, er, honeymoon phase ourselves," he added wryly.

Barnaby let out a breath. "Louis, that's awfully good of you. Are you quite certain, though? I'd be glad to give my staff a bit more time to prepare for me turning up with a wife. They'll be running about like headless chickens as we speak and that… well, assuming Torie is happy, that would be wonderful."

Louis patted his shoulder, looking pleased. "Of course I'm certain. I could not be happier. This is excellent news, for we shall celebrate Christmas together."

"Thank you, Louis, you're a good friend," Barnaby said, meaning it. "And I'm sorry, for being so stubborn before. I know you were only trying to help and—"

Louis laughed and waved this away. "Think nothing of it. I am only happy you are celebrating this wonderful day here at Heart's Folly. Perhaps I am getting sentimental in my old age, but I feel the house has been sadly alone for too long. It needs filling with people and happiness and celebration. I can almost feel the place sigh with relief that it has a family under its roof again."

"You are getting sentimental," Barnaby said with a laugh. "But, as I cannot help but agree, I shan't tease you about it. Come along, then. At this rate, Torie will be there before me, and we can't have that."

His nerves suddenly gone, replaced only by an impatient desire to see his bride, Barnaby practically ran down the stairs to the great hall, where everyone was gathered for the ceremony.

"Good heavens," Emmeline exclaimed, before smothering a laugh as her older sister Florence turned to stare at her.

"I know," Flo said with a wry smile as she put a fretful baby Mabel on her shoulder and patted her back to soothe her. "The Reverend Martin in all his glory. Isn't he beautiful?"

"He's the vicar?" Emmeline demanded in shock, staring at the man Evie had just shown into the room.

Tall and broad-shouldered, he was an imposing figure in his clerical gown and did not look like the sort of reverend Emmeline was accustomed to seeing. The vicar at the church they attended was about ninety, smelled strongly of mothballs, and had a tendency to forget where he was in the service. Sometimes this was handy as he skipped large sections, other times it meant listening to the same sermon twice. Emmeline did not think this would be a problem with the Reverend Martin. Truthfully, she doubted any female with a pulse would hear a word of what he said. They'd be too busy gazing into his warm, brown eyes and thinking wicked thoughts.

"He is indeed the vicar, and it's impossible to get a pew on Sunday if you don't turn up early. Every woman for miles around is there. Some aren't even from the parish! The poor man has the devil's own job going about his business, for everywhere he goes there's some female making sheep's eyes at him. Henry thinks it's hysterical. Well, he does now he believes I'm not among the smitten… but it must be very trying for the poor man."

"Isn't this outside his parish?" Emmeline demanded.

"A little, yes, but the vicar for Heart's Folly and the surrounding area is very elderly and won't come out in this weather, so Henry had a word with Harriet, and she asked a special favour. They've just committed to restoring the church roof, so Mr Martin couldn't really refuse."

"What's he like?" Emmeline asked, curious as to why the beautiful man had not set her pulse a-flutter, for he was exactly the kind of handsome, romantic figure that usually attracted her attention and invaded her daydreams. An obviously handsome, yet sober and intelligent man of the cloth ought to be the stuff of her dreams, and yet whilst she could admire all his many, *many* charms, she *was* only curious, not… interested.

"Thoroughly decent, sincere, and completely baffled why he has such an effect on the female population. It's rather adorable, actually. He's so serious about everything and tries so earnestly to do his job, and yet he's thwarted at every turn by young women turning up to bring him cakes, or to do the flowers in the church. The to-do there was over the Harvest Festival was quite the scandal in these parts. There have been a few rather awful scenes, you know, between jealous rivals. Oh, we may prefer to rusticate most of the year these days, Em, but it's never dull."

"So it appears," Emmeline said, shaking her head. "I had no idea Sussex was such a hotbed of intrigue and romance."

"Well, that's because you've not given it a chance. Never mind London, come and stay with me, my girl, and I'll open your eyes to life in the raw." Flo nodded knowingly, easing an increasingly fractious Mabel from one arm to the other.

Emmeline snorted. "Fibber. You just want me to help with the children."

"Lord help me, yes! Please come," Florence wailed, making Emmeline give a loud bark of laughter as Flo snorted.

She did not know if it was the laughter, or the snort, but Reverend Martin looked in their direction, his expression puzzled and rather disapproving, making her and Flo dissolve into giggles.

Evie hushed them with an amused glint in her eyes. "Barnaby is here," she hissed. "Behave yourselves, you dreadful girls."

Solemnly, Emmeline and Flo nodded, and sat silently side by side, shoulders shaking.

Barnaby stood at the front of the room, whilst the gathering behind him all chattered animatedly and took their seats. He gave the vicar a double take, for the Reverend Martin was not what Barnaby had expected at all, but the fellow was polite and had an air of authority about him, which was reassuring to Barnaby's leaping nerves.

"A pretty fellow," Louis observed, watching the vicar as the man readied himself for the ceremony.

"Yes, certainly. Don't fret, though, he's not prettier than you," Barnaby said dryly.

Louis quirked a dark eyebrow, blue eyes glinting. *"Évidemment,"* he replied, feigning outrage. "Or I should never have let him in."

Barnaby laughed, and then the room fell suddenly silent. He turned, all the air leaving his lungs in a rush as he saw Victoria, his bride, and was overcome with a wave of pride and love and such happiness it was impossible not to smile. He knew it was supposed to be a serious ceremony, that their vows were not to be taken lightly, but he had never believed it possible this moment would happen, and to see the answering, giddy smile lighting up his beloved's face only made him grin all the harder. A soft ripple of laughter filled the room, but Barnaby didn't give a damn. In any

216

case, it was a warm sound, affirmative and full of affection from all the people in their lives that loved them best and approved wholeheartedly of their happiness. Belatedly, Barnaby noticed the duke, upon whose arm Victoria was walking. As they reached him, Bedwin raised his daughter's hand to his mouth, smiling at her with pride and affection. Then, somewhat reluctantly, he offered her hand to Barnaby.

"Take care of her, Mr Godwin. I am putting my trust in you," the duke said, his expression grave but encouraging.

"I will, your grace. Don't ever doubt it," Barnaby replied sincerely, before taking his bride's hand in his.

"Good day to you, Mr Godwin," Victoria said, blushing shyly, her lovely green eyes sparkling.

"It is a very good day, Lady Victoria. The best day that ever was," he replied, lacing their fingers together and turning to face Reverend Martin.

The reverend was not so stuffy as most vicars Barnaby had come across and returned a good-natured expression, his dark eyes warm as he looked at them both.

"Dearly beloved," he began, his voice deep and carrying, and Barnaby swore he heard several women behind him sigh, but then the ceremony was underway, and he didn't give a tinker's cuss for anyone else in the room.

There was no one else in the world but his bride, and the quicker he could get the ring Louis was looking after on her finger, the better he would like it.

Torie looked about the room and experienced such a burst of happiness she did not know how she could contain it. Evie had done her proud. Her wedding breakfast was a glorious affair. She had adorned the enormous fireplace with candles and the most splendid mantel dressing, with huge boughs of pine and bay, decorated with red ribbons and Christmas roses, apples and nuts and cinnamon sticks. The scent of pine and spices filled the room and mingled with the mouth-watering smell of every dish that was brought in to please the guests, each more lavish than the last. The table was heavy with crystal and shining silver, and outside the snow had begun again.

Many of the guests were leaving after the meal before it was too late. Mama and Papa had commitments and needed to return to Beverwyck for Christmas—something Torie suspected Barnaby was relieved about, not wanting to face her father over the breakfast table tomorrow. The Knights were staying for Christmas, though, with Lady Helena and Gabriel Knight having arrived just that morning.

"Happy, love?"

Torie turned to Barnaby—*her husband*—and nodded. "Very, but I'm a little overwhelmed, honestly."

"It's been something of a whirlwind," he agreed, taking her hand and lacing their fingers together. "No regrets?" he asked, lowering his voice.

Torie shook her head at once. "Not a one, I'm just trying to keep up. My head is spinning. I can't believe it's real, but it is, isn't it? I'm not going to wake up?"

"No. It's too late now. You're stuck with me."

Torie laughed, leaning into him. "I'm glad."

"I think a lot of the guests will be going soon, before they get snowed in," he whispered. "So, if you wanted, we could, er… get a bit of peace too, by ourselves."

Torie bit her lip, avoiding his gaze and feeling suddenly shy, for she knew quite well what that meant. She nodded though, glancing back at him and smiling. "I should like that."

"That's good," Barnaby said, raising her fingers to his lips and kissing her knuckles. Her stomach gave an odd little flutter at the warmth in his eyes, and the soft way he spoke to her. "For I should very much like to have my wife all to myself for a bit."

The chink of metal on crystal silenced the gathering and everyone looked up as Louis César stood, a full glass of champagne in his hand.

"*Mesdames et Messieurs*, the hour grows late, and some of our company must leave us shortly, though it saddens us to say goodbye. But whilst we are all still together and enjoying this splendid dinner that my lovely comtesse has so beautifully designed for us, might I ask that you all charge your glasses and raise a toast to our newlyweds. Lady Victoria, you are the picture of loveliness, and Barnaby is a lucky man indeed. And Barnaby, my dearest friend, no man was ever more deserving of such happiness. *Félicitations, mes amis*, we wish you health, happiness and good fortune, and thank you both for allowing us all to share in this wonderful day. *The bride and groom.*"

"The bride and groom!"

The toast echoed about the room as everyone raised their glasses and drank to their health. There followed more toasts after that, as the champagne flowed, and everyone got thoroughly over excited. Then some bawdier toasts flew about the room, as Jules and Leo had imbibed rather too deep, and were both subsequently skewered with a warning glare from the duke. Felix laughed uproariously at their goings on until his big sister dumped a baby in his arms and told him not to be such a lummox in company.

Finally, those that were going home reluctantly left to gather their belongings. Carriages were loaded, and those who were staying sought more comfortable lodgings in armchairs by the fire, or took themselves off for a little snooze in private.

Victoria and Barnaby frowned as they saw the doorway clogged with people, including Leo and Jules, who were still chatting and deciding what it was they were doing. A game of billiards seemed to be in the offing as Leo tried to persuade Jules to stay with him for Christmas.

"Dash it all, why must they stand there?" Barnaby said with a huff, and Victoria took his arm, knowing he did not want to embarrass her by pushing past and make a spectacle of them wanting privacy.

She knew her wicked brother and Leo would enjoy making sport of them and was no keener than Barnaby to give them the opportunity.

A throat clearing behind them had them both turning to see Louis standing there. Silently, he crooked his finger, signalling them to follow. Walking to the far end of the dining room, he opened a hidden door and handed them a lamp, for the passageway was dark.

"Turn right when you get to the top. It will come out three doors down from your room," he said quietly.

Quite overcome, Barnaby took Louis by the shoulders and kissed him on both cheeks as Louis was wont to do to him.

"Thank you," he said fervently, took the lamp, and hurried Victoria up the stairs.

They could hear Louis' soft chuckle follow them until he closed the door behind them, and all was silent but for their footsteps.

Chapter 17

Dear Miss Milly,

Please do not go putting ideas in poor Humboldt's head. He's hard enough to manage as it is, without him getting misty eyed notions about the Zoological Society of London. He's become very uppity since receiving your letter and only this morning made an extremely rude comment about monkeys.

As for not resembling a billet doux, my sweet Milly, you are too innocent yet to understand when you are flirting with a fellow, but I shall let that go as I can feel Humboldt scowling at me and hear his irritation in the way his pen scratches so furiously upon the paper. However, I am well aware my charms are limited and not at all what they once were. My hubris is not so great that I consider myself a marvellous prize. I have been cut down to size most publicly, and more than once since losing my sight, and have had my shortcomings explained to me in depth. If you think I do not know it is only the sweetness of your character that bears my clumsy attentions with such good humour and grace, then I must be a greater fool in your eyes than I had supposed.

Still, I am a wretchedly selfish fellow with little left in the way of tender feelings and I will impose upon that sweetness further, Miss Milly, for I am at my wits' end, and I do not know who to trust. Outside of the estimable Humboldt and my sister, Delia, I am quite alone. Yet I trust you. May I trust you? Tell me I am not wrong in believing it so.

Will you remain at Heart's Folly into the New Year? For we <u>must</u> speak privately.

Yrs etc,

—Excerpt of a letter to Miss Emmeline Knight (daughter of Lady Helena and Mr Gabriel Knight) from The Most Hon'ble Leander Steyning, The Marquess of Wrexham.

22nd December 1844, Heart's Folly, East Sussex.

Barnaby sighed as he finally closed the bedroom door behind them.

"Made it," he said, and with such obvious relief that Torie could not help but laugh. "It's not funny, you wicked girl. I thought we were done for when I saw my aunt round the corner. Good heavens, I don't think I could have stood that. You know what she is for plain speaking. I wouldn't put it past her to give me advice."

He looked so thoroughly appalled by this prospect, Torie snorted. She slapped a hand over her face, as it wasn't a terribly elegant sound for a bride to make.

He gave a mournful sigh.

"Oh, I see how it is, making sport of me already and the ink not even dry on the marriage certificate," he said, trying and failing to look severe and advancing on her.

"Oh, n-no, Barnaby, I wasn't," Torie insisted, trying hard not to laugh. "Truly. Only you looked so horrified, it was rather f-funny."

"Funny, am I?" he said, grasping hold of her waist and pulling her into his arms. He stared down at her, his eyes warm with affection as he gave a sad shake of his head. "Just what a fellow wants, getting laughed at on his wedding night."

"Barnaby, stop teasing," Torie said, lightly smacking her hand on his chest. "I was doing no such thing. You know very well that I adore you."

"Do you, love?" he asked, serious now. "Because I'm head over ears for you. Are you really mine? I'm still having trouble believing it."

"Really and truly, and yes, I adore you. I told you that ages ago, you just didn't believe me," she scolded him.

"I was a fool," he said ruefully, but Torie couldn't have that.

"No, you were guarding your heart. I know that, and I don't blame you in the least."

Barnaby lowered his forehead to hers. "I was never in love with her," he said, his voice low. "It wasn't like this, Torie. You're the only one I want, the only one I shall ever want. There's something I want to say to you, and I know a fellow ain't supposed to talk this way on his wedding night, but I think that's a lot of nonsense. I ought to be able to speak to you about anything, just as you can talk to me about anything, and you ought to know I'm the faithful kind. I won't ever take a mistress, or flirt with other ladies. You can depend on me, always. I won't let you down."

"I knew that already, Barnaby," Torie said, blinking hard, for he was so earnest and so dear, and she loved him a quite ridiculous amount. "But I'm glad, and I shall never flirt with anyone either, or give you any reason to doubt me. And I'm glad I can talk to you about anything, for I'm a bit outspoken—well, you know that by now—and if I can't talk to you without minding my tongue, then who can I talk to?"

"Well, that's that sorted, then," Barnaby said, grinning at her.

"Yes."

"So, can we stop talking now? For I'd rather like to kiss you, if you don't mind?"

"I don't mind," she said, breathless now, fighting back a silly smile as he cupped her cheek, his palm warm against her skin.

"You are so very beautiful, my lovely Victoria. I was never so proud as when I saw you walking down the aisle towards me today."

And Victoria might have returned the compliment, might have told him he was the handsomest man in the room and her stomach had erupted with butterflies when she'd seen him standing waiting for her, but then he was pressing his mouth to hers and so she kissed him back. Because who needed words when she could express her feelings just as easily like this?

The kiss went on, lingering, tender, as Barnaby held her close, in no hurry to do anything more than this. When he finally released her, Torie gave a little gasp, breathless and vividly remembering everything he had made her feel the night they had been so rudely interrupted by his aunt and the duke.

"My shoes and stockings aren't the least bit wet," she said, affecting a mournful sigh.

"Oh, dear," Barnaby said, immediately understanding. "That's a pity. Might I take them off anyway, do you think?"

"Yes, please," she whispered.

With a low chuckle, Barnaby led her to a comfortable chair by the fire and bade her sit down.

"Now," he said, his eyes glinting with amusement. "Where was I?"

He knelt before her and leaned in for a kiss as his warm hands encircled her ankles.

"I think you were a little further on than that," Torie pointed out, feeling the first stirrings of impatience.

Barnaby quirked an eyebrow. "I'm in no hurry, love. Such dainty ankles you have. They deserve my full attention."

Torie watched as he carefully removed her shoes, his warm hands massaging her feet until she sighed, though with pleasure rather than impatience. Slowly his hands moved higher, up over her silk stockings, past her knees, where he paused.

"No drawers?" he asked, looking rather shocked.

Torie blushed. "Flo told me not to bother with them today," she said, watching his face to see if he was pleased or scandalised.

She decided it was an equal measure of both, just as Flo had suggested, and relaxed as his hands continued on their path to her garters, which he removed with splendid alacrity. Torie's heart quickened as he reached for the lace top of her stocking, and tugged first one, and then the other from her, casting them aside.

"I seem to remember you played a part in this last time," Barnaby said, caressing the backs of her knees until Torie wanted to purr like a cat. She had never known such an inauspicious place as the backs of her knees could be so very sensitive.

"Did I?" she asked, struggling to think at all as her nerves leapt beneath his touch.

He nodded, and so Torie gathered her courage and reached for him, pulling him to her, widening her legs so he could fit between them. Barnaby kissed her again, his hand stroking up and down her thighs in a way that was at once both soothing and maddening.

"I'd never hurt you, Torie, you know that, don't you?" he whispered, nuzzling at the sweet spot beneath her ear that made her shiver, before nipping at her earlobe.

Torie's breath caught. "Of course I know that," she said, impatient now. "Touch me, Barnaby. Like you did that night."

He made a low, approving sound as his fingers traced up and down her thighs, then moved lower, tickling through the soft nest of curls. Torie held her breath, closing her eyes as his touch teased her senses, never coming quite to the place where she wanted him. She opened her eyes then, about to protest, only to find him watching her, smiling.

"I think we ought to take that lovely dress off you and take this to the bed. More comfortable."

For a moment she considered scolding him, but Flo had explained that a good lover was likely to tease a little, and so she bit back her impatience and nodded, allowing him to help her up. Doing her best not to fidget with impatience, Torie turned this way and that as he undid the fastenings on the deep emerald gown she had worn to get married in.

He paused suddenly, staring at her. "Did you mind? The wedding, I mean. I was in such a hurry to marry you I never.... Would you have wanted a huge, splendid affair in a church with hundreds of guests and—"

Torie shut him up with a kiss, lingering until he sighed, and she pulled back. "Better?" she asked.

"Much," he agreed, nodding.

"Our wedding was perfect. I would have wanted nothing more, even if I'd had months to plan it all."

Apparently satisfied, he carried on until the dress sagged and Victoria stepped out of it. She shivered, though the room was far from cold, and Barnaby smiled.

"I'll warm you up soon enough."

Suddenly, Torie could not stand it a moment longer. She was not a passive creature by nature, and she was impatient now. She reached for the buttons on his waistcoat, tugging them undone one by one with fingers that were clumsy with nerves. Barnaby did not seem to mind, though, and shrugged off his coat, tossing it over the nearest chair and then sending his waistcoat after it once she was done.

"Well, there's me trying to be patient and not spook you, and now you're wrestling with me," he said, laughing as she tugged his shirt from his trousers. "Steady on, love, you'll do me a damage."

"I don't spook easily. I'm not a skittish horse," she objected, striving to sound tart to hide the fact she was fizzing with nerves, just as he suspected.

"I had noticed," he replied gravely.

Torie ignored the comment, too caught up in trying to undo the blasted cravat which seemed to have been tied using some arcane law of physics that defied her understanding, and all her efforts to remove it. "Oh, really! Who tied this? A magician?" she demanded.

"Louis would have you believe so. It was his blasted valet, Elton. Honestly, love, I don't know which of them reveres the other more. Here, let me…."

He tugged and muttered at the starched cloth, and then yanked and cursed and got a bit red in the face, but finally, he was free of it and flung it aside in triumph. He pulled his shirt over his head too and sent that after the cravat.

"Think I need a lie down," he said, chuckling.

Torie bit back a giggle and tried to send him a stern look, but was too distracted by the more interesting pastime of staring at his chest. She had been held close enough by him to have understood that he was far more powerful and substantial than he appeared. Somehow his mild manner and modest personality put one so at ease it was effortless to be comfortable around him, and not pay proper attention to quite how well-made he was. Now, though, stripped of the layers that hid the real Barnaby, the strong chest and muscular arms of the man before her were rather a shock to behold. She studied him for a long moment before lunging for his trouser buttons, her patience all used up. Barnaby danced away.

"Hold a moment," he scolded, though his eyes were alight with laughter. "I'm not standing about in the altogether whilst you've got all that lot on."

He waved at her corsets and the mountainous layers of petticoats frothing about her ankles.

Frowning, she huffed, and reached behind her for the ties, undoing each one before she kicked the petticoat aside. Barnaby watched, never taking his eyes from her, his expression veering from delighted amusement to something darker and more intent with each layer she removed. Finally, she tugged at her corset strings. It was a front opening style that she could manage on her own and, having loosened the laces, she sent it flying. It landed with a thud beside the frilly lace of her petticoats.

"There!" she said, breathless and triumphant, standing in only her shift.

"There, indeed," Barnaby said, sounding far more breathless than she was as he stared at her, the way his gaze lingered on her breasts making her blush. She fought the urge to cover herself, torn between modesty and the wicked pleasure of enjoying his admiration, revelling in the lust she saw darkening his eyes.

"Your turn!" she exclaimed, to cover her confusion, reaching for his trouser buttons once more. Her breath caught as her knuckles grazed his belly, the dark hair that arrowed beneath his waistband tickling her fingers. There was more on his chest too, and she was seized by the sudden impulse to kiss him there. So she did, finding the hair coarse and wiry, but the skin beneath silky soft like her own. Surprised, she tried the skin of his shoulder, brushing her lips over it, then noticed the flat, male nipples and tried kissing those too, darting out her tongue to touch the tiny nub that puckered beneath her teasing caress.

Barnaby sucked in a breath, gooseflesh rippling over his skin. Intrigued, Torie looked up at him. He stared down at her, still and silent, wanting in his eyes. Torie undid the last button on his falls. Not taking his eyes from hers, Barnaby moved to sit on the edge of the bed and tugged off his boots, then stood again and pushed his trousers down, kicking them to one side, leaving him in only his smalls.

"Who's going first?" he asked, his mouth kicking up into a smile.

"You!" she said at once.

He snorted. "Well, I expected that, wicked girl. Very well, here I go."

With an expression so grave Torie could not help but snigger, he pushed down his small clothes, leaving him naked.

"Really, Torie. Very bad form to snigger at a fellow when he takes his unmentionables off for the first time. Likely to give me a complex," he complained, though she heard the laughter in his voice. Barnaby followed her gaze and stared down at himself, and then back to Torie, who was far from laughter now, riveted to the sight of him, already aroused and standing proudly erect. "Will I do?" he asked, a teasing note to the question, for he must be able to read the naked desire in her eyes.

She nodded. "You're very fine, Barnaby."

He looked pleased by that and moved closer to her. "Well, then, it's your turn," he said softly. "May I?"

Waiting until she gave an answering nod, he reached for the hem of her shift and pulled it up, over her head. He let out a ragged sigh as he gazed down at her.

"Died and gone to heaven," he murmured, sounding a little dazed, a state she understood well enough as he cupped her breasts in his hands, stroking and gently squeezing, rubbing his thumbs over her nipples until they were taut and aching. "Too lovely for words," he whispered, ducking his head to trail his mouth over the generous mounds.

Tentatively, Torie stroked his hair, sinking her fingers into the warm silk and holding him in place as he explored. Her fingers tightened as he drew her nipple into his mouth and gently sucked, sending explosions of sensation ricocheting around her body like tiny fireworks. He lavished equal attention on both breasts before looking up at her. A smug smile tugged at his lips.

"Like that, did you?" he asked, though she suspected he did not need an answer.

She could barely stand, her blood fizzing in her veins as if it had been replaced with champagne. Torie nodded anyway, just to be clear. Before she had time to actually speak—not that she was certain she *could* speak—Barnaby picked her up. She gave a little shriek of surprise.

"Well, we're off to a good start, then," he remarked, carrying her to the bed, the covers of which were already turned down.

He laid her carefully on the mattress. Torie snatched for the covers, pulling them up, but Barnaby tugged them down again.

"No hiding," he scolded. "I want to see. I'll keep you warmer than any blanket, anyway."

Torie shivered, though in anticipation rather than from any chill in the room, but Barnaby kept his word. He lay down beside her, drawing her into his arms, and the sensation of his hot skin against hers was so delicious and so shocking that it stunned her. Still, she wanted more, and so she curled her limbs about him, holding on like ivy coiling around an oak tree. Time passed in a haze while they lost themselves in the slow caress of hands over silken skin, with kisses that slid from languid to passionate and back again as they explored and mapped out all the delightful places their bodies touched.

When they finally paused for breath, Torie felt dazed, alight with so many new sensations she hardly knew what time it was, though the room was dark now. The dim light of the late afternoon had long since fled. The warm glow of the fire and a single lamp that burned on the bedside table bathed the room with a soft, warm glow, making it feel cosy and intimate despite the snow falling silently in the darkness beyond the walls.

"Don't stop," Torie whispered, consumed by the clamouring ache of need tugging at her core, wanting more of him.

"I'm a long way from stopping, love," he promised her, kissing her again, before trailing kisses down her neck, over her breasts and belly.

She caught her breath when he did not stop, but carried on down. She was not shocked—Mama had always been frank with her children about such intimacies, and Flo had filled in any gaps—but knowing such a thing might happen and experiencing it were quite, *quite* different.

Torie raised her hand to clutch at the pillow beneath her head, needing to hold on to something as awareness rippled through her, It made her shiver and her skin burn all at once, made her arch towards the sinful mouth that covered her most secret place, to cant her hips harder against the wicked tongue that teased the tiny nub of flesh that throbbed and demanded more even as it shrank from the overwhelming sensation. But there was no escape. Barnaby held her hips, holding her in place so that there was nowhere to go but over the edge. The force of the cry that escaped her might have mortified her if she had wit enough to register it, but she'd been flung into the night, floating with the snowflakes dancing outside in the darkness.

She was warm and sated, and she found herself once more in Barnaby's arms. Blinking hazily, she found him staring down at her with such an expression of smug masculine pride she could only laugh, beyond feeling either embarrassment or regret for her wanton behaviour. After all, he seemed well pleased with her, and she certainly wasn't about to complain.

"Heavenly," she murmured dreamily, still drunk on pleasure. "I'm a snowflake."

"Are you now?" he said, amused. "You're very warm for a snowflake."

"Hmmmm," she sighed.

"Found something else you like, did I?" he asked nonchalantly.

She nodded, grinning stupidly and wrapping her arms around his neck. "Now I need to find something you like."

Barnaby snorted at that, obviously amused. "Oh, I liked that plenty. I like everything about you."

He shifted, settling his body between her thighs so his arousal pressed firmly against the part of her that still throbbed and flickered with tiny fireworks. Torie gasped at the new pressure as a bolt of sensation lanced through her, sweet and hot.

"See? I like it too. I like the way you feel, the way you taste, everything about you pleases me, love. I want to be inside you now, Torie, darling girl. Can you let me?"

He positioned himself against her, nudging gently and for just a moment Torie's body locked down defensively, but then she stared up at the man above her. She saw the tenderness in his eyes and the willingness to do whatever she wanted, to be patient, to take as much time as she needed. He would never take what she was not ready to give, and then it was all perfect, because it was Barnaby, and she trusted him to be kind, to give her everything she needed, to do whatever it was he could to make her happy. All at once she relaxed, her body pliant, welcoming him in. She gasped as he thrust inside, waiting for pain, or discomfort, but it was only rather strange and new, and as he began to move even that strangeness fled. Instead, she felt nothing but loved, nothing but close to this wonderful man, and she knew, as she had known from the start, that he was the one she would love for always.

She was neither shy nor anxious as he loved her, and let her wandering hands go where they pleased, mapping the contours of his strong shoulders, the sleek expanse of his back and the curve of his buttocks. She welcomed his kisses and revelled in the breathless endearments, the praise that might have made her blush had she not felt just the same, finding him lovely and wonderful, and as perfect as he found her. When his rhythm faltered and she felt his muscles lock down, a fine tension singing through his limbs, she understood that he approached that splendid peak that he had taken her to. The knowledge made her own body tighten. That joyous, sparkling sensation began anew, making her hold her breath and chase it, determined to reach the heights again as he was. Barnaby groaned, a deep sound of such pleasure that it reverberated through her, sending her crashing over the edge with him as his body shuddered and he spilled inside her, his breathing harsh and ragged as pleasure held him in its grip.

Somehow, Barnaby had wit enough to roll to the side and didn't crush his bride by collapsing on top of her. It was about all he could manage, though. This woman had always melted his brains and turned his senses inside out, but now—after *that*—he didn't think he'd ever be the same again. Not that he cared. Poor Torie might find herself married to a halfwit, but if she kept loving him like that, she'd just have to put up with it. What was a fellow to do in the face of such incandescent pleasure? It was astonishing and lovely and… By Jove, he was a lucky dog.

He heard a soft snort of laughter in his ear and turned his head to see Torie watching him, one hand covering her mouth as she tried to smother her amusement.

"What's so funny?" he demanded. "Haven't I told you about laughing at your beloved during intimate moments? You'll give me a nervous disposition if you keep this up."

His feigned indignation only made her snort all the harder and Barnaby propped his head on his elbow, staring at her in consternation. "What *is* so funny, you dreadful creature?"

"Y-You," she stammered helplessly. "You had this daft smile plastered to your face, and you looked so p-pleased with yourself."

Barnaby snorted too, not doubting it for a moment. "I shan't even deny it," he said, rolling onto his back and pulling her against him, gratified when she snuggled close. "I am daft. You've turned what little brain I possessed to treacle, and I don't care. I'm very pleased with myself for choosing my bride so wisely."

"Oh ho! You chose, did you?" she said, sitting up at that and poking him in the chest with her finger. "That's such an infuriatingly *male* thing to say. *I* did the choosing, if you remember. You did a lot of running away!"

"Now, Torie," he said reproachfully. "You really ought not point such things out to your husband."

"Why not?" she demanded with a laugh. "It's true."

"Yes, but now we're married, you must at least *pretend* that I'm the one who does everything right and never makes a mistake. It's the law."

"Oh, you poor deluded fool," she said, giving a sad shake of her head. "You are quite out of your depth, you know."

"I know." He sighed heavily, and then pushed her onto her back, making her gasp as his body made it clear he was already quite willing to carry on where they'd left off. "But it will be a dashed lovely way to drown."

And he smothered her outraged laugh with a kiss to illustrate the point.

Epilogue

Dear Cat,

Oh, yes, my mama was so happy to see yours! Not only did she chatter nonstop while they were together, but she talked my ear off all the way home, too. Do you think we shall be that way when we are old, discussing our children and their friends and all the gossip? I hope so. It's a nice thought, isn't it? Like a circle fulfilling itself, ties of friendship and family that go through generations.

I'm sorry I couldn't stay at Dern longer. I did want to, but the good news is that I shall be at Holbrook earlier than I expected, in January, so if you are allowed to, I should be so happy to see you there too. It's such a dismal time of year, after Christmas and before the season begins and nothing interesting ever happens. But I know if you come and stay, we can find some fun if we put our minds to it.

I have decided this is <u>my</u> year. You see, I've been feeling very low of late. I feel so guilty about breaking things off with Ollie, even though I know it was for the best, but I have *promised I shall forgive myself and move on this Christmas. My New Year's Resolution is to find joy in all things and look for happiness. I am certain that if I keep an open mind and search for it, I can find it. And by that I DO NOT MEAN A MAN. I have no interest in finding my forever for some time, yet. I am going to enjoy my freedom and ignore everything that makes me cross and unhappy. I will not lose my temper or be impatient. I shall be a blue sea of serenity, and everyone will wonder at my poise and tranquillity.*

Eighteen forty-five is going to be the best year ever and everything is going to be wonderful.

—Excerpt of a letter to The Lady Catherine 'Cat' Barrington (daughter of Lucian and Matilda Barrington, The Most Hon'ble Marquess and Marchioness of Montagu) from Miss Alana Cadogan (daughter of Mr Jerome and Mrs Bonnie Cadogan).

25th December 1844, Heart's Folly, East Sussex.

"Have a mince pie," Axton said, waving a plate beneath Louis' nose.

"Mon Dieu, have mercy. I cannot face another morsel. I shall not eat again until March," Louis complained with a groan.

Evie snorted and snatched a mince pie for herself. "Ignore him, Alfie. He's French. You know how they like to go on about how heavy English food is, yet I saw him take two helpings of the plum pudding. Don't you deny it," she said, wagging a warning finger at her husband before biting into the pie.

"Well, now I pay the price," he retorted. "I shall have to send for Elton to make me a restorative."

"As his restoratives are usually ninety percent brandy, I shall save you both the trouble and pour you a glass myself."

"Ah, *mon amour*, you are very good to me," Louis said with a sigh.

Evie fetched him the brandy, handed it over and then gave a squeal as Louis pulled her into his lap.

"Oh, you must stop doing that! What will everyone think?"

"That it is an excellent idea, considering the company," Louis retorted.

Torie suspected he was not wrong, for it was late in the evening and everyone had gone to bed. Now only the duke and Aunt Hester—as the lady insisted Torie address her—Louis and Evie, and she and Barnaby remained. Barnaby was half asleep, his head tipped back, his arm holding Torie tight as she snuggled close. It was very informal, more than they would have dared in anyone else's company. Louis and Evie were so obviously besotted with one another, however, it seemed impossible for them to stick to the rules among friends. Since they'd both achieved rather scandalous reputations, they'd dispensed with much of the formality that most people saw as proper, even within the security of their own homes. It was wonderfully relaxing to be in their company. It had been a marvellous day, with lots of laughter and silly games, present opening and far too much food. Then Emmeline had played the piano for them, which had been exquisite, but so very soothing that, as everyone had been so well fed and watered, they began dozing off. Happily, she hadn't taken the least bit of offense.

Now, the duke eyed Louis and his contented expression as he cuddled his wife close.

"I agree with you, by Jove," he said to Louis, setting down the plate of mince pies before sitting in the chair opposite Louis and

Evie by the fire and giving his lap an inviting pat. "Come along, Hester."

Aunt Hester glared at him. "Don't be ridiculous, Axton. What on earth are you thinking?"

"I'm thinking it's about time we announced our engagement. Barnaby and his lovely bride know, so why not everyone else?"

"Because such tarradiddle is for the young and we did not want to overshadow their celebration with our own news. There's really no need for a fuss," Hester scolded him, blushing as Evie and Louis made exclamations of delight.

"Hester!" Louis exclaimed. "You little minx. You have been holding out on me. Do you mean to tell me you have caught yourself a duke, and you never let on?"

Her mouth fell open as she stared at Louis in consternation. "I certainly did not 'catch myself a duke,' as you so vulgarly put it, you devil!"

The duke gave a knowing chuckle. "Now, now, Hester, don't be modest. You know very well you set your cap at me, and I fell hook, line and sinker. Didn't stand a chance."

"Set my cap—" Hester repeated, outrage vibrating through her elegant frame. "Alfred Grenville, you take that back. You pursued me, you dreadful, dreadful man, and why on earth I gave in, I really cannot remember. I must have been out of my wits!"

"Perhaps," the duke allowed, gazing at her fondly. "And I shall thank my lucky stars every day for however many remain to me. Of that, you may be certain. Now, come along, my dove. Make a wicked old duke happy."

He gave his lap another encouraging pat and Hester blushed scarlet.

"Really, Axton. It's most undignified."

"Poppycock."

"And you know very well your knees wouldn't stand it," she added.

"Nonsense," the duke said, indignation flashing in his eyes. "I'm still in my prime, woman. Strong as good old English oak. As if a little slip of a thing like you could do me any harm. Now come here and obey your husband-to-be."

Hester huffed, clearly torn between wanting to cuddle up to her betrothed and finding the entire thing rather mortifying. "Oh, very well, you old goat. Make a spectacle of us, why don't you? And as for me obeying you, enjoy the moment, for it shall be the last time, I promise you."

"I know, my treasure, and I shall adore every moment of your disobedience."

With as much dignity as she could muster, Hester got to her feet, crossed to where the duke sat, and perched gingerly on his knees. Axton wasn't having that, however. He grasped her about the waist and hauled her back until she was leaning against his chest, his arms wrapped securely about her.

"I may never speak to you again," she warned him, looking thoroughly flustered, but not entirely displeased. "And if anyone breathes a word of this—"

"As if we'd dare," Barnaby retorted. "And I shall be watching you, Axton. You're not married yet," he grumbled, skewering the duke with a disapproving expression.

Axton returned a toothy grin. "Don't you worry, son, I'll get the paperwork in order first thing. And you're all invited to Royle House for the wedding, should you wish to attend."

"We'll be there," Torie promised.

"Sadly, we will not," Louis replied with obvious regret. "For Evie ought not to travel to Derbyshire in her condition, but we shall be with you in spirit, and we would love to see you here again, perhaps later in the year, once our new arrival is with us."

"We would love to," Hester agreed. "Wouldn't we, Alfie?"

"Certainly we would. I'll bring something special to wet the baby's head when we do. I owe you, Villen, for the invitation. Reckon you knew the way the wind was blowing, eh?"

"I had an inkling," Louis said dryly. "I just decided to, er… give you both a little nudge."

"Interfering busybody," Hester remarked.

"Just as you say, my dear," Louis replied serenely, looking unbearably smug. "But you must admit, my first attempts at matchmaking have gone rather splendidly. Hester and Axton, *and* Barnaby and Victoria. I believe I have found my vocation. I wonder who I should turn my attentions to next?" he added thoughtfully.

"I think we've had enough meddling for the time being," Evie said firmly, though she was laughing at Louis' sulky expression.

"You spoil my fun."

Evie bit her lip and then bent to whisper something in her husband's ear that made him smile. Torie looked hurriedly away, having a fair idea of what Evie had said to make it up to him. The duke also appeared to be murmuring sweet nothings to Hester, judging from the colour her cheeks were blazing. Deciding everyone was happily engaged with their own priorities, Torie reached down the side of the sofa, to where she had hidden a small present, waiting for the right moment to give it to her husband.

"Barnaby," she said softly, nudging him awake.

"Hmmm?" he said sleepily, cracking open an eye to look at her. "Time for bed?" he asked, a hopeful glint chasing away the drowsiness from his expression.

"Soon, but first, this one is for you," Torie said, handing the small, wrapped package to him. "It's only a token," she added, as he sat up straighter and scowled at her.

"You little wretch," he said crossly, staring at the present in consternation. "I thought we agreed, as we had no time to get to the shops to buy presents for each other before we wed, there wouldn't be any until after Christmas."

"It's only very small, Barnaby," Torie said, laughing at his indignation. "And I brought it before we even came here, just in case."

"Well, I say!" he exclaimed with a huff. "You were very sure of yourself, weren't you, miss?"

"No," she said, taking hold of his hand and raising it to her cheek. "But I was very sure of you."

If it were possible to see a grown man melt into a puddle of mush in front of one's eyes, Barnaby did a fair approximation of the state. His expression softened, and he sighed, shaking his head.

"You turn my brains to treacle," he grumbled, though there was no heat in it.

Torie leaned in and kissed his cheek. "I know," she said soothingly. "Open your present."

Barnaby undid the red ribbon and opened the paper to reveal a small leather-bound case. "I hope you know I am going to shower you with presents once the snow lets up in revenge for this," he said, slanting her a wry smile.

"I think I can endure that," she said, leaning into him. "Now hurry and open it."

Carefully, Barnaby lifted the lid on the box and made a soft exclamation as he saw the silver cravat pin topped with a tiny carved ivory trotting horse. The workmanship was exquisite, every detail finely wrought. from the feathers on the animal's fetlocks to the swish of its tail.

"Well, now. Would you look at that?" he said, turning the pin this way and that with admiration. "Ain't that just the finest thing I ever saw."

"You like it?" Torie said, tucking her arm through his as he stared at the little horse.

"Course I like it. I love it. I love that you chose it for me, especially as you didn't know about the stud back then. What made you choose it?" he asked, curiosity in his gaze as he turned back to her.

"Papa and I rode past you in town a while ago and I saw the way you looked at his horse. Of course, I had no idea Trooper was one of yours then, only that you looked so pleased when you saw him, and even I can see how splendid he is. I just thought then that, even though you never kept horses in town—that I knew of—you must like them a good deal, to admire one so obviously."

Barnaby turned to look at her in wonder. "What a brainbox you've got, Torie, to notice such a thing. But you do that, don't you? You notice things other people don't. You're clever like that, putting things together. I admire that. Couldn't be prouder of you. You know that, don't you?"

Torie blinked hard, suddenly emotional, too happy to find words to express it.

"Yes," she managed, sounding choked. "I know that, and I feel the same way. I'm so proud of you, Barnaby, and... so h-happy."

"Well, don't cry, then!" he said in alarm, hurriedly putting the cravat pin aside. He gave a surreptitious look around, to see the two other couples cuddled up and murmuring softly to each other before reaching for his wife. Lifting her into his lap, he held her close and kissed her. "No crying," he scolded her, frowning.

"But they're happy tears," Torie protested, sniffing.

"Even so, unsettles a fellow," he said awkwardly. "It's Christmas, and we're newlyweds, and I want you to be happy, for everything to be perfect for you."

"It is," Victoria said simply. "You are. I've had a marvellous time. Just think, Barnaby, a Gothic adventure in a magnificent house, ghosts and a ruined chapel, underground tunnels and a treasure that showed us how very loved Mrs Payne was, and her beautiful home. I think Evie and Louis will be very happy here."

"And what of us, love?" Barnaby asked, gazing at her with adoration.

Torie cupped his dear face, smiling at him. "I think we will be happy wherever we go, Barnaby, whatever we do, and I cannot wait to begin. Merry Christmas, my love."

And she kissed him.

Next in the Daring Daughter Series …

Indecently Daring
Daring Daughters Book 16

To be revealed …

Available February 24, 2023. Pre-Order your copy on
Amazon at: https://mybook.to/IndecentlyDaring

And coming in **2023**, an exciting new series based on the male children of the Girls Who Dare…

Their mothers dared all for love.
Their sisters did the same.
Something wicked this way comes…

The first book in the **Wicked Sons** series….

The Devil to Pay
Wicked Sons, Book One

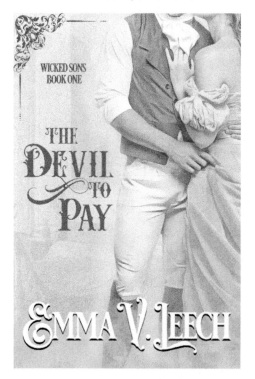

To be revealed

The Peculiar Ladies who started it all...

Girls Who Dare—The exciting series from Emma V Leech, the multi-award-winning, Amazon Top 10 romance writer behind the Rogues & Gentlemen series.

Inside every wallflower is the beating heart of a lioness, a passionate individual willing to risk all for their dream, if only they can find the courage to begin. When these overlooked girls make a pact to change their lives, anything can happen.

Twelve girls—Twelve dares in a hat. Twelves stories of passion. Who will dare to risk it all?

To Dare a Duke
Girls Who Dare Book 1

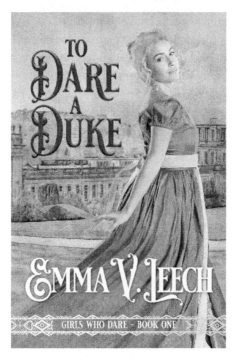

Dreams of true love and happy ever afters

Dreams of love are all well and good, but all Prunella Chuffington-Smythe wants is to publish her novel. Marriage at the price of her independence is something she will not consider. Having tasted success writing under a false name in The Lady's Weekly Review, her alter ego is attaining notoriety and fame and Prue rather likes it.

A Duty that must be endured

Robert Adolphus, The Duke of Bedwin, is in no hurry to marry, he's done it once and repeating that disaster is the last thing he desires. Yet, an heir is a necessary evil for a duke and one he cannot shirk. A dark reputation precedes him though, his first wife may have died young, but the scandals the beautiful, vivacious and spiteful creature supplied the ton have not. A wife must be found. A wife who is neither beautiful nor vivacious but sweet and dull, and certain to stay out of trouble.

Dared to do something drastic

The sudden interest of a certain dastardly duke is as bewildering as it is unwelcome. She'll not throw her ambitions aside to marry a scoundrel just as her plans for self-sufficiency and freedom are coming to fruition. Surely showing the man she's not actually the meek little wallflower he is looking for should be enough to put paid to his intentions? When Prue is dared by her friends to do something drastic, it seems the perfect opportunity to kill two birds.

However, Prue cannot help being intrigued by the rogue who has inspired so many of her romances. Ordinarily, he plays the part of handsome rake, set on destroying her plucky heroine. But is he really the villain of the piece this time, or could he be the hero?

Finding out will be dangerous, but it just might inspire her greatest story yet.

To Dare a Duke

Also check out Emma's regency romance series, Rogues & Gentlemen. Available now!

The Rogue

Rogues & Gentlemen Book 1

The notorious Rogue that began it all.

Set in Cornwall, 1815. Wild, untamed and isolated.

Lawlessness is the order of the day and smuggling is rife.

Henrietta always felt most at home in the wilds of the outdoors but even she had no idea how the mysterious and untamed would sweep her away in a moment.

Bewitched by his wicked blue eyes

Henrietta Morton knows to look the other way when the free trading 'gentlemen' are at work.

Yet when a notorious pirate bursts into her local village shop, she can avert her eyes no more. Bewitched by his wicked blue eyes, a moment of insanity follows as Henrietta hides the handsome fugitive from the Militia.

Her reward is a kiss, lingering and unforgettable.

In his haste to flee, the handsome pirate drops a letter, a letter that lays bare a tale of betrayal. When Henrietta's father gives her hand in marriage to a wealthy and villainous nobleman in return for the payment of his debts, she becomes desperate.

Blackmailing a pirate may be her only hope for freedom.

**** **Warning**: This book contains the most notorious rogue of all of Cornwall and, on occasion, is highly likely to include some mild sweating or descriptive sex scenes. ****

Free to read on *Kindle Unlimited*: The Rogue

Interested in a Regency Romance with a twist?

A Dog in a Doublet

The Regency Romance Mysteries Book 2

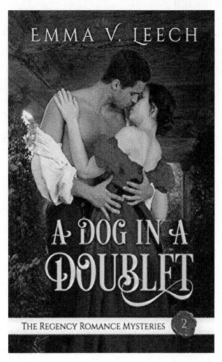

A man with a past

Harry Browning was a motherless guttersnipe, and the morning he came across the elderly Alexander Preston, The Viscount Stamford, clinging to a sheer rock face he didn't believe in fate. But the fates have plans for Harry whether he believes or not, and he's not entirely sure he likes them.

As a reward for his bravery, and in an unusual moment of charity, miserly Lord Stamford takes him on. He is taught to read, to manage the vast and crumbling estate, and to behave like a gentleman, but Harry knows that is something he will never truly be.

Already running from a dark past, his future is becoming increasingly complex as he finds himself caught in a tangled web of jealousy and revenge.

A feisty young maiden

Temptation, in the form of the lovely Miss Clarinda Bow, is a constant threat to his peace of mind, enticing him to be something he isn't. But when the old man dies his will makes a surprising demand, and the fates might just give Harry the chance to have everything he ever desired, including Clara, if only he dares.

And as those close to the Preston family begin to die, Harry may not have any choice.

Order your copy here. *A Dog in a Doublet*

Lose yourself in Emma's paranormal world with The French Vampire Legend series…..

The Key to Erebus

The French Vampire Legend Book 1

The truth can kill you.

Taken away as a small child, from a life where vampires, the Fae, and other mythical creatures are real and treacherous, the beautiful young witch, Jéhenne Corbeaux is totally unprepared when she returns to rural France to live with her eccentric Grandmother.

Thrown headlong into a world she knows nothing about she seeks to learn the truth about herself, uncovering secrets more shocking than anything she could ever have imagined and finding that she is by no means powerless to protect the ones she loves.

Despite her Gran's dire warnings, she is inexorably drawn to the dark and terrifying figure of Corvus, an ancient vampire and master of the vast Albinus family.

Jéhenne is about to find her answers and discover that, not only is Corvus far more dangerous than she could ever imagine, but that he holds much more than the key to her heart…

Now available at your favourite retailer.

The Key to Erebus

Check out Emma's exciting fantasy series with hailed by Kirkus Reviews as "An enchanting fantasy with a likable heroine, romantic intrigue, and clever narrative flourishes."

The Dark Prince
The French Fae Legend Book 1

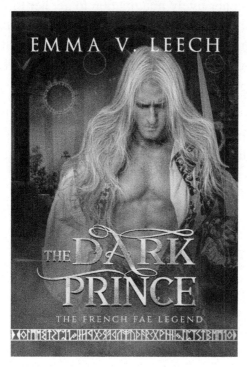

Two Fae Princes
One Human Woman
And a world ready to tear them all apart

Laen Braed is Prince of the Dark fae, with a temper and reputation to match his black eyes, and a heart that despises the human race. When he is sent back through the forbidden gates between realms to retrieve an ancient fae artifact, he returns home with far more than he bargained for.

Corin Albrecht, the most powerful Elven Prince ever born. His golden eyes are rumoured to be a gift from the gods, and destiny is calling him. With a love for the human world that runs deep, his friendship with Laen is being torn apart by his prejudices.

Océane DeBeauvoir is an artist and bookbinder who has always relied on her lively imagination to get her through an unhappy and uneventful life. A jewelled dagger put on display at a nearby museum hits the headlines with speculation of another race, the Fae. But the discovery also inspires Océane to create an extraordinary piece of art that cannot be confined to the pages of a book.

With two powerful men vying for her attention and their friendship stretched to the breaking point, the only question that remains…who is truly The Dark Prince.

The man of your dreams is coming…or is it your nightmares he visits? Find out in Book One of The French Fae Legend.

Available now to read at your favourite retailer

The Dark Prince

Want more Emma?

If you enjoyed this book, please support this indie author and take a moment to leave a few words in a review. *Thank you!*

To be kept informed of special offers and free deals (which I do regularly) follow me on *https://www.bookbub.com/authors/emma-v-leech*

To find out more and to get news and sneak peeks of the first chapter of upcoming works, go to my website and sign up for the newsletter.

http://www.emmavleech.com/

Come and join the fans in my Facebook group for news, info and exciting discussion...

Emma's Book Club

Or Follow me here...

http://viewauthor.at/EmmaVLeechAmazon

Facebook

Instagram

Emma's Twitter page

TikTok

Can't get your fill of Historical Romance? Do you crave stories with passion and red-hot chemistry?

If the answer is yes, have I got the group for you!

Come join myself and other awesome authors in our Facebook group

Historical Harlots

Be the first to know about exclusive giveaways, chat with amazing HistRom authors, lots of raunchy shenanigans and more!

Historical Harlots Facebook Group